She didn't *want* to care for him, didn't want to worry about him.

He'd left her carrying his baby with nary a care for her. How could she even think or worry about him now when it was her own life that was in such turmoil?

Her attention must be toward her own future and that of her baby. Brandon didn't deserve it, and yet...and yet he was her baby's father, the man she had loved. How could she ignore what had changed him so?

* * *

Texas Wedding for Their Baby's Sake
Harlequin® Historical #961—September 2009

TEXAS WEDDING
--•FOR•--
THEIR BABY'S SAKE

KATHRYN ALBRIGHT

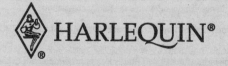

HARLEQUIN®

TORONTO • NEW YORK • LONDON
AMSTERDAM • PARIS • SYDNEY • HAMBURG
STOCKHOLM • ATHENS • TOKYO • MILAN • MADRID
PRAGUE • WARSAW • BUDAPEST • AUCKLAND

Recycling programs
for this product may
not exist in your area.

ISBN-13: 978-0-373-29561-6

TEXAS WEDDING FOR THEIR BABY'S SAKE

www.eHarlequin.com

Printed in U.S.A.

Prologue

Caroline Benét searched through her basket of ribbons for the length of burgundy silk she had saved to decorate the veranda's front post. It had been here only moments before. She was getting flustered with all the last minute details she'd had to contend with before the start of the benefit social. Something tightened around her waist and suddenly warm lips pressed to her neck, just below her right ear, sending a shiver down her spine. "I believe I missed this spot the other night," whispered a rich, baritone voice. "Now, you're my hostage."

The strength in her knees wavered. *Brandon.* He'd finally arrived. Caroline checked her waist and found the burgundy ribbon wrapping her mid-section. With a tug, he spun her around to face him. His eyes, the deepest blue of the Charleston Bay water, twinkled with warmth. She wanted to return the kiss much more intimately than the present public site would allow. However, she settled for pretending to straighten the silk bow tie she'd given him for Christmas.

"I've missed you." His smile was for her alone as he pulled the ribbon at her waist to bring her closer yet.

She pushed halfheartedly against his chest. "Not here, Brandon. Anyone could see." Guests milled about the plantation's front lawn and through the gardens in the back. It was nearly time to start the festivities.

He didn't budge, but seemed to loom even closer. A proprietary smile eased his angular features. "Not until you admit you missed me, too."

The veranda railing pressed against her spine. She sniffed the air. "Is that liquor on your breath?" she asked, stalling, making him wait as he'd made her wait and wonder the past few days.

"You're avoiding my request."

She hadn't fooled him. He knew exactly what she was doing. "If you'll give me room, I'll answer."

He stepped back. Waiting. Confident. Downright cocky in fact and most likely due to her sudden lack of moral strength three nights past. The look on his face both thrilled her and worried her. Now that she had succumbed once, it surprised her to realize how easy it would be to do so again. It also alarmed her. A barrier had crumbled that she had no desire to rebuild. She wouldn't let it happen again. She had a reputation to uphold as a Benét.

She sighed. "You could have sent a note, something to reassure me. I...I thought you might be displeased."

His dark brows drew together. "I'll never understand women. Why in the world would I be displeased with you?"

"Well." She struggled to order her thoughts. "I haven't heard from you for days! And after we'd..." She couldn't say it out loud. Anyone could hear.

"You received my flowers?"

"Yes."

The crease in his forehead smoothed. He took her hand in his and pulled her around the corner, away from the eyes of her guests. "I thought of you every moment we were apart."

His admission released a coil in her gut that had been tense for days. "I missed you, too."

A smile played across his face—the mysterious one she loved. It conveyed an intimate promise for her future. He touched his lips lightly to hers. "I had no idea my proper fiancée would be so passionate. When I get you alone again…"

A thrill coursed through her at the thought his words conveyed, but with it came a stab of worry. "Brandon. No. You mustn't press me. Not until we are married."

"Then we had better announce our plans today, because I don't want to wait."

"I confess I feel the same way." Her cheeks warmed with the admission. "Are you shocked?"

Before he answered, a commotion on the lawn drew their attention. Brandon grimaced. "I see my brother has arrived."

"Your brother?" The black sheep. "When did he get in?"

"Three days ago. A full month late. Says he didn't receive word of Father's illness." A deep, buried anger seemed to boil up as Brandon spoke. His knuckles blanched with his grip on the porch railing.

"Do you believe him?" she asked.

He didn't answer for a moment. "It doesn't matter now."

But obviously, it did matter. Brandon had come to her the very night his brother had returned after a ten-year absence—and then he'd mentioned nothing about him.

Caroline watched as two of her friends blushed at something Brandon's brother said. So this was Jake. She studied the man who was seven years older than Brandon and who'd caused him so much ambivalence over the years. Most likely he was completely unaware of the pain he'd brought.

He wore dark trousers, a cotton shirt and a vest—yet still he looked more the rugged frontiersman than anything she'd ever seen in Charleston before. He didn't seem concerned that he was underdressed without a coat and tie for the occasion and decidedly out of his element. Indeed, he oozed self-assurance to the brim and, having seen and admired that same trait in Brandon, Caroline wondered if such was the trait of any Dumont man. She watched as a group of Brandon's friends cast interested glances at the newcomer and walked over to meet him.

"Looks like he has made a few conquests already." Brandon turned his back on the scene and faced her. "He keeps asking about the will. After being gone for ten years that's all he cares about—his share."

"It must be awkward for you."

"I can't welcome him home. It's just not in me. Besides, he already told me he's not staying. Just wants his money."

"He *said* that?" She hardened her heart toward the man. She couldn't believe he was so callous.

"It's the feeling I get."

"Has he owned up to why he left in the first place?" She knew Brandon had always wondered. It would be good if they could clear up some things between them.

"No. But Jake had every right to take off back then. I would have, too, if I'd been older."

"You showed stronger moral character by staying."

He huffed. "I was only twelve at the time—hardly old enough to run away. And Father had me under his thumb."

"He trained you well. You're the best surgeon on the coast." She unloosed the ribbon from her waist with a saucy smile, hoping to lighten his mood. "And just look where that's brought you—to my veranda."

He smiled. "I guess I do have him to thank for that." He tugged a tendril of hair that had escaped from her crocheted hairnet. "You always see the best in things."

"Is this Caroline?" A deep voice came from the stairs.

Brandon's jaw tightened. He stepped back indicating the tall man behind him. "Caroline Benét, may I present my brother, Jake Dumont."

Jake moved up the last two steps to the veranda and surprised her by taking her hand and bowing slightly. "A pleasure, miss."

She could understand her friends' sudden entrancement with this man. He had charisma to spare. However, she could read between the lines. Jake had caused Brandon grief and hurt over the years with his selfishness. Caroline wasn't about to openly accept him. He would have to prove himself to both of them. She pulled her hand away.

"Welcome, Mr. Dumont. I hope you'll enjoy yourself today. I imagine our little benefit is a far cry from the excitement you are used to."

He straightened at her reserved tone, his eyes narrowing. "Just wanted to spend time with my brother. Meet his friends. See which particular filly had caught his eye."

She didn't care to be equated with a horse. "Brandon tells me you are good with a rifle. Perhaps you would enjoy entering the shooting competition today. It's for a good cause."

"Thanks, but it wouldn't be a fair match. It's better that I just watch."

His lack of humility annoyed her. It would do him good to have a comeuppance. Several of the men here were quite accurate. And as far as she knew, Brandon was the best shot of all of them.

"You're that sure you would win?"

"I've made a living with my gun, scouting for wagons going west. It's an unfair advantage."

"Aren't you interested to learn what the prize will be?" She looked from one brother to the other.

"You're not…" Brandon began. She'd let him in on her plans a week ago.

"I am." She felt an impish grin forming. "The winning prize is a kiss from Abigail Satterly, the prettiest girl in the district."

"That privilege belongs to you," Brandon argued. "But you can be sure I won't have you giving away kisses to anyone."

Her heart thrummed. He was just too perfect, defending her looks that way.

"Are your parents going along with this? For that matter, are Abigail's?"

"It's all for a good cause. They understand that."

Brandon shook his head. "I don't like it."

The sound of polite clapping interrupted them. Brandon offered his elbow. "Sounds like your father's opening speech has started."

She took Brandon's arm to join the guests on the front lawn, conscious of Jake following behind her. Everything was going to be perfect in spite of his intrusion into their lives. She wouldn't allow it to be any other way.

The weather was just right—sunny and cool for the start of February. The Spanish moss draping the cypress trees swayed in the light breeze. It would be wonderful to meet the goal her fledgling organization had set of one thousand dollars. With the bake sale, the games of croquet, the shooting match and the generous amount of liquor, surely the guests would feel inclined to open their purse strings.

As her father's speech continued, Caroline considered what would be the best time today for Brandon to announce their engagement. Having already given their consent to the marriage, her parents wanted a date set. Mother had dropped hints that the governor would be invited along with Charleston's mayor and she was anxious to start the process of invitations, deciding on a caterer and all the other minutiae that went into creating the perfect wedding. Mother was at her best when planning and putting on extravagant parties—and as her only daughter, Caroline knew she would spare no expense. Caroline could just envision the guest list—the elite of the East Coast, the associates of Brandon's recently deceased father and her own parents' colleagues.

However, her parents were not nearly so anxious as she was. Just thinking of the passion she'd shared with Brandon…why it made her insides turn to liquid fire. She would not be able to stand a long engagement now that she'd sampled what life with him would be like. That same intense passion that he had directed toward his studies and then his career had suddenly been focused on her. It had been the most intoxicating experience of her life—so far.

After her father welcomed everyone, he turned their attention to Caroline. She was in charge of the baked goods auction. Brandon had promised to bid for her chocolate cake creation and win it no matter what. As anticipated, his friends increased the bid relentlessly to an outrageous sum. With a wide grin on his face, he stepped forward to claim the cake and then good-naturedly ordered that it be sliced and distributed among the guests.

At the end of the auction, Caroline covered the desserts and noting that the large punch bowls of mulled hot cider and brandy had been depleted, excused herself and went to the cookhouse to remedy the situation. She found the building deserted. Apparently the two maids were busy elsewhere.

She stirred the cider in the large caldron and then used a pitcher to dip out the liquid and fill two empty bowls.

"Would you like some help?"

She looked up to see Jake at the door. "No. I can manage. I'll be out in a moment."

Instead of leaving, he walked further into the room and removed his black felt hat. "I get the feeling you are managing very well. My brother is smitten with you."

Something about his tone cautioned her. She stopped pouring and set the pitcher down. "Is there something you want to say?"

"Guess I'm wondering where this relationship is headed. Brandon hasn't told me much about you, but I did hear he'd spoken for you."

"That's right. We're betrothed, although it hasn't been officially announced yet."

"Why is that? What's stopping him?"

"Look. I don't feel comfortable discussing my relationship with Brandon, with you. Why don't you ask him?"

"Because he's not talking to me. In my limited experience, most women are after only one thing."

She frowned, not liking his tone or his words. "And what would that be?"

"Money, of course. Although, I've got to admit it looks like your family is sitting well already."

She gasped. Had the man no manners at all? One didn't discuss finances like this—or speak of women so. "I happen to care deeply for Brandon. We've been good friends the past two years—not that you would have any idea since you haven't been around."

He shrugged. "Couldn't be helped, but I'm here now and I don't intend to see the Dumont estate fall into the hands of just *any* woman."

"You have a strong aversion to the opposite gender, Mr. Dumont? I find that hard to believe considering the way my friends have been throwing themselves at you since you arrived."

"Again, from my experience, women tend to be fickle."

"Then why did you come today if you are so ready to condemn half of the human race?"

"I told you. I wanted to meet the woman who had her sight set on my brother."

"To see if I measure up to your standards?"

"Yes."

Anger welled up inside, nearly choking her. How dare he talk to her like this? He had no idea how she felt about Brandon. Hands on hips, she squared off with him. "Since you are being quite frank, I will be, as well."

"That's how I like it."

"I don't know who gave you such a low opinion of women in your past, but some of us actually do have a heart. I happen to love Brandon, and I think my actions show it, which is more than I can say for you."

An amused smile played about his lips and eyes as he looked down at her.

She clenched her hands into fists, not liking at all the disadvantage of her shorter height. What was he up to?

A grin worked its way onto his face. "Just had to be sure, Miss Benét, and getting a woman riled up tends to make her say what's really on her mind. I needed to know my brother isn't being hoodwinked. I still plan to keep my eyes on you, but I think we understand each other better now."

"You're saying that in some strange way you have been looking out for Brandon by frustrating me?"

"Guess you could call it that. Brandon and I have the estate to settle. I'm sure he's made you aware of that. A stipulation in the will states that we have to be together to learn what it contains."

"All he has said is that you are interested in getting your share and that you planned to leave then."

"Seems like the best choice. I don't exactly feel welcomed—but then I never did. Doesn't mean I don't care what happens to him."

Apparently there was more to Jake's leaving than simply being selfish. If Brandon was aware of it, he certainly hadn't told her, but it was something they should address. The sooner the better. "Jake, I think you should talk to Brandon. You two need to talk before you leave."

His face hardened. "Don't you think I've tried?"

"Caroline!"

At Brandon's call, she turned quickly—and so did Jake. So quickly that they collided with each other. Jake grasped her shoulders, steadying her.

"Caro— What's going on?"

Brandon stood at the door, the surprise on his face transforming into a closed, guarded expression. He looked from Jake to Caroline.

Heat suffused her face despite the fact she wasn't guilty of anything. "Nothing. I'm getting more cider for the guests."

"Getting to know Caroline." Jake stepped back and tipped his hat to her. "I'll see you at the match."

She turned back to filling the bowl and took two deep breaths to calm herself. She couldn't very well tell him what his brother had said.

"Jake couldn't be satisfied with every other woman here today—he had to count you among his conquests?"

"Of course not. I have no interest in him other than as your brother."

"It didn't look that way."

She faced him. "Brandon…how can there be any doubt in your mind after the other night?"

He studied her face for an interminable time, and then finally his shoulders relaxed. "Guess it took my brother coming home to find out I was the jealous type."

"You're head and shoulders more than him."

He pointed at the cider with his chin. "Let's get that out on the table. I'm in need of a partner for the games."

The games on the lawn eventually wound to a close and the men headed toward the gardens and the canal in back where the shooting match would take place. Jake and Brandon stood like tall bookends on each side of her brother, Tom, who showed off the new pistol he'd just purchased. Her parents had tried to dissuade him, but Tom was determined to leave for Texas territory by the end of the week. He and another friend were anxious to prove themselves in the fight for freedom there. He'd tried to talk Brandon into going. Thank goodness, Brandon would rather heal people than shoot at them.

Jake studied the weapon with a practiced eye. He stroked down the cherrywood encased iron barrel, pausing to note the fancy stamped patterns in the brass casing, before checking the sighting.

"Try it out," Tom urged. "Won't hurt to break it in a little before I use it in a real skirmish."

Jake shook his head. "No, thanks. I'm satisfied with my own pistol. It's old, but it shoots straight."

"You should enter the match, Mr. Dumont. You'll make it much more exciting. Brandon here always whips us."

"He does, does he?" Jake looked at his brother with renewed interest. "I did teach him everything he knows about guns."

Brandon huffed. "That was a long time ago. I've learned a few tricks since then."

"That so? I might have to enter at that."

Brandon narrowed his gaze, first on his brother and then on Tom. "I'll give your pistol a try. That'll put me at a disadvantage—unfamiliar gun and all."

"What's the entry fee?" Jake asked.

"Three dollars."

Jake handed the pistol to Brandon. "Think I'll take you up after all. Haven't seen my brother shoot since he was twelve."

Ten men entered the shooting match. Bets were placed—all with the intention of a portion being dedicated to the new hospital addition.

Caroline joined the other ladies in the gazebo. From this vantage point she could see the shooting event in spite of the stovepipe hats worn by many of the men. Her unease grew as each of the local men eventually lost to either Jake or Brandon. It didn't take long. Within the hour, the match had been whittled down to the two brothers. The others good-naturedly bowed out.

Caroline seemed to be the only one to feel the underlying animosity that existed between the two men. They'd covered their emotions well, chiding each other, playing to the crowd. But now, although Brandon still seemed to be at ease, the tension had escalated to a palpable level. They stood, shoulder to shoulder, waiting while the target was moved back ten more paces for the final round. This was no longer a game.

Without speaking, they reloaded their guns, each man concentrating on their final shot and probably playing it out in their mind. A baby cried out among the crowd. At the sound, neither brother flinched.

Caroline could barely breathe. Brandon had to win. He just *had* to.

Brandon took his stance first. He loosened his tie and then set his legs wide, his right shoulder closest to the target two hundred yards down the dirt path that lined the canal. He raised his arm to shoulder level, aiming through the crosshairs of Tom's new pistol. The crowd hushed. The only sound was that of the breeze rippling the cattails along the water.

He fired. A flash of smoke puffed up from the gun.

Tom raced to the target, checked the shot and turned back to the crowd. "One inch from center!"

Caroline let out her breath. Her heart started beating again. It would be near impossible for Jake to shoot any better at such a distance with such an old gun. Brandon had as much as won the match. He stepped back, his shoulders relaxing, his gaze centered on his brother.

Jake took his position—identical to his brother's stance. His right foot sank deep into the muddy bank, soaking his leather boots, but he seemed oblivious to the distraction. The crowd quieted.

With a loud crack, he discharged his pistol. Then he turned toward Brandon, meeting his eyes. Together they walked to the target while Tom ran from the tall grass to join them there. Everyone waited for the verdict.

Suddenly Tom grabbed Jake's arm and held it up.

Men closed in, clapping Jake on the shoulders and taunting Brandon, who held back, helping to gather the targets. Caroline was proud of him. He hid his tension remarkably well. It couldn't be easy for him to be bested in front of his friends and colleagues by his older brother.

"Now, about that prize you mentioned..." Jake said with a grin as he approached the gazebo. "Time to claim it. Where is this Abigail?"

"There's been a change," her mother said, coming to her side. "I'm afraid Abigail was unable to stay. Caroline will be handing out the prize."

Caroline's jaw dropped in shock. "Mother!"

Mother patted her arm. "Like you said, dear—it's for a good cause. You're the next logical choice among the ladies here."

"But Brandon..."

"This is an unforeseen emergency. He'll understand."

Someone in the crowd hooted. "Come on, Dumont. Take your prize. None of the rest of us has had the privilege."

From behind the crowd of onlookers, Brandon stopped gathering the targets and straightened to listen.

Her face warmed. This was getting out of hand. Perhaps it was best to get it over and done with. She put on her most gracious smile for the crowd. "I hope you have all paid up on your wagers."

"All but you, Caroline!" one of her married girlfriends called. "Pay up."

It's all in good fun, she told herself. All in good fun. But she couldn't bring herself to glance at Brandon. She stood her ground while Jake stepped inside the gazebo. With the exception of a boy under the mistletoe when she'd been ten, she'd never been kissed by anyone other than Brandon.

A good-natured grin split Jake's face when he stopped before her, but his eyes held concern. He must know he wasn't making his brother happy, but didn't quite know how to gracefully extricate himself from the situation, same as her. She nearly stamped her foot in frustration. If Brandon had announced his intentions toward her earlier no one would have expected her to kiss another man.

She raised her face, acutely aware of how Jake's lips matched Brandon's in design. Perhaps she could pretend it was Brandon kissing her…

The moment his lips touched hers, she knew there was no comparison. Where Brandon's lips had been soft and giving, Jake's were firm and stiff. They broke apart quickly.

"Ah! That isn't any kiss!" a man yelled. "Kiss her again and make it worth the three-dollar entry fee!"

Caroline's face flushed.

"You be quiet," the man's wife said, cuffing him on the shoulder. Soon everyone got involved, urging Jake and Caroline to kiss once more. At the edge of her vision, Brandon approached, looking perplexed at what was occuring.

Jake's Adam's apple floated up and then dropped in his throat as he swallowed hard. Beneath the brim of his suede hat, his eyes glinted in the hazy afternoon sunshine. "All right, Miss Benét. Let's give'm what they want."

He snaked his arms around her and pulled her flush against him. She gasped, her lips parting in surprise, unable to keep from comparing the two brothers. Where Jake's body was rock-hard from constant work out-of-doors, Brandon's, though firm, was more yielding. As their lips met, she heard a few twitters from the audience, and then she felt…

Nothing.

Oh, his lips were softer than she'd first thought. He plastered his mouth against hers and for a moment she was worried he might do something with his tongue, but instead he arched her backward, supporting her with his arms, and continued the chaste kiss.

Jake straightened and pulled away. He was no longer smiling. In fact, he looked confused just before his eyes hardened. He was mad as a hornet. "All for a good cause, right?" He released her abruptly and she stumbled a step.

Someone behind her giggled.

She regained her footing and as her brain cleared, her first thought was of Brandon. She glanced at him. His scowl dashed any hope that he might consider announcing their engagement now—after what had just occurred. Tom shouldered him good-naturedly but it did nothing to shake the shimmering anger in his eyes. Suddenly he spun on his heel and strode away.

Caroline wanted to chase after him, but her upbringing held her back. A genteel woman didn't just dash after a man—especially with all these guests watching.

Beside her, Jake grumbled something about hotheaded young men and then pinned her with his dark gaze. "I hope you are content. You just got the charity event of the season."

Dumbfounded, she watched as he, too, stormed off in the opposite direction.

Three days passed. Three days of her mother saying Brandon would eventually come to his senses, and three days of remorse. No one knew where he'd gone. Even Brandon's butler, Franklin, had been to her house asking if she knew his whereabouts.

During that time, her brother departed for Texas. Her parents didn't support him in this quest of his. Neither could Caroline, but she could understand it. Tom needed to separate from his parents and this was his way. At his age, he craved adventure before Father tried to mold him into a copy of himself.

Just after breakfast on the fourth day, a young boy came to the door bearing a message in Brandon's handwriting. Caroline snatched it from him and broke the wax seal.

Caroline—
Today you made it obvious you want a different kind of man than me. One more like my brother. I'm going to Texas with Tom. It will give us both time to think things through. The fight should only last a few months and then I'll be back. Who knows? Maybe I'll be a better shot—for both of us.
Always,
Brandon Dumont

Her knees gave way, and she sank to the floor.

"Miss!" The courier's eyes widened in alarm. "Miss!"

She glanced at the note—no date anywhere. Clutching his shirt, she waved the paper before him. "When did you get this?"

If it was possible, his eyes widened further. "I didn't do nuttin' wrong, miss. Man told me to wait three days. Just doin' what I was told."

Three days! Too late to stop him. She crushed the note in her fist. What was he thinking? He had no right to leave her like this!

It was all Jake's fault. She wished he'd never come to town. All that had happened since had led to this horrible moment—Brandon's unusual moodiness…the kiss. Her stomach clenched at what else Jake's appearance had led to—the night Brandon had made love to her. She held herself, rocking back and forth on the floor. How could Brandon do this to her? How could he leave after the promises he'd made?

As much as she hated the thought, she had to find Jake. He must go after Brandon and bring him back. She would beg if it came to that. Brandon had to return. He just had to.

Chapter One

Texas Territory—July 1836

Brandon whipped the rope above his head in a circle until it felt "right," leaned in cautiously on his weak leg, testing its ability to handle his full weight and then launched the rope toward the spindly pine thirty feet away.

Missed. For the third time.

He yanked off his hat and with his forearm wiped the sweat from his brow. A low chuckle sounded to his right.

Great. Witnesses.

He spun around and immediately regretted the quick move as a bolt of fire raced through his right ankle. Tall and solid, his brother sauntered up, an older, rougher version of himself—without the limp.

Brandon resettled his hat on his head. "Thought I was far enough from the hacienda to avoid an audience."

Jake dropped the reins to his horse. With a practiced hand, he whirled his rope overhead, letting loose at just the right moment. It sailed through the air and landed neatly around the young tree.

"Playin' to the gallery," Brandon mumbled. *As always.*

Jake shrugged his shoulders and dismounted. He strode to the tree to remove both lines and then tossed Brandon's back to him. "You're thinking too hard. Gotta get that big brain of yours out of the way."

Easier said than done in Brandon's case.

"Just takes repetition—doing it so much that your body takes over naturally."

"I can think of only one thing that comes to me like that—and it ain't lassoin' a tree."

Jake grinned. "Well now. That so? Didn't think that was a part of your medical education. Must be more to your past than I figured." He nodded at the pine. "Give it another go."

Brandon didn't want an audience. Not even his brother. He gathered in his line. "No, I'm finished. What are you doing back from Bexar so soon?"

"Got done early. Couldn't stand stayin' longer. Lot of sickness there."

Brandon pressed his lips together. He figured the doctor in town could use his help, but he couldn't bring himself to go. His doctorin' skills weren't what they used to be—not since the war. "So how'd you find me?"

"Followed your tracks," Jake said. "Gotta admit it was a hell of a lot easier than last time.

"A rabbit couldn't hide his tracks in all this mud."

"The rain did help," Jake admitted.

"Next time I'll give you more of a challenge."

Jake had come after him when he had taken off for Texas to fight with the freedom fighters. Now they were both stuck here—for different reasons. Jake's reason being infinitely better than Brandon's—and prettier.

"Picked up some ground mustard and laudanum in town."

Brandon frowned. "What for?"

Jake shrugged. "Just thought it might help you earn your keep."

"Who says I'll keep on doctorin'?"

Jake studied him with those penetrating blue eyes. "Well, while you're making up your mind, someone might need the medicine. Seems to help enough with your leg."

Laudanum took the pain away all right—of more things than just his injury.

"We need to make plans." Jake ignored his surliness. "Franklin will be here any day now."

"I figured he'd stay with us, although I can't quite imagine him using my table as a bed." Just the thought of his formal, impeccably dressed estate manager lying prostrate on the exam table gave Brandon the willies, his mind conjuring up the image of a funeral wake.

Jake looped his rope on his saddle horn. "He could stay in the cabin."

"Considering his feelings about dust and disorder…the cabin would be a disaster." Tidiness had never been one of Jake's virtues—he'd actually never owned enough things to bother with keeping tidy. Brandon, on the other hand, had grown up under Franklin's tutelage and knew everything had a place—a concept even further ingrained with his medical training. However, since coming to Texas, he'd let that compulsion slide quite a bit. "He'll be more comfortable at the big house."

"My thoughts, too," Jake said. "Juan has a lot going on with Victoria's family staying until the wedding. One more shouldn't break him."

"It's decided, then." Brandon strode to his horse and fixed the rope to the saddle. He didn't particularly want to talk about Franklin. He figured he'd hear more than his share of criticism when the man arrived. "I see you got your ears lowered in town."

"And a shave. A haircut wouldn't hurt you, too."

Brandon swiped a hand through his hair. He'd never worn it this long when he lived on the coast. It just didn't matter anymore, but apparently it was important to Jake that he clean up a bit for his big day.

"Being my brother and all, you're gonna have to think of a toast." Lines crinkled around Jake's blue eyes. "Say something great about me. Lie if you have to."

"Well, that makes it a whole lot easier," Brandon said sarcastically, but inside he was truly honored to be part of his brother's wedding. Eight months ago, at their father's funeral, he would have never thought it possible. They had both been too stubborn, too mule-headed to make the first move after a long line of subtle rejections.

He picked up Jake's hat from the ground, slapped it against his thigh to dislodge the dust and then tossed it to him. "Victoria has no idea what she's getting herself into."

Jake's smile widened. "One big adventure. That's me. Let's find Diego."

Brandon mounted his sorrel and once Jake was on his horse they headed west across the prairie to the hacienda. The air after the storm had lightened considerably, and the sun peeking through a hole in the clouds promised to dry things out.

"You given any thought to what you're gonna do after the wedding?" Jake asked.

"No." And he didn't want to think about it now.

"Considerin' going back with Franklin?"

Brandon shot a dark look at Jake. He couldn't return to the life he'd once had. Too many things had changed.

"Just wondering. You don't talk about it."

"I'll let you know when I sort it out myself."

"Suits me. Just thought you had a job waiting. Figured you'd take over Father's practice."

At one time, that had been Brandon's dream. Not now. Not ever. That life was officially over. "Nothing I have to get back to," he said, keeping his voice even.

"Aren't you curious about who Caroline married?" Jake persisted.

Brandon pressed his lips together. She'd had plenty of choices among his friends and colleagues. For her to accept another so quickly after he'd left for Texas…well, he still reeled from the news. He'd been stunned. Thought they had an understanding, especially since she'd sent Jake to find him. All the while he'd been fighting Mexicans in Texas he'd believed he had something to go back to once the territory was free. The entire thing left a sour feeling in his stomach. He'd trusted her and she'd thrown it back in his face—and hadn't even had the decency to write him a letter.

"Caroline and I…" Brandon started, and then stopped. No point spending time thinking on it. "It was over a long time ago."

"That's not the way it sounded to me."

"It's the way it was." He cast a sharp look at his brother. "Believe me."

"Humph."

"For the record, I'm glad she's married. She's someone else's worry now."

"Well, you're better off without her. If you can't trust her to wait a few months, you can't trust her at all."

"Just back off, Jake," he said, his voice hardening. He'd come to the same conclusion—especially now that he couldn't return to his old life. He was lucky to be rid of her.

In moments of lucid honesty, his conscience would

squeeze him, telling him that he'd played a part in losing Caroline. After all, he could have stayed in Charleston and swallowed his pride, could have confronted her. He didn't have to leave.

Like hell, he grumbled.

Turning away from his brother's probing, he concentrated on the slope of the hillside to the hacienda. From this distance the large U-shaped house looked inviting and well kept. It was only as they drew closer that evidence of the Mexican Army encampment there several months ago marred the landscape. Ruts from heavy artillery bisected the expanse of prairie to the east. Where the tents and campfires had been, weeds had grown up and choked out the prairie flowers. Nearer the house, trees had been destroyed for firewood.

He closed his eyes and took a deep breath of the sweet air, clean now since the rain had come. Here, for a brief moment, he felt at peace. If only it could stay like this. If only Franklin weren't coming and bringing remnants of his past life with him.

Brandon set his jaw. It would only be for a week or so. Just long enough to settle their father's will and get Jake hitched. He figured he could deal with it that long.

A shout sounded from the cluster of pines near the house. A rider appeared—white horse, big hat.

Jake whistled through his teeth, piercing the afternoon quiet with an ear-shattering noise. "Diego!" He stood in his stirrups, grabbed his hat and waved it over his head.

Diego spotted them on the ridge and kicked his mount into a gallop, riding bareback so fast that his hat slipped off his head and bounced against his back.

"He's riding hard. Something's wrong," Brandon murmured. He adjusted his seat, pressed his knees to his mount's flanks and urged his horse down the slope.

As soon as Diego pulled up on the reins in front of them, Brandon realized the man's cotton pants and shirt were soaked through. "What is it?"

"A wagon's stuck in the river."

"Anybody hurt?"

"An old man is caught up. His head is above water, but I don't know how long he will last."

"Water level is too high. It's made that crossing dangerous." Jake glanced over at Brandon, his gaze resting momentarily on Brandon's injured leg before turning once again to Diego.

A knot of anger lodged in Brandon's throat. It wasn't like Jake to hesitate because of him. Leaning forward in his saddle, he kicked his sorrel. The horse lurched into a gallop down the slope.

They raced toward the river. A mile north of the big house they rounded the bend in the dirt road and slowed. Through the cottonwoods, they caught sight of the wagon half-submerged in the water. The ears on the two lead horses flicked forward nervously as the newcomers approached.

From the high bank, Brandon surveyed the surrounding hills, checking for signs of trouble—most notably Comanche or hostile Mexicans. He didn't fancy getting ambushed in the middle of the river where he and his brother would be easy targets. Reassured of their safety, he headed toward the wagon. Only it wasn't a wagon, but a black carriage tipped halfway on its side against a large boulder and held there by the pressure of the current.

He dismounted and strode to the shoreline. The water sluiced by, crashing over large boulders as it raced downstream and created a terrific roar. The elegant crest on the carriage door lay half-submerged under the frothy surface and looked strangely out of place in this raw country.

Brandon swore suddenly under his breath as he recognized the fancy ornament. "That's Franklin out there!"

Jake's gaze shot to the crest on the carriage.

Brandon stepped into the rushing water, tensing against the slap of the current against his injured leg. Pain raced up his shin and stole his breath away in a gasp. A hundred white-hot needles jabbed at his ankle. He clenched his teeth together. Once he acclimated to the pain he'd be all right. At least he hoped so.

"Head back!" Jake growled in passing. "I can't worry about you, too."

"I'm not asking you to."

Slowly he made his way toward the carriage as Diego splashed into the water and raced ahead of him, catching up to Jake. The water coursed around Brandon as he maneuvered between a few boulders and sought to find stable footing on the smooth and slippery rocks in the riverbed. Although the day was warm, the water still felt as cold as ice.

Jake made it to the carriage first. A shriek echoed from inside the conveyance and bounced off the rock walls on the far bank. A woman's solitary enraged cry.

What the hell was a woman doing riding with Franklin? If in fact the man in the water was Franklin.

Brandon reached the carriage just as Jake thrust a bundle of wet sky-blue material and soggy blond hair at him. "Here! Take her! She's not making any sense with her ranting."

Momentum arched the woman halfway over his shoulder. Reacting in surprise, Brandon grabbed on as his weaker leg gave in and he lost his footing. They both slipped under the water. Her voluminous skirt tangled around his arms and face as he wrestled with the cloth, trying to establish a solid stance and get them both above the surface. His arm butted against a hard object. He grabbed the carriage wheel and steadied himself.

The minute their heads emerged above the surface another scream rent the air right next to his ear. The woman struggled and pummeled his back. "Put me down!"

"As soon as I get you to shore, ma'am," he said, trying to ignore the woman's hysterics and look for Franklin. He didn't have time to consider what the man was doing traveling with this she-cat, but he'd sure expect some answers later—banking on the fact that Franklin was all right.

Jake appeared on the far side of the carriage.

"Franklin?" Brandon asked.

"He's all right, but he's stuck under the carriage. Diego and I can get him."

Brandon nodded. "I'll head to shore." He turned, taking one step toward the strip of sand on the bank when something stopped him, nearly pulling him over backward.

"What the…"

The woman held tight to the cloth that disappeared under the coach.

"Let it go, ma'am."

"Noooo!"

"Let it go or we'll both go down again."

Still she wouldn't release the fabric.

"I gave you good warning," he said through gritted teeth. Quickly he whipped the knife from his belt and slashed through the cloth.

For a second her outraged gasp was all he heard—that and the roaring of the water. Then she found her tongue.

"How dare you! You don't know what you've done." She beat his back with her fists. "Put me down! You…you imbecile!"

"Don't tempt me," he muttered. It would serve her right.

But it just didn't seem the thing to do when he was trying to rescue her. He took an unsteady step toward the shore. This direction, the force of the water was stronger on his ankle. Thankfully by now both legs were nearly numb. The woman wasn't much weight, but her wiggling didn't make the going easy. He had half a mind to spank her since she was acting like a child. Too bad it wasn't in his nature. Heck, in the current situation, rather than quieting her, it might make her that much more of a wildcat.

Halfway to shore, he shifted her on his shoulder and off balance a moment, he stumbled. His foot came down crooked on a large stone. His ankle twisted and white-hot pain seared through him. His vision blurred. He forced himself to take three more unsteady steps. The small beach loomed close. He might make it. On his last step he teetered and went down face-first on top of the woman. Her extra layers of clothing along with what strength was left in his arms, softened the fall onto the sand—for him at least.

Momentarily stunned, she lay quiet—for the space of a second. Maybe, just maybe, he would get a thank-you out of her. Then she pushed at him with renewed strength. "Get off me you big oaf!"

In this horizontal position, the blood returned to his head in a rush and her high-pitched words registered. He rolled off and sprawled onto his back, letting his head drop back on the coarse sand. Slowly the throbbing pain in his leg subsided. Stars spun on the edge of his vision. When they stopped moving he opened his eyes.

The woman sat next to him, looking toward the carriage, her energy spent, gasping for new air. Pale golden hair hung in wet, snarled hanks down her back to her waist. Her satin dress, the color of the sky, clung to her bodice and twisted around her legs. Fool of a woman. She would have drowned in all that material. He'd saved her life and her screeching was the thanks he got.

"I have never been treated so deplorably!" she began.

He could tell she was gearing up for a considerable rant and mentally braced himself while an uneasy premonition built inside. The voice. The form. They were all too familiar.

She pushed the hair from her face and then turned, her green eyes snapping fire as she readied her arsenal of words.

"Hello, Caroline."

Her eyes widened and her cheeks, already pale from the cold water, drained further of color. "Oh, dear," she began awkwardly. "Oh…dear…"

In the two years he'd known her, he'd never seen her flustered. She'd always known the perfect thing to say on any occasion. He didn't think he'd find anything amusing about this situation, as mad as he felt, but there it was.

"What? No words for me?" The sarcasm rolled off his tongue easily enough.

She clamped her mouth shut and glared at him.

He'd forgotten how beautiful she was—the flawless skin, the straight nose and the generous rose-colored lips made for kissing. No, that wasn't correct. He'd tried hard to forget ever since he'd learned of her engagement, shoving her memory to the back of his mind. She belonged to another time, another life—in Charleston. Definitely not in Texas.

And as far as he knew, she belonged to another man now. What the hell was she doing here?

His chest tightened with anger. He'd come to the conclusion that he'd never cross paths with her again, that they'd gone their separate ways. After her betrayal, Texas had seemed like a safe bet that he'd never lay eyes on her again. This country was no place for the proper Miss Benét or whoever she was now. What had Franklin been thinking to bring her and where was her fool of a husband?

"What the hell are you doing here? Is Franklin all right?" he asked gruffly, purposely ignoring the fact that she'd started shivering.

At the mention of his butler's name, her anxious gaze flashed back to the river. "He's pinned on the other side. The carriage tipped over just as we tried to free the wheel and his foot got stuck. Those men…they need your help."

Brandon grimaced. Another trip through that water and he'd end up a casualty as sure as the carriage, but Franklin was more important than his own comfort. Franklin had seen him through all the good times and many of the rough times in his life. The one man he could always rely on. Shouts passed back and forth between Jake and Diego, their voices muffled by the water's rushing. He rose to his feet and headed toward the water, glancing back once at Caroline. Her censoring gaze didn't help matters.

Just then his brother and Diego emerged from the underbelly of the carriage carrying Franklin between them. They dragged him across the top of the water, keeping his head above the surface as they stumbled over submerged rocks and around boulders in their path toward the shore. Once there, they laid him, pale and shivering, at Brandon's feet.

"Might want to take a look at that right foot," Jake said. "It was wedged tight." He straightened, his gaze shifting to Caroline. His eyes narrowed and grew ten degrees colder. "Welcome to Texas territory, Miss Caroline."

She nodded cautiously, picking herself up from the ground and brushing the grainy sand from her palms. "Mr. Dumont."

She broke eye contact first and turned to Franklin. Wringing out a portion of her skirt, she knelt beside him and wiped the excess water from his face and neck.

Jake glanced at Brandon, his brows raised. Brandon had caught the fact that she hadn't corrected her name, but that didn't mean anything. Obviously she was shook up—the evidence being her ministrations to a man she had at one time considered beneath her station. A man she had gone out of her way to avoid.

"M-M-Master Brandon," Franklin said through chattering teeth. "How good to see you."

He clasped Franklin's large hand. "Hair's a bit grayer than the last time I saw you," he said gruffly.

"If that's the case," Franklin returned, glaring at him through his shivering, "it's your fault."

Brandon's eyes stung. "Let's get you into the sun to dry off."

He motioned to Diego and Jake and together they dragged him a few yards up the bank, out from the shadow of the cottonwoods. There Brandon knelt on one knee and examined the man's foot. "No swelling. No evidence of a break," he murmured. He checked the range of motion, flexing Franklin's foot. "Any pain when I do this?"

Franklin shook his head. "A little."

"Give it a day or two. You'll be fine."

"I tried to tell Master Jake that, but he wouldn't listen."

"He never does. And Franklin—out here it's just Jake and Brandon. We're not masters of anything."

"A hard habit to break, I'm afraid."

"Obviously since you never could adjust to addressing me as Doctor, either. Just Brandon. Please. Otherwise I'll be looking over my shoulder trying to figure out who you're talking to."

"To whom."

He'd heard the automatic corrections all his life from

this man. At one time it would have made him grin and he'd have riled Franklin all the more, just to egg him on. Now he ignored it and rose awkwardly to his feet.

He limped to his horse, conscious of both Franklin's and Caroline's gazes on him and removed the coiled rope. He handed one end to Jake. "Once you get your end secured and are ready behind the carriage, give me a shout."

He secured his end of the rope to his saddle and did the same with another line that he received from Diego. When the carriage was all trussed up and ready, Brandon called orders to the lead horse as Jake flicked a bullwhip at its rump. It started with a snort, tossing its head in surprise. With a concerted effort the carriage rocked from its position against the boulders. But they couldn't budge it further.

Noticing again the material caught in the wheel spoke, Brandon yelled to this brother. "That cloth is hooked on something."

Jake nodded in agreement and with the quicksilver flash of his knife, he cut through the fabric and let it float away.

Brandon ignored the moan at his side. No doubt the material was a favored shawl or some such nonsense. Well, out here you couldn't let such things stop you from acting. You did what was necessary. Sentiment got you nothing but misery.

The release of the material freed the carriage. On the men's fifth attempt, the conveyance righted all the way and the horses started, and then pulled it to the bank.

Once there, Brandon grabbed the old quilted bedroll from Jake's horse and spread it across the seat for a dry space. He held the door open. "I'll drive to the hacienda, Franklin. You rest that leg. And elevate it."

He tipped his hat to Caroline. She followed Franklin

into the coach, pausing at the door long enough to let her gaze sweep down to Brandon's leg. "When did it happen?"

He hadn't had the limp when he had left Charleston, so he'd expected the question eventually. It was the open concern in her green eyes that caught him off guard and made him remember her soft side, made him remember why he'd been drawn to her in the first place. He didn't want those memories—not after all that she'd done. She could just keep her concerns to herself from now on.

He grasped her elbow and helped her into the carriage. "It's not important."

For once, she didn't start another battle of wills. "Perhaps later then," she said and seated herself.

The acceptance that flashed in her eyes confused him. She'd always been one to push to get her own way. The whole fact that she was here now confused him. Just what was she up to?

He slammed the door after her and tied his horse to the back of the carriage. Jake watched him with a grim expression as he climbed into the driver's seat and took up the reins.

Brandon clamped his jaw together and jerked the reins, urging the matched pair forward. Whatever her reason for being here, it was over between him and Caroline. That's all there was to it. But it didn't take much to figure things were going to change with her around. Caroline would learn soon enough—it would be on his terms—not hers.

Chapter Two

The dark-haired Mexican who had first discovered their coach stuck in the river grabbed her trunk and escorted Caroline to the front door of the big house. Behind her, Brandon helped Franklin down from the coach, then with a shoulder under his arm and Jake supporting his other side, they assisted him slowly toward the house.

The size of the hacienda spoke of better times. Weeds and thistles choked the flower gardens near the door and the few struggling flowers did not look like they would survive unless nursed carefully.

She stepped inside the impressive structure. The floor tiles of the spacious front hall gleamed with a recent washing. It looked…vacant…she realized. No furniture at all. A few tiles were broken. The plaster on the walls had several large, spidery cracks.

"Diego? *¡Ven aqui!*" A pleasant soprano voice called from up the staircase.

Diego cocked his head. "Excuse me, *señorita*." He flashed a smile and set her trunk on the tile floor. She judged him to be a bit younger than herself, despite the fact that he was taller by six inches. His loose cotton shirt and worn brown pants were still damp from river water, but not nearly as wet as her dress.

He took the stairs two at a time, stopping to speak in Spanish to the woman on the stairs. The woman glanced her way and then after another word to Diego, descended to meet her.

"Welcome. I am Victoria Torrez."

Petite and dark-haired with large, expressive brown eyes, Victoria Torrez had intrigued Caroline ever since Franklin had spoken of her on the journey west. Instead of the tough-as-leather, boots-and-spurs image she had pictured for a woman who'd battled alongside Jake at the Alamo, Victoria stood before her now in a flowing and very feminine pale yellow dress. She had twisted her shiny near-black hair off her neck into a fancy chignon and secured it with a silver comb.

Caroline remained still, acutely conscious of her own bedraggled appearance and the water dripping from her traveling dress into small puddles on the tiles. "Señorita Torrez. Thank you for your hospitality. I know you were not expecting me."

"I am happy to have you here." The sharp assessment in her eyes belied Victoria's gracious tone and voice. "However, this is my cousin's house—Señor Seguín's. He is the one to thank. He will greet you at supper. Is this all?" she asked, indicating the trunk.

"Yes."

"Then follow me and I'll show you to your room." She looked over Caroline's shoulder. "Jake, you can help Mr. Penderton to the room prepared for him on the west hall." She turned, and started back up the stairs.

Caroline followed her to a doorway that overlooked the

entry hall. She stepped inside the room and looked about, impressed with the beautiful Spanish architecture. The white plaster walls and arched doorways made the room feel spacious and cool, despite the heat of the late afternoon. Twisted ornamental iron hooks protruded from the wall by the door—Caroline could only guess at their use. A large cherrywood bed pressed against one wall. Next to it stood a matching stand with a pitcher and bowl for washing. On the opposite wall a small fireplace had been carved. The hearth was clean now and devoid of kindling. A simple, straight-backed chair sat in the corner.

No wardrobe cabinet, no desk.

Well, what did she expect? With her decision to come on the journey so rushed, she hadn't given any thought to where she would stay once she arrived. This was adequate—actually much better than a few of the inns she'd stayed at on the way here where she'd had to sleep on a pallet on the floor.

Victoria stepped to the window and surprised Caroline when she drew up her skirt and removed a small dagger from her garter. She cut a dead vine from the pink flowers on the wide sill, threw it outside and then replaced her knife. She turned back to Caroline as she adjusted her dress.

"You will be staying for the wedding?"

"Y-yes," Caroline stuttered, shocked at the casual display.

Diego arrived with Caroline's trunk and deposited it on the floor at the end of the bed.

"*Gracias,*" Victoria said to him. She turned to Caroline. "I'll let you get settled. Leave your damp things on the chair and I'll have them aired."

"Thank you." Caroline shut the door after her. She leaned back against the wood and closed her eyes, relieved to finally be alone.

What kind of barbaric place had she come to where women had to protect themselves with hidden knives? Hadn't the war taken care of any hostile situations?

And so much for the greeting she had hoped for from Brandon. Apparently their five-month separation had done nothing to ease his anger. Not once had she deluded herself into thinking he still cared for her, but truth be told, she had expected some civility on her arrival. His treatment bordered on rudeness. She shouldn't be surprised, though— the cad had deserted her.

She stamped her foot in frustration which only served to wrap her wet skirt about her legs and send a chill through her. Her teeth chattered, despite the warmth of the day. She opened her trunk and removed a dress. As her hand squeezed the fabric she gasped in dismay at the dampness. Tossing the dress aside she rummaged to the bottom of the trunk. Everything was wet!

It was bad enough she'd had to live without her usual toiletries for the duration of the journey. She'd made a point not to complain, but without her creams and special soaps, her skin had dried out and was darkened from the sun despite her constant use of a hat. Her bonnet, more ornamental and stylish, simply hadn't had the wide brim necessary to protect her face.

She plopped down on the bed. What more could go wrong? She'd wanted to make a good impression with Brandon. Actually she'd wanted to make him regret ever leaving her, to feel a fraction of the pain he'd caused her, although she'd never admit that to him. She sighed and turned her dry hands over in her lap, studying her ragged nails. She'd botched the entire thing already.

Spying her brush on the top of her clothes, she began the task of detangling her long hair. Voices drifted up from outside—one particularly familiar. She walked to the window and peered out, her strokes slowing when she spied Brandon speaking to Jake in the yard below.

She stood there unable to look away, absorbing every nuance of the man. No longer was Brandon the slender, ropy boy she'd met two summers ago at her father's encouragement. Now he seemed so much taller, so much wider at the shoulders. A day's growth of dark beard shadowed his face. The days in the sun had darkened his skin, much like the fishermen on the wharf back home. Odd, how on a man, that could be so appealing, whereas on a woman it was considered base and unrefined.

And his clothes! She was used to seeing him in dark woolen trousers with a waistcoat over his tailored shirt. The way he dressed now a person could not even tell he was a doctor. His buckskin pants hugged his legs, and his butternut cotton shirt, still damp and clinging, fell open at the neck. He looked more the frontiersman or cowboy than the doctor she knew him to be.

She frowned as he pulled a rifle from his horse's saddle boot. The array of weapons on his person was an even bigger change. At his waist he toted a gun similar to her brother's. And in a leather sheath at the small of his back rested a sinister-looking knife, the blade as wide and long as her forearm. She couldn't have been more surprised if she'd seen a bow and arrow in the assembly. What sort of uncivilized place had she come to where weapons were a person's constant companion?

She tried to put the disturbing thought from her mind. She was determined to view this trip—the entire ordeal—as an adventure that would eventually be over. Many people from the east had come to the Texas territory and stayed—women as well as men. Something here drew them. Whatever it was, she couldn't understand it and had no desire to. Her mind was made up. She would stay only as long as necessary and then return east.

Finishing their conversation, Jake mounted his horse and headed down the trail through a stand of pines. Brandon turned to gather the horses' reins, leaning upon a makeshift cane. He glanced once at the hacienda. She pulled back from the window.

Somehow, over the past months Brandon had become a man's man. She saw the difference in the way he held himself. She heard the difference in the quiet tone of authority when he spoke. When he'd carried her across the river, the muscles in his shoulders and arms had tensed firm and unyielding against her. Even now, just thinking of the solid feel of his body made something womanly curl in her center. Her cheeks flamed hot. Definitely a man.

And a stranger to her.

In the next second he turned away and favoring his right leg, led the horses, now free of the Dumont carriage, to the stable.

He'd never told her he was injured. Even her brother, Tom, had neglected to mention it. How had it happened? And when? Surely something so minor couldn't possibly have prevented him from returning home.

He might have denied it in his only letter to her, but all she could believe was that he hadn't forgiven her for her kiss with Jake. What a chain of events that had set in motion. Had she known at the time, she would have done everything in her power to avoid the charity shooting match. She would have begged illness—anything. The kiss had been for a good cause, but even so, she'd given up far more than one kiss.

They would have to talk of it. He had no excuse for his behavior. He was the one who had left her. Oh, his rationale at the time had been honorable enough—to help fight for Texas freedom. But it hadn't been his fight. And she had needed him to stay in Charleston more than he could possibly know. She was the one who should be angry with him. She had every right to be.

She huffed out a breath, trying to release some of her frustration. Well, it wouldn't be forever. She'd be careful to keep that in mind. All she had to do was convince him to come back to Charleston with her. It shouldn't be too hard. He'd always had an ambitious streak and her father had quite a carrot to dangle. Once Jake's wedding was over they could both return to the coast.

Another shiver trembled through her and she moved from the window and began to peel out of her wet dress. She couldn't think about it now. Exhaustion was taking its toll. Her arms and back ached as she poured water into the bowl from the pitcher. At first she couldn't remember why her arms were so sore and then she remembered she'd held Franklin's head above the water for a good amount of time before figuring a way to attach the cloth to the wheel. The make-shift sling had worked, thank goodness. She didn't want to think what would have become of Mr. Penderton if it hadn't.

Dipping her hands into the tepid water she began washing herself off. She wanted to be ready, refreshed and looking her best by suppertime. Mentally she began to prepare herself for the dialogue ahead. She would wait for a private moment. Brandon deserved that much. She would be calm, in control, and would have her say.

That evening, she dressed in her mint-green gown with the deep forest-green fitted bodice. Maria, the maid, had aired out the dress while Caroline napped. Although the bodice was still slightly damp, it was wearable for the evening. She waited in her room for Maria's knock announcing supper, pacing back and forth. Each time she neared the window she couldn't help checking to see if Brandon was in the drive below. She'd gathered that he wasn't staying at the hacienda, but somewhere nearby. The setting sun streaked purple and pink clouds across the sky and she was, for a moment, entranced by the landscape, the rolling hills to the south and the whispering stand of pines to the west.

At a knock, she opened her door and found Brandon standing there. He'd taken time to change into dry clothes—a white cotton shirt and black jeans. He'd also shaved. A wave of deep brown hair, still wet from a quick combing, dipped low on his forehead just above his blue eyes. She'd never seen his hair so long—had not realized it would curl slightly at this length. The sudden urge to reach up and touch a swirl of it on his shoulder annoyed her. She held the urge in check.

Brandon stood rigid. "I trust you had a good rest," he said formally. At her nod, he continued. "They are ready for us at supper."

His closed expression cut her to the quick. Why was he being this way? He wouldn't even look at her. "Brandon?"

The muscles in his jaw worked. "I know we have things to discuss. However, not tonight."

"My appearance has been something of a shock to you."

He didn't answer. Didn't do anything. He was hard as stone.

"What is wrong with you? Aren't you the least bit curious as to why I'm here?"

"Not now. What I want you to do for now is to put on a good face at the table. You should be able to do that much."

She frowned. "Meaning?"

"Meaning that what's between us isn't for anyone else's ears."

She bristled at his criticism. "I know how to conduct myself at a supper party."

His gaze was cool on her. "So I remember—parties and shooting matches in particular. Anywhere you have an audience."

She inhaled sharply. A retort formed on her tongue—

He silenced it with a dark stare. "I don't want to see my friends here caught between us."

Pressure built inside her chest. She hadn't come all this way for a dressing down. Her skills as a hostess in Charleston were sought after. Along with her parents, she'd entertained the governor for goodness' sake. People vied to be invited to a dinner party of hers. "I won't embarrass you, Brandon, if that's what you mean."

"Then we understand each other."

He offered his arm. Of course it was only for appearances—only because propriety dictated it, but after the things he'd just said, she hesitated before accepting his gesture.

"I won't bite."

"You have no idea," she shot back at him. She stifled her urge to continue the conversation. The slow burn in her chest had everything to do with how perturbed she was at him.

But he was right—now, while everyone waited supper on them was not the time to discuss things. She looped her arm through his. The warmth and strength of his muscle radiated into her. Unwittingly pleasure stole over her. She clamped down on the thought, blocking the sensation. It wouldn't do to let her feminine emotions overrule her head where he was concerned. She'd done that once before and look where it had brought her—to this rough, uncivilized territory. It would not happen again—ever.

They descended the stairs and continued down the hallway. When they stepped through the open doorway to the dining room, conversation stopped and every face turned toward her. It was then Brandon extricated himself and moved slightly away. She braced herself against the subtle rejection, refusing to look up at him.

A chair at the head of the table scraped against the tiled floor and an older gentleman stood and bowed formally. "Welcome to my home. I am Juan Seguín." He proceeded to introduce his wife and three children and Victoria's parents before indicating the two empty seats at the table for her and Brandon.

"Mr. Seguín—Señor Seguín, I must thank you for your hospitality," she said.

As she sat, Brandon slid the chair in under her. It was a small gesture and one he'd done countless times in the past. Why then did it seem intimate? Why did the slight tingle on her neck from his breath continue long after he'd taken the seat beside her? He was only performing a gentleman's duty, she told herself. He would have done the same for any woman.

During the dinner courses, Caroline gratefully accepted Franklin's domination of the conversation. He answered many questions from the others, describing his and Caroline's journey and speaking about the estate in Charleston. For her, it seemed her nerves were pulled taut. She noticed every movement of Brandon at her side, whether he picked up his fork or put it down. It was as though an invisible rope bound them together.

The very cadence of his deep-timbered voice the few times he spoke brought a rush of warm memories—the picnics at White Point Gardens, boating on the canal and his tender murmurs when she'd given herself to him in the boathouse. Thank God he'd survived the battles here. Thank God he still lived no matter their strained circumstances now.

Halfway through the meal, she inadvertently dropped her napkin. He reached for it with a swift motion, nearly bumping her head as he returned to a sitting position.

"Thank you," she said, taking it from him.

"You're not eating."

The way he said it, it was an accusation. She couldn't help herself. Although the food looked delicious, the strange spices made her stomach roil. She picked up her fork and moved the food about on her plate, looking for something bland.

The conversation continued without her participation as she tried to disguise her growing distress, looking anywhere but at the food in front of her. She gripped her hands together in her lap, her skin clammy, her stomach rebelling. Brandon had wanted this supper to be as uneventful as possible. She mustn't draw attention to herself.

However, it wasn't long before Victoria noticed. She spoke quietly to a servant who then removed Caroline's plate and brought a custard dessert.

Others at the table noticed, too. "You do not care for the flan?" Juan asked Caroline.

She would make light of it if it killed her. "I'm afraid my stomach is upset from all the traveling. I close my eyes and still feel as though I'm bouncing in that coach."

"A bit of ginger might help," Victoria said, motioning again to the servant. "Maria?"

"No," Caroline said quickly. "I don't want to trouble anyone. I'll be fine by tomorrow."

Jake, sitting across from her, leaned forward. "Caroline, now that we are all together. Tell us what brings you here?"

The challenge in his voice had the others glancing silently between themselves and then at Brandon. The dark look in Brandon's eyes countered any questions they might think of asking, but of course, that didn't stop Jake. Jake had never let etiquette keep him from what he wanted.

"I take it you didn't marry after all," he continued. "Or if you did, it must be to Franklin here."

Her gaze flew to Franklin, who had stopped eating. A frown marked his face. Over the course of the journey, Franklin had become quite dear to her. She would not have him talked about this way, especially by the very man who had asked him to come.

Victoria put her hand over Jake's forearm. "Perhaps now is not the time."

"Now is the perfect time, darlin'," he answered, placing his large hand over hers. "My pardon, Franklin, but we all want to know." He turned back to Caroline. "Last thing we heard was that you were halfway down the aisle at church."

Caroline put down her napkin. Married? How had that news traveled here? No one knew of her proposal outside of her social circle. She glanced at Brandon. Hadn't he said anything to his brother? Why was she being put on the spot like this?

"I take it you don't believe I have come to see you properly married, Jake," she said.

"Just didn't think we were on that good of terms when we parted. I'm tickled pink that you're here."

He said it politely—for the children's sake—she realized as she looked about the table, yet she heard the undercurrent of sarcasm. She hadn't come here to be badgered and she could give as good as she got. "No. I remember you promised me to bring your brother back to Charleston. Apparently that has gone by the wayside."

"I promised to try. I wasn't about to force him to do something he didn't want to do."

Brandon hadn't wanted *to return home?* The words were a slap in the face. He had a future there—his father's practice just waiting for him! More than that—*she* had waited for him! It couldn't be true.

Jake took advantage of her hesitation. "Besides, I wanted him at my wedding."

Awareness of the man at her side had her choosing her words carefully. "After Brandon left—after you both left—for Texas, my parents introduced me to an acquaintance of my father's. For some time they had been anxious to have me meet him. He is a lawyer presently, working with land development in and around Charleston."

"He sounds perfect for you."

She frowned at his comment. "He is a very nice man, but I never agreed to…I don't know how you received word that I was betrothed." She couldn't control the slight tremble in her voice.

Franklin cleared his throat. "I believe that message came inadvertently through me, miss."

He hadn't mentioned that in the four weeks they'd traveled together. His omission cut her to the quick. It spoke volumes of his earlier hope that her relationship with Brandon would be severed by his race to Texas.

"I regret not telling you. I should have said something. You see there was no point in sending another letter. We would be here ourselves in the time it took to get a note across the country. I knew we could straighten things out then. Now."

Her smile felt strained. "Well, of course. It was a wise decision."

Abruptly Brandon scraped back his chair and stood.

"This conversation can wait until later. Miss Benét and I deserve a chance to speak alone first."

Jake narrowed his gaze. "I don't think a few *honest* answers are uncalled for. We all want to know."

"Keep to your own business, Jake," Brandon ordered forcefully. "She's here for a wedding. She's here as our guest. Leave it at that unless she wants to say more."

Those sitting around the table looked to her—waiting. A stifling silence filled the room, so thick that she couldn't move for a moment. She took in a shaky breath, thankful for Brandon's intervention, albeit late. The best thing for now perhaps was retreat. As graciously as she could muster, she stood. "Excuse me. I'm not as hungry as I thought. Thank you for the delicious supper."

Chapter Three

Midmorning of the next day, Caroline joined Franklin in the courtyard. Sunlight dappled through the branches of the large oak in the center of the garden and sparkled on the water in the fishpond. The scent of mesquite from the kitchen fire wafted through the air. Before sitting down, she surveyed the two flower gardens—so ill kept compared to the vegetables growing in the other two plots.

Franklin put aside the legal notes he'd been reading while he sat on the long wooden bench. "You weren't at breakfast with us."

"No," she said, yawning in a most unladylike fashion. She didn't need to explain to him that she'd had trouble sleeping. He'd noticed it often on their overland journey. "I wasn't up for another interrogation from Jake."

"He was rough on you last night. I should have stepped in."

"He was unkind to you, as well."

"Don't trouble yourself about that. I know Jake—how he thinks. He didn't mean anything."

"No, just goading me any way he could to get an answer." She sat down beside him and smoothed out her chocolate-brown skirt. "I asked the cook for a bit of bread."

"You need more than that."

"At noon will be soon enough."

Franklin grunted.

A shout rose from the proximity of the stables along with the startled neighing of a horse. Jake shouted something—and then Brandon joined in, too.

"They're working a new horse," Franklin said, leaning his head back against the short adobe wall that surrounded an ornamental fishpond and crossing his arms over his chest. "Go on with you. I'm not moving so long as the shade keeps me cool. This foot needs another day to heal from the abuse it received yesterday."

"You're sure? I don't mind staying."

Franklin chuckled. "I'm content to stay in one spot today. And I'd think you would have had enough of my company after traveling together for the past month."

"Touché," she said, but there was a friendly lilt in her voice.

His face sobered. "I haven't thanked you for what you did at the river yesterday."

"No need." Her arms were stiff, but less sore today.

"You deserve more than a word of thanks. What you did took spirit."

Spirit. Most people would consider having spirit something to be commended. Her only regret of her actions yesterday was that it had resulted in the loss of her cloth when Jake slashed it free with his knife. She had been embroidering the design during the entire journey. "You would do the same for me. Actually you have—simply by bringing me with you."

"You gave me little choice in that matter, young lady. You were quite persuasive waving that pistol so nervously."

"Well, we're even."

"Not really. But I'll leave it alone for now. You have enough of other things on your mind at present."

She laced her fingers together in her lap, nervous how the morning would progress. "Now that I'm here. I don't know how to tell him."

"It will come to you."

"He doesn't care for me anymore. Maybe that's why he left in the first place—he just didn't know how to tell me." The words tumbled from her, her heart aching with their release. "He never did announce our engagement, even after…" *they'd made love.* "Jake was right last night. Brandon would have returned home after the war if he'd really wanted to. Hearing Jake say it out loud— well, it hurt."

"You don't know Brandon's mind."

"But his actions…"

"You don't know his mind," Franklin emphasized once more, his tone sharp. "He has a brilliant career waiting in Charleston if he chooses. Remind him of that."

She wasn't convinced. "He shouldn't need reminding or coercing. Like Jake said, he should *want* to return."

"He will. Once he learns your condition he'll do the right thing."

She bit her bottom lip as a yearning started in the pit of her stomach wondering what the "right thing" entailed. Brandon could have quite a different concept than she did. "You can't be sure of that. I'm not."

"All you can do at this point is to say your piece. Offer him the job your father has prepared for him. After that, it's up to him."

She picked at the purple flower growing next to her, hardly aware that she held it. "He's changed."

"I warned you that might happen. War can do that to a man. It's not pretty."

"He's so hardened. So distant even when I'm right next to him. As though we never were close to begin with." She rose and paced the short path between the two flower beds. "Honestly, after all this time, I'm not sure how I feel about him anymore."

"I thought that didn't matter."

"It doesn't," she said defensively. Her hand tightened over the small mound of her abdomen. The whole purpose of this trip was to let Brandon know about their child. She needed his help. Desperately. Her parents would not let her return home with a baby and she wouldn't leave it to someone else to raise. At one time, she had hoped—naively—that Brandon loved her. That hope had been dashed when she received his letter saying he wouldn't be coming back to Charleston. No, she didn't have the luxury to believe in love anymore—on her part or his. She just hoped he would help her.

"Talk to him, Caroline. Better for it to come from you directly than to have him discover it from someone else later."

"You're right. As much as I'd like to, I can't control everything."

His gray eyes twinkled. "You try harder than most."

Bolstered to a degree by the man's matter-of-fact attitude, she squared her shoulders and walked to the tall gate at the end of the courtyard. Through the iron bars she could see Diego in the corral, working a horse. He snapped a line lightly on the animal's buttocks as it circled around him. Sweat glistened off the sleek black body of the horse.

At the railing Jake and Brandon called out directions

and advice. Brandon wore the same cotton shirt he'd had on yesterday, the sleeves rolled up past his elbows. A red bandanna circled his neck. His buckskin pants rode low on his hips, along with the gun and belt strapped there. He was Texan today. No trace of the East Coast Charlestonian remained.

She took a deep breath. He looked every bit as handsome this way. She felt a tug deep inside as she looked at him. If only they could go back to the way things had been before. If only…

She pushed the feeling aside. There was no room in her life for such emotions—not anymore. She opened the gate. The iron hinges creaked. With the sound, everyone turned and stared at her. She swallowed hard. "Good morning."

The horse snorted, tossing its head. Jake stared at her a moment and then turned back to the corral. A look passed between the men—some unsaid code. Brandon pulled away from the railing. "Thought I'd take you riding," he said stiffly. "Show you the lay of the ranch."

"I'd like that. I like to ride."

Under the brim of his deep brown hat, his eyes glittered, a midnight-blue against his tanned face. "I remember."

"But not as much now. I'm not quite so adventurous," she admitted.

A soft snort blew from him. "Then how do you account for the fact that you're here?" He studied her briefly. "Where's Franklin?"

"In the courtyard."

"Will he want to join us?"

She swallowed past the sudden lump in her throat. So Brandon wasn't interested in being alone with her—in talking. "He's resting. His foot still bothers him."

"I'll speak with him." Jake pushed away from the corral

railing. "I have some business to discuss with him before the wedding. Now is as good a time as any."

"Father's will?"

"No. Those details can wait for you. I have a few other things I need to speak to him about."

That Brandon even mentioned the will so easily told Caroline the brothers' relationship had indeed changed. In Charleston, he had refused to talk about it with Jake. What had happened to mend the rift they'd once had? she wondered. Things were definitely different between them now.

Brandon led the way to the stable where the pungent odor of straw, horse and leather nearly overwhelmed her. Several of the stalls were empty, but with evidence of use and in need of cleaning. Passing those, she came to another and recognized one of the carriage horses. Brandon gave the gelding a rub and pat on the neck before moving on to the next stall where he pointed out a pretty piebald mare for her use. "This one's lady broke. She'll do for you."

"You've made amends with your brother," she said. "Last night at the table, the things he said were as much for your benefit as for him."

"We're civil," Brandon answered.

"It's more than that."

He threw on a blanket and lady's saddle, cinching them tight. Turning to face her, he paused. "We've cleared up a few things."

"I'm glad."

His jaw tensed, but then he led the horse outside, gripped her waist and helped her mount. He was perfunctory and businesslike, with no lingering touches or glances.

Silently he adjusted the stirrups. His head bobbed close to her knee and the urge to reach out and push back the shock of brown-black hair from his eyes came over her again. She leaned down and raked her fingers through his hair. At her touch, he stilled for a moment, but then continued lengthening the stirrups for her use as if nothing had happened.

Silly. What had she expected? The intimate gesture, so commonplace during their courtship, no longer stirred him. The firm set of his mouth indicated he felt nothing.

Well and good, she told herself. She knew where she stood with him. Any illusions she'd had were just that—illusions. That helped smooth the course for her. The sooner she explained why she was here, the better for all of them. Then she could make plans for her future with a clear conscience.

He untied his horse from the corral rail and mounted.

Taking the lead, half a horse-length ahead of her, he started on the path through the pines. The summer air was warm and windy with just enough humidity to suggest that it was a benevolent respite from the normal amount. At the first bend in the trail, they passed a cabin nestled in the pines. A creek ran a short distance behind the log house, the sound of gurgling water both fanciful and calming at the same time.

"Jake and I stay here," Brandon said.

"May I take a look?"

He shrugged. "It's not much—a small, one-room office."

Obviously he didn't want to show her. "Perhaps later, then." His attitude perturbed her. In Charleston, he'd gone out of his way to accommodate her.

He kneed his mount and they headed toward the meadow beyond the trees. A sweet fragrance intermingled with the scent of pine drifted through the air. When they emerged into the sunlight, Caroline realized what it was—a field of flowers of every hue swayed in the light morning breeze. Bright red phlox dominated the landscape, interspersed with yellow primrose. Every so often breaking the monotony of the colorful carpet a thistle or milkweed bush sprouted up over the shoulders of the other flowers.

She watched Brandon riding ahead of her and wished the tenseness would drop from his shoulders. He held it around him like a shield. She had expected questions and demands for answers today and she was ready for them—anxious even to have the whole matter out in the open and done with. Yet she wondered now if she could penetrate his toughened exterior.

She studied his back, the way he sat his horse as though he were one with the animal. "You've taken to riding easily enough."

He held himself rigid, not answering her, but he slowed his horse and waited for her to move up beside him.

"In Charleston you used a carriage. You said it was more fitting for a doctor."

"Those were your father's words."

"But you used one."

"I prefer to ride."

Why was he being so…so brusque with her? What had become of the young man she'd once loved? The easygoing boy who'd dared the other medical students to swim the channel just to win a chance to take her home. What had happened to him?

He'd become a man, the answer came to her. A man with secrets she no longer shared. A man closed off from her.

"Let's cut to the crux, Caroline. Why are you here?"

He said it so suddenly she nearly jumped in the saddle. She took a deep breath, ready to talk, but something didn't seem right. *He* didn't seem right. She couldn't bare her soul to this…this stranger.

"It's complicated," she said instead.

"Everything with you is complicated," he grumbled. "You leave a swath of complications behind you as long as the Rio Brazos."

"That's not so! You're being monstrously unfair. You want answers from me when you have yet to tell me how you were injured. How can you expect me to be frank and sociable when you bark at me like that?"

He stared at her coldly. "You are the one who came to see me, not the other way around."

"And what a wonderful welcome I received!" She urged her mount forward, angry at Brandon's rude behavior and angry with herself, too. Frustration pounded through her.

They rode on, neither one speaking for a time. Both of them trying to rein in their emotions.

Brandon broke the silence first. "Franklin guarded you like a cougar would her cub last night."

"You noticed."

"I noticed that he is not so bent on your removal from my life now. What happened?"

She darted another glance at him. "Perhaps he realizes he has no concerns on that point anymore. You and I are not the same impetuous couple we once were. We've matured."

"Sometimes that only makes things worse."

He couldn't know how close he was to the truth. "Franklin and I...we just became better acquainted with each other on the journey here. Did you know he was raised in New Orleans?"

"Yes, and you're changing the subject. How did it come about, Caroline? You coming here. I expected Franklin—not you."

In other words, *she* wasn't invited—or welcome. She'd

understood that all along, but to have it said out loud, and by Brandon, hurt. "Can't you just be pleased to see me?"

A scowl crossed his face. "I didn't mean that the way it sounded. It's just that you are a surprise."

"Six months ago, you would have welcomed such a surprise."

"Look, Caroline. The last I heard, you were set to marry someone else. By now, I figured the deed was done. I'll admit it took getting used to, especially after the things we promised each other." His thick, dark brows drew together and for a moment she caught a glimpse of vulnerability before his blue eyes hardened to stone. "Suddenly you show up here and you're not married at all. Seems like you're the one trying to twist me every which way and I'm supposed to accept whatever comes. Well, I don't."

Her piebald danced sideways, sensing the taut emotions. "I didn't realize the news propagated by my parents would extend all the way to Texas, although if I had known I doubt I would have tried to rectify it. At the time I was furious. You left so suddenly, Brandon, and without a proper goodbye! It was as though our betrothal meant nothing to you. Even though you hadn't announced it to our friends, between us it was real—or so I thought." Her eyes burned with tears she refused to shed. How dare he twist this around to be her fault. Hadn't she hurt enough because of him?

He had the grace to look away.

"My parents said you'd abandoned me, that any promises we'd once made to each other were null and void. That is why they tried so hard to dissuade me from waiting for you."

He reined in his horse and stared at her. "You waited?"

"I told you last night that I refused the proposal. Why do you think I said that?" Of course there was more, much more, to the story. She'd loved Brandon and him alone. To give herself to another man was beyond unthinkable—an ugly hypocrisy of the worse kind. "I realized after weeks of not hearing from you that I was being foolish—that I was hoping in vain for you to return. When Tom arrived home bearing your note, I finally understood once and for all that you would not be coming back."

They rode on in silence before Brandon spoke again.

"And Tom? What did he think?"

"He's your friend as much as my brother. He was disgusted with my father for forcing his own agenda."

His jaw tensed. "Your father didn't want me to come back?"

"With the news we received regarding the conflict here, he didn't *expect* you to come back. There's a difference. And he was looking out for me."

"His only daughter."

"You would do the same in his place."

"I might," Brandon conceded. "Can't fault him there."

He rode on another half mile before speaking again. "Tom gave you my note, then."

"Yes," she said quietly. She didn't tell him how the things he'd written had hurt her. How she'd had to harden her heart to keep it from breaking. How she'd lost all hope of ever seeing him again until she'd learned of Franklin's plans.

"So who was this man your parents wanted you to marry? Did I know him?"

"Does it really matter?"

His lips pressed into a thin line before he answered. "Perversely—yes."

"Graham Barstow."

"Barstow! He's ten years your senior!"

The way he said it, as though Graham were horse

fodder, annoyed her. "He's stable, respectable, and charming—and might I add rich."

"And dull as a game of Twenty Questions. You would have been miserable with him."

Secretly she agreed, but at the time, there had been other things to consider—such as Graham's financial solvency and his steadiness. "It makes no difference now. I refused him. It's over." Taking a deep breath, she nudged her horse forward.

They reached the far side of the meadow and Brandon took the lead once more, taking her to the top of a knoll that looked over the river. "This runs along the border of Juan's property. You can follow it until you come to that third hill."

The area that incorporated Juan's land was huge—farther than she could see. "What is that there at the base of those two hills, where the hawk circles?"

"That grouping of trees and boulders?"

She nodded.

"It's a natural spring. Good swimming place."

After all her traveling, a dip sounded heavenly—especially where the water was calm—much preferable to the river yesterday which had tried to tear her apart. "Can we go there?"

"Not now. It's too far," he said gruffly.

"We have all day, don't we?"

She was prepared to cajole him or argue with him, whichever would change his mind, but he turned from her and pointed out the dirt road leading away from the river on the far bank. "Yesterday, you crossed upstream. There."

A flash of white caught her eye. She urged her mount closer for a better look. Far out in the water, draped across a half-submerged tree, her swath of material floated. Perhaps it hadn't been lost to her. "Look! Brandon!"

He studied the river and the distance to the object.

"Can we retrieve it?"

"No, Caroline."

"But…but it's mine."

"Maybe in August when the water level is down—*if* the cloth is still there."

She glanced from his uncompromising face back to the river. "I won't be here in August." If she had her way, hopefully by then she and Brandon would be back in civilization, back in Charleston.

Without waiting for his assistance, she slipped from her saddle and hurried toward the bank. There had to be a way.

He caught up to her at the water's edge and grabbed her elbow. "Now hold on. I know that look in your eyes. Be sensible about this. We've had a bucket-load of rain. The river is too deep and too fast."

"But…"

"It's not worth it."

"It is to me," she insisted, frustrated at his practical manner. "I can swim. You remember what a good swimmer I am, don't you?"

"Not that good. You're crazy to even think it."

He didn't know what that cloth meant to her or he wouldn't say that. She'd spent hours working the stitches.

"What's so important about it anyway?"

When he would have turned away and mounted his horse again, she gripped his arms, improvising—

"If you must know…it is a wedding gift for Jake and Victoria."

"The thing is still not worth the risk involved," Brandon repeated, his voice hardening. "I'm sure it's dirty with mud by now and probably torn, too. Besides it's more than fifty feet out there."

"Bran—"

A twig snapped.

His head jerked up, his gaze sharp as he pulled her close. She held her breath, listening hard. "Was it a deer?"

"More likely a bear," he allowed. "Deer aren't noisy." He released her and took a few steps downstream, studying the surrounding foliage. When he turned back he drew the pistol from his holster and handed it to her. "Stay here. I want to check on it."

He grabbed his rifle from its boot, tore a cartridge with his teeth and poured the powder into the barrel. Then he fished a lead ball from his vest pocket and rammed it into the barrel.

Something had him worried. She was suddenly grateful for the arsenal of weapons he kept with him. Dumbly she nodded her head in agreement.

Chapter Four

He strode away, anxious to put a bit of distance between them. The minute he'd pulled her close, her light perfume had wafted over him. She'd clung to him, seeking protection. She couldn't know what a heady thing that was after all the months of feeling weak, feeling inadequate. How strong it made him feel.

Truth be told, it was hard facing her again. He'd done some pretty selfish things in his life—asking her to wait for him while he went off to fight in Texas territory being the worst. It wouldn't be right to hold her here—not someone like her.

When he'd pointed out that swimming hole a vision of her floating in the water like a water sprite filled his thoughts. He knew her too well. She would have been utterly feminine and tempting. And he'd be hard-pressed to keep his hands off. He'd want to touch her—a lot. That was *not* the direction he intended to take this little reunion. Jake's wedding couldn't come soon enough.

Not more than one hundred yards from where he'd stood with Caroline, he came across recent bear scat and paw prints in the dirt heading away. That didn't disturb him. What did was the campfire in the clearing—recently used since the heavy rains—and near it, the broken hull of a Brown Bess musket—evidence that Mexican renegades still roamed the land.

The sound could have been an animal or a trespasser. He should get back to Caroline. She was defenseless in this country. He turned and started back.

He couldn't have been gone more than five minutes— just long enough to satisfy himself that whatever had caused the sound was gone. Even so he wasn't prepared for the picture that greeted him when he broke through the brush.

Caroline straddled a fallen tree, halfway out over the water, reaching for all she was worth for that damn cloth.

"What the hell are you doing?" he shouted.

Startled she jerked back and then gripped the tree to keep from tumbling off into the river. "Brandon! You gave me a start."

"I gave you a start?" he said, incredulous. "You are willing to get washed away for that rag?"

Her chin jutted out. "It's important to me. And what do you care anyway? It's obvious you cannot stand the sight of me."

"That's not true."

"I'm not stupid. You don't want me here. You didn't want me to come. You're angry at everything I say."

Good grief. Here he was half scared out of his mind for her safety and she wanted to have a heart-to-heart. "Caroline. Come back here. We'll talk when you are on solid ground."

"I don't want to talk. You've been nothing but horrible to me. At the moment, I consider you quite a bore. I—I want to get that cloth."

He would have laughed had it not been for her precarious position over the water. She might be angry with him for what had transpired, but she certainly didn't think him a bore, not if that stroke of his forehead earlier meant anything.

"Caroline! You are going to get yourself killed if you're not careful and then where would I be?"

"Happier, I'm sure."

"You don't mean that."

"You wouldn't understand. Not that you really care to."

"Try me."

She quit reaching then and glared at him. She wasn't scared at all, he realized. She was angry with him and frustrated, but she wasn't scared.

"If you'll hand me a long stick," she said, "perhaps I can reach it."

"Why don't you come back here and I'll get it. My arms are longer than yours. I have a better chance. Besides, I'm the stronger swimmer."

"Even with your injured leg?"

He inhaled sharply. No one talked about his leg. No one. Only she would dare to, he realized. He fisted his hand and then slowly released it, meeting her gaze. "Yes," he said fiercely.

She studied the cloth once more. "Very well." Finally she pulled back.

The tension in his gut uncoiled a degree.

She started making her way, inch by inch, back to the bank. He wondered how she could move in her heavy skirt at all, the way the brown fabric twisted around her legs. He caught a flash of white cotton stockings and shapely ankle in her maneuvering. As soon as he could grab her he caught her waist and set her on solid ground.

The look on her face spoke less of being thankful than of mutiny. Quickly she pulled from his grasp and searched the surrounding ground. Finding a four-foot branch, she thrust it into his hands. "Don't set it loose to drift further downstream."

He was a bit more secure now that she was safe. "I wouldn't dream of it," he mumbled. Stubborn woman. Maybe he didn't know her as well as he thought he did. The thought, at first disconcerting, held a certain appeal. He hadn't expected her to climb out on a tree limb.

He took the stick and shimmied out onto the tree until he was within a few yards of the cloth. As he leaned out, he felt the tree give, bowing low over the water's surface—something Caroline, with her lighter frame, hadn't encountered. It would be just his luck to fall in. The water was freezing and fast enough to take him downstream for some time before he'd be able to make it to the safety of the bank.

"Oh! Do be careful!" Caroline called.

He gritted his teeth and reached again for the cloth, feeling the tree bend perilously close to the water. What was he doing? And all for a bit of fluff. She owed him after this.

He stretched further.

"You're nearly there! Don't give up!"

The tree limb dipped into the current. He hung on as his perch jostled dangerously. Getting his bearings once more, he reached again with the stick, but to no avail. A good three feet separated the end of the stick and the fabric.

He relaxed back onto the tree and sat upright. "It's too far out, Caroline. I'm coming back."

He slid backward on the trunk until he touched the dirt on the bank and stood. They were both ridiculous—her for risking herself for the silly cloth and him for doing the same thing. Luckily nobody else had come upon them. He threw the stick aside in disgust and started for her horse.

She stopped him with a hand on his arm. "I know you thought it was a fool's errand. Thank you for trying anyway."

This time he couldn't ignore the contact. He looked at her long-fingered hand on his arm. His skin tingled where she touched. Her touch had always done that to him. He studied her face—the high-boned cheeks, the sweep of her long, dark lashes against her flushed skin. "I'm sorry it's lost to you. I do remember how well you could swim. You were like a mermaid," he said quietly. "I remember... everything."

His gaze dropped to her lips.

She stilled, her green eyes big.

"How soft your skin was. How good you felt." Somehow, one arm ended up around her waist. "*Especially* how good we felt together." His heart beat faster. The image of her naked on the tarp in the boathouse was burned into his brain forever. He'd tried to eradicate it from his memory, but one touch from her was all it had taken to call it back full bore.

He stared at her full, half-parted lips, knowing how giving they were, how smooth the skin on her cheek felt. His body thrummed with the need to rub his mouth against her there, near her ear where he'd once pressed kisses that drove her wild. He'd been intoxicated with the power he felt at the time, drunk with the thought that he could make her shiver with merely a touch.

He grasped her upper arm. She watched him with a curious look in her eyes. If what she'd been saying was true, if she had denied Barstow and waited for him, she deserved a better man than he. Besides he couldn't just take up where they'd left off before he'd departed for Texas territory. It was impossible. Too much had happened and she didn't know the half of it. The war...the fighting...he'd seen too much. He was a broken man now with nothing left to give her.

He took a steadying breath, holding himself in check. Be quick and to the point, he told himself. Blunt. That was the only way to address this wisp of attraction that wouldn't let go. "You won't like the way this will end—and there is only one way it can—with you returning to Charleston alone. So let's not start anything we'll regret later."

She jerked from his grasp as if stung by a scorpion. Her bosom heaved under the crisp white blouse. "I have no trouble controlling myself. I merely said thank-you. You assumed anything further." She handed back his gun, which he holstered.

"Fine. Then we understand each other."

She was silent while he led the way back to the hacienda. He kept a watchful eye for any signs they might be followed and chose a different path than the way they'd come, skirting the meadow in favor of keeping to the cover of the trees near the small bluff. Safer for her.

He didn't want to worry her about what he'd seen. He wouldn't have given the campsite much thought if it hadn't been for that musket. Renegades—Mexicans who'd fought under Santa Anna. They'd caused all kinds of troubles since the war. He needed to tell Juan and Jake. Soon.

"Brandon!"

Adrenaline shot through him. He grabbed his pistol, ready to protect them both if necessary. At the same time, he heard the bellow of an animal to his left. Fifty feet away in the center of a pond they'd been rounding a longhorn struggled in his prison of mud. The beast's glazed, white-eyed stare spoke of its fear of them, but its weak movements spoke of exhaustion.

"What should we do?" Caroline asked, lifting her reins to move closer.

Brandon released his grip on his gun and grasped the bridle on her horse, holding her mount in place. "Don't go any closer, Caroline. That's not some milk cow from a farmer's meadow. He's wild."

"Then he's too dangerous to help?"

Brandon dismounted and ground-hitched his horse, studying the situation. "I didn't say that."

He grabbed his rope, moving closer. Seeing as how the bull was on Juan's spread made it Juan's. With the mess the rebellion had made of the land and Juan's livelihood, one bull could be a very valuable asset. He glanced back at Caroline. "Stay back out of the way. If he gets loose, he could run in any direction. Most likely will if he feels threatened."

He inched around the stand of cattails, going slow to keep from alarming the longhorn. He was crazy to try this, especially with his injured leg. He'd probably end up forfeiting his good rope—and that's if he was lucky.

His fingers curled around the looped cord in his hand. The buzz of dragonfly wings swooping over the brown, rucked-up water was drowned-out by the bull's occasional thrashing, followed by a snort that vibrated through the water. Lukewarm ripples lapped against his leg and sloshed into his boots. He slowed his movements…slowed his breathing…inched closer…

Glancing over his shoulder to make sure his horse waited quietly, he checked that Caroline had done as he asked and stayed back. His sorrel had lowered his head and munched on the tall summer grass at the base of an oak, whereas Caroline watched in breathless anticipation, her eyes alight with excitement.

He unwrapped a good fifteen feet of rope and checked his slipknot. "Now would be a good time to benefit from all my practice," he mumbled to himself. Vainly he didn't want to look bad in front of Caroline, didn't want her going back to Charleston with tales of his ineptitude, because she *was* going back. The evidence of the renegades had only strengthened his resolve. Texas was too dangerous for the likes of her.

He set his feet as best he could on the muddy pond bottom, then swung the rope overhead once, twice, and on its third journey let it go. It arched over the water's surface and landed around the longhorn's head and one horn.

He stared in surprise. How'd that happen?

Startled, the bull snorted and looked around, for a moment bewildered. Brandon slogged from the water and strode toward his horse. He knotted the rope over the saddle horn just as the longhorn, with one toss of his strong head, snapped the line taut. "Brace yourself," he murmured, for his own benefit as well as his horse's.

The bull thrashed in earnest in a gigantic attempt to be free of the restraining muck, brambles and rope. The stupid cuss didn't have a clue he was being rescued.

Striding forward, Brandon grabbed the line with his hands. "Back!" He jerked on the rope and lent his strength to that of his horse, pulling with all his might despite the way his sweaty hands slid along the rope.

The bull tossed his head and with his eyes rolling wildly jerked Brandon forward into the cattails. He landed, face-first, in the muck. "You pea-brained cow," he said, struggling to his feet with the water and mud streaming from him. "You'd buck a helping hand as soon as a coyote not knowing the difference."

Gripping the cord again, he pulled hard. The longhorn

rose in the water, and then his front legs, coated with mud, thrashed through the surface in an attempt to meet solid ground. Straining against the rope, Brandon whistled to his horse.

The rope tightened further and the young bull moved toward him. The animal struggled again, this time releasing his hindquarters and legs from the mud, but his strength was waning, his attempts to fight the rope weaker. At a sound behind him, he glanced back and found Caroline grasping his sorrel's bridle, urging his horse back.

"It's now or never, you cuss," Brandon said under his breath and strained with all of his might.

The beast thrashed one last time and suddenly all four legs came free of the bottom muck. The animal struggled forward awkwardly, confused at first to be out of the mud. Then, his hooves on solid ground, it stared straight at him.

Brandon swallowed. The stupid thing looked as if it might charge him.

Slowly Brandon stepped backward until he felt the warm hide of his horse at his back. In one quick motion, he pressed the rifle against his shoulder, sighting the longhorn in the crosshairs. "Don't do it…" he murmured under his breath, speaking to the bull. "Not after all that. You're free now. Don't do it."

He had sworn he'd never kill another living thing after the war. He'd been forced to modify his oath—once when a rattler had threatened Juan's daughter and another time when he and Jake had been hungry and came upon a deer. Never a person, though. And he didn't want to kill this bull if he could do otherwise, but there was no way he'd let it hurt Caroline.

He set his stance and targeted the irregular-shaped splash of white on the animal's chest. Mud smeared the area, but it was a vulnerable spot. Then he made the mistake of glancing into the bull's face.

A rivulet of blood trickled from the longhorn's nostril, so similar to the nightmare Brandon had had last night that it unnerved him. Then more blood came until all he saw was blood. It spurted from the beast's nostrils, coating its entire hide and then it kept on spreading, covering the ground in an ever-enlarging circle.

It couldn't be real. It wasn't real. Yet still his heart hammered in his chest. Suddenly he couldn't get enough air. He lowered the flintlock. The trees spun around him. The blood couldn't be real…but he stepped back as it flooded toward him in a thick carpet of dark red.

The animal charged.

Caroline's scream shattered the early-afternoon quiet, and reverberated through his head.

Startled, Brandon reacted without conscious thought. He focused on the longhorn racing toward him and fired. Mud flew everywhere as the beast collapsed at his feet, stunned, but not dead—and still dangerous. In fluid motion Brandon grabbed his knife and straddled the bull's thick shoulders. He pulled back on one horn to expose the soft underside of its neck and slashed its throat. The longhorn twitched once, twice, and then was quiet. As the jugular emptied out, the sticky blood ran in a small stream toward the pond, discoloring the muddy water's edge.

Brandon blinked. The pool of red had disappeared.

His heart thumped painfully in his chest, the adrenaline still churning through him, making his stomach roil. He leaned against a boulder and ripped the bandanna from his neck. *Just breathe. Relax.*

The spells were getting worse. This one happened in daylight. He checked his hands. They looked steady so far.

He didn't want Caroline to be here when the shakes came—and they always did as soon as his heartbeat slowed to normal.

"Brandon?"

Oh, God. Caroline. He mopped the sweat from his forehead and straightening, faced her. "Are you all ri—?"

The look of shock on her face told him otherwise. She looked like she might fall off her horse. He helped her dismount and walk to a small boulder. "Here, sit down."

Her lips were pale where usually they held a soft pink color. He crouched beside her, more concerned when she shrunk away from him. "You look like you're going into shock. What's the matter?"

"The way you handled that knife…like it was part of you. You've done this before, haven't you?"

"I've learned to do a lot of necessary things."

"But slitting a throat?"

He was getting anxious now. She had to leave. "Would you rather I waited for the beast to get up and attack again? I might not have had time to reload the rifle before that happened."

"You had a pistol."

"Which wouldn't even slow such a strong animal." Why was she questioning his methods? He'd gotten the job done.

He stared at the still form of the bull, wishing they hadn't come across it in the first place. "It's never comfortable—seeing something die. I'm sorry you had to witness it. But it's a fact of life. Maybe we saved the stupid animal from a worse fate, like slowly starving—or living."

Her eyes flashed to his, alarmed.

He'd crossed the line, said too much. He clamped his mouth shut. She had to leave.

"I want you to ride back to the hacienda and tell Jake or Diego to come help with the butcherin'."

His terse order bewildered her.

"Now. Not Sunday."

Hurt tightened her face, but she turned toward her horse.

He strode up behind her, grabbed her waist and set her on her mare. "It's just beyond that rise ahead."

She took the reins from him. "You could have been killed. Why did you wait to shoot?"

He wasn't about to discuss the real reason with her. "Just acting like a normal longhorn. I told you they were ornery. I hoped he'd turn away at the last minute."

She opened her mouth to say more but he interrupted. He didn't want any more questions. There wasn't time.

"Be careful heading back. Stay to the trees, not out in the open. And once you're there, stay there."

"Why?"

"Just do as I say, Caroline."

"But…"

He turned on her, suddenly angry at her constant pushing. "Is it necessary for you to challenge everything I say? Everything?"

Her eyes widened and unwittingly she pulled back on the reins, making her mount back-step. Good. He'd struck some fear in her. She might as well learn now that out here she'd have to be tough—and she wasn't tough enough—not with the way she'd reacted.

He turned back to the carcass, shutting her out. He didn't want to scare her with news of the renegades. He just wanted her safe—and away from him.

Resettling his rope around the animal's neck, his fingers started to tremble. He gripped the bull's horns, willing his hands to stop shaking, but it didn't help. He glanced up, hoping by now Caroline was long gone. She was just disappearing into the trees on the far side of the pond.

Relieved, he sank down on a nearby boulder and let the

shuddering overtake him. It always started in his hands and worked its way up his arms. No matter how hard he fought, nothing he did controlled it. He just had to wait for it to pass.

By the time Jake arrived Brandon had scouted out a patch of earth that hadn't turned to mud in the last three days. With the longhorn roped to their horses, they dragged it twenty feet to the grassy area. Jake knelt beside the carcass and whipped out his knife, quickly setting to the business of saving what meat and hide they could before the buzzards found them. Brandon watched for a moment, bracing himself, and then started in, too.

They stripped the hide and then packed the meat into it for ease of carrying. As they worked, Brandon told his brother about the cold campfire and the musket. "We should check on it—at least make sure they've moved on."

His brother nodded. "Is that why Caroline looked so shook up when she found me?"

Brandon paused in his work. Her mood could have been because of any number of things that had happened that morning. "I didn't tell her about the camp. She wouldn't have known."

"Wonder what had her bloomers inside out, then."

Brandon shrugged, keeping his eyes on his task. "This bull charged. That could have done it."

Once the horses were loaded, Jake looked Brandon over and a slow grin came to his face. "You could use a bath."

Suddenly on guard, Brandon stepped back. "No more'n you."

Jake sauntered toward him, a gleam in his eyes. Then he locked arms with Brandon and wrestled him to the water. Brandon fought back, but being of slighter build, he got the worst of it. In the end, they both ended up soaked—

but the tension that had coiled inside him all day like a snake had eased.

Jake yanked him from his seat in the water and together they sat against a boulder to empty their boots of the pond water. Brandon pointed with his chin at the bull's head lying in the grass. Buzzards or coyotes would strip it clean by morning. "Stupid animal," he mumbled. "He didn't have to die. Didn't have the sense to know I was trying to help."

"Yeah." Jake threw him a look. "I've met people like that, too."

It didn't take a genius to figure who he meant. Brandon chose to ignore him and mounted his horse, reining it toward the hacienda.

Chapter Five

After having told Jake where to find Brandon and why, Caroline entered the hacienda by the kitchen door. She was anxious to get to her room. The incident with the bull confounded her. The entire morning confounded her. Something was going on with Brandon—something he did not want to share with her. What had happened to him in the months since he'd left Charleston? What had the war done to him?

The kitchen wasn't empty, bringing her up short. Victoria and her mother watched expectantly while at the table Franklin used an iron bar to pry open a slatted crate. She recognized the crate as one that had traveled with them in the carriage boot.

With a loud creak, the lid toppled off. Victoria reached in and removed the delicate hand-painted teacup, brushing off the remains of straw packing. "These made it all the way here without breaking!" She examined the china with delight and then turned to hand the cup to her mother.

Caroline wondered how in the world Victoria handled the rough-hewn Jake with her petite frame and soft voice.

After Caroline's interrogation at supper last night, just speaking to him a moment ago had unnerved her.

Deep voices in the hall drew her attention. It couldn't be Brandon or Jake. They'd still be busy with the longhorn. These men spoke in rapid Spanish. One voice in particular was unique in its gravelly tone.

Victoria rose and stepped to the arched doorway. She listened a moment before returning. "Men looking for work. There are many drifters since the war. Juan is speaking with them."

"Did the Mexican soldiers come through here?" Caroline asked.

Victoria motioned about the room, her expressive eyes sad. "This was not the way the hacienda looked when I was younger. The *soldados* used the furniture for firewood. Books, too. They left scars everywhere—on the land, and on the people."

Caroline looked about with new understanding. "What a great loss for Juan and his family."

"It has been very hard for them. I don't know if they will ever recover completely."

"Are they happy to be living free of Santa Anna now?"

Victoria nodded. "I hope that preparing for my wedding has helped them look forward and not back." She pulled another teacup from the crate. "*Gracias,* Señor Penderton. I know it is because of your expert packing that they did not break. I will treasure these."

"They are from Jake's mother—an heirloom of the family."

"Then I will treasure them all the more."

He dusted his hands on his pants. "I'll leave you women to the rest."

"*Gracias.*"

After Franklin left, Victoria continued unpacking, talking to Caroline at the same time. "Tomorrow, I am going into town with Jake and my parents. There are a few things I must purchase for the wedding party. Perhaps you would like to accompany us?"

Caroline would rather get things worked out with Brandon. She still hadn't told him the real reason of her visit. "Actually I think I will stay here."

"As you wish."

"It's just that I am so tired of traveling," she hurried to explain. She also had to confront Brandon. She was sure that if she hadn't cried out, that longhorn would have trampled him. "As a matter of fact, I'm tired now. The ride this morning…"

"I understand completely, Señorita Benét. Please. Go. A *siesta* before supper is just what you need."

Caroline left the kitchen and climbed the stairs, glad that the men in the front entrance had gone. Just before closing the door to her room, she heard Brandon's uneven gait on the entry tiles and left it ajar to listen.

Victoria met him in the hall. "What do you think you are doing coming in here soaking wet?"

"Caroline all right?" Brandon replied brusquely.

"She is upstairs. Resting."

A pause followed Victoria's words.

"Should I announce that you wish to see her?"

Another pause. "No. I've got work to do."

Caroline closed the door softly. What was going on? One minute Brandon pushed her away, wanting nothing to do with her, and then the next he wondered if she was all right? She paced back and forth, unable to get the morning ride and Brandon's actions off her mind.

Her clothes had been removed from her trunk and taken

to be cleaned and aired. Thinking it would be good to air the inside of the trunk, too, she opened the lid and wedged a dowel in place.

In the corner a familiar piece of paper caught her eye. She took it out, carefully unfolding it, remembering the day her brother had returned from fighting in Texas and delivered it. She'd been so excited to finally hear something from Brandon, only to fall into despair after reading it. The page was wrinkled from frequent handling and now the indigo ink was smeared across the damp paper. Each time she read it she wished the words were different, that something more would appear.

Caroline,

I hope this letter finds you well. The fight is over. I'm as fit as can be expected. Jake explained to me about the kiss. It happened so long ago I hardly remember being angry, but I guess I was since I am here and you are there. Funny thing…after staring down a musket barrel with a bayonet pushed against my chest, that kiss seems like a pretty silly thing to get all fired up about.

I promised before that I'd be home after Texas won its freedom. I don't think much of a man who breaks his word—so you know I'm not high on my own list—but I won't be coming back. Sorry I can't say more than that. It's best if you forget about me. Take care of yourself.

Brandon Dumont

Caroline's fingers curled into fists as she read the note again. He must have written the letter after the war but before learning of her betrothal—a betrothal that never actually happened. The letter from Franklin must have crossed in the post. If Brandon had thought she was marrying another he probably wouldn't have bothered to write at all.

There was no mention of love, but the very fact that he'd taken the time to write said that he held some feelings for her or else he felt guilty for not coming back as he'd promised. At least at that time he did. He seemed to have gotten over it now.

There was no obvious emotion at all in the note—and this from a man who had been so passionate about helping the sick of Charleston at one time and then helping the Texans in their fight for freedom. He'd been a man of noble ambitions, vision and passion.

Where was that man now? Not once this morning had he mentioned anything about medicine or being a physician. It was as if he'd shut the door on his past life—including her. Then again, there'd been no talk at all about his future, either.

He'd been passionate in other ways, too. She smoothed her hand over her growing abdomen, remembering the warm slide of his body against hers, skin to skin, the one and only time they'd lain together. Passionate, attentive, tender—he was everything she'd ever dreamed of in a lover, in a husband. Her body resonated with the unforgettable sensations.

How would she live never knowing his touch again? At times her chest ached from wanting him even though at the same time she was angry at his abandonment. She would always remember that night even though the memory hurt in ways that cut deeply. Every time she felt the movement of his child inside, she was reminded of him.

She would not give this baby up. She couldn't. No

matter what her parents said. They couldn't be so cruel as
to force her hand. She already loved the little one.

She had to convince Brandon to go back to Charleston
with her. He was her only hope. Finding him so changed
scared her. What would happen now? Could she depend
on him at all?

She folded the note to put it away and suddenly the
damp and worn paper ripped down the center. Her breathing stilled. She stared at the two halves while a strange sensation came over her. She had never been one to believe
in superstition, yet an uncanny sense that this was an ill
omen settled inside.

Chapter Six

~~~~~~

Caroline knocked on the door to Brandon's cabin. A small sign boasted the word "Doc/Médico" painted on the wood.

"Is he expecting us?" Franklin asked, standing beside her and peering through the dirty front window.

"Actually. No. I haven't seen him since the ride yesterday." A fact that bothered her. After waking from her nap, she'd wondered where he'd disappeared.

"Were you able to talk to him?"

She paused in knocking a second time. Franklin was asking about the baby. "No." She tried the door. It opened easily. "Brandon?"

She wrinkled her nose as she stepped inside onto the puncheon floor. "This room needs a definite airing."

There was no sign of Brandon, but she could tell he used the place. A battered desk, the wood darkened with age, sat in the corner. Papers scattered the top of it along with a scale containing weights and measures. A near-empty cabinet stood against the wall shelving two tomes of questionable relevancy to medicine and five amber apothecary jars. Behind one cabinet door leaned a bone saw.

Opening a drawer, she found only long-handled scissors. There were no forceps, no scalpel and blades. Further searching established the absence of a mortar and pestle which were staples of her father's practice. She picked up a strange accordion-type iron implement and held it up for Franklin's inspection. "I wonder what this is used for." Considering the odd assortment of tools in the drawer, if this was all he had—ancient, rusty instruments and few at that— it was a far cry from what he'd worked with in Charleston.

A thick layer of dust and grime covered the top of the cabinet. She rubbed her fingers across and then stared at her fingertips in distaste. Clapping the dust from her hands, she met Franklin's gaze. "He has never accepted sloven-liness in the past."

She wandered toward the back of the one-room abode. Behind a curtain lay two straw pallets for sleeping. Not even a proper bed. After living at the estate in Charleston, how could he stand this for any length of time?

Sighing, she turned back to the center of the room and removed her bonnet, searching for a dust-free place to deposit it. Unable to find any clean horizontal spot, she finally spied a wall peg and hooked it there.

A scraping noise came from behind the cabin.

"Let me go first," Franklin said with a warning in his voice.

Before he could investigate, an expletive shot from the front of the cabin.

Brandon stepped through the door. He wore his buckskin pants and little else. Sweat gleamed on his torso, tanned from the sun and sculpted from hard work. He'd always had a decent physique before and had been a cut above the other men who'd vied for her hand, but now…now Caroline quite had the breath knocked out of her.

Awkward, especially with Franklin standing there, Caroline felt a blush start at her toes and work its way up her body. She really didn't know quite where to look when all she could think was how smooth and strong he looked, and of the one time she'd pressed against that chest quite intimately. She shouldn't look, for heaven's sake, but couldn't seem to drag her eyes away.

Brandon strode into the cabin—*his* cabin, he reminded himself—and looked for the pitcher of water he'd set on the counter. It was no longer there. His head pounded, reminding him he'd overindulged last night trying to keep the dreams at bay. Dreams of the war. Dreams of the nameless Mexican soldiers he'd patched up and ultimately buried. Dreams of Caroline. The liquor hadn't helped. He'd still woken at dawn, his mood foul from lack of sleep.

Turning back he looked directly at Franklin, whose lips pressed together in mute disapproval. Brandon growled another expletive and headed outside. He had work to do today and didn't need anyone criticizing him. And it was too damn hot to put on a shirt.

The impeccably dressed Franklin followed him.

Brandon grabbed the hoe and started in on the garden he'd been weeding behind the cabin. "What? Now you are suddenly her guardian?"

"I have always behaved as a gentleman. Despite my initial feelings, I was never rude, which, by the way, you just were to her. And it wasn't that I disliked her. You simply weren't ready to settle down."

"Didn't want to see me hog-tied before my time, is that it? Franklin, sometimes you are more like a parent to me than Father was."

Franklin studied him with an uncanny look in his gray eyes. "Caroline has grown up since you last saw her. She's been forced to."

Brandon mopped the sweat from his brow with a swipe of his forearm. He hadn't missed that she'd filled out nicely, curving in all the right places—especially her breasts. He'd noticed the snug fit of her bodice on the ride yesterday.

"While you were off playing soldier—"

"I wouldn't call it playing," he interrupted darkly, his voice full of warning. He attacked a particularly large weed with his hoe.

"My apologies. However, you still might try to consider her side of the situation."

"I haven't noticed much of a change. Considering that she finagled her way here, she still acts before she thinks, just like she did in Charleston. I'll bet jaws are flapping on the home front with both of your departures."

"She went to great lengths to avoid any social misstep. For your information, with the exception of one aunt, no one is aware that she's here."

"Guess there's no way of knowing until you return," Brandon said evenly. "You could be going back to a shotgun wedding for all you know."

Franklin's lips twitched. "I doubt it will come to that."

"So tell me—how did she corral you to her wishes? How did she end up coming in the first place? Her parents couldn't have approved."

A rueful smile came over Franklin's face. "I'm embarrassed by my part in it—or rather my lack of foresight."

Intrigued, Brandon leaned his hoe against the cabin.

"I've always prided myself in being more alert than the next man and more adept at anticipating situations before they occur. Preparation is the key, you see, to being ready for anything."

Now he really had Brandon's attention, confused as it was. "What in the deuce are you talking about?"

The man's face was a peculiar shade of crimson. "She stopped the coach and pulled a gun on me."

Brandon's mouth went dry. "What!"

"Impulsive, yes," Franklin hastened to say. "I'll concede that point. But apparently only where you are concerned."

Brandon snorted. Why Franklin was trying to explain away Caroline's action and take some of the responsibility off her shoulders was anybody's guess.

"She'd heard from her brother that I was traveling here for Jake's wedding and she was determined to see you. Taking me hostage was the only option she could think of to get her way. She has a good head on her shoulders. To tell the truth, I was impressed with her gumption."

"You could have been shot!" Brandon could throttle her! She had no experience with firearms and one slight bump of the carriage could have sent the blame thing off. It had to have been a ruse. "She wouldn't have used it. The entire idea is preposterous."

Franklin's brows shot up. "Surprisingly I believe she might have. She seemed a bit desperate in her actions. However I didn't give her much of a chance. She had the upper hand for only a few seconds."

"Long enough to have shot you through."

"In her defense, she aimed at my leg."

"Take it from me—it hurts no matter where the plug ends up," Brandon said sarcastically. But as he thought about Franklin, a man of goodly proportions, held hostage by Caroline, the image suddenly made him want to laugh. He didn't, though—that feeling being as foreign to him now as Charleston was. "The little chit. She does like to have her own way."

"Don't we all." Franklin's lips twitched again. "I found her to be quite resourceful and very determined. As I said—full of spirit."

Brandon had been drawn to that spirit from the first time they'd met. She took such delight in all things. As a doctor, he was constantly pushed against the ugly side of life. A physician's curse. He'd seen so much in his chosen profession of the sick, the sad, the lonely, the dying. Too often there was nothing he could do but provide comfort in place of a cure, a few hours of pain relief in place of eradication of the cause of the pain. While a student it had frustrated him. Knowing Caroline waited for him at the end of the day made it bearable. Believing that she waited while he'd been a captive in prison had made that bearable, too. But now even her presence couldn't hold back the nightmares. Nothing could.

Obviously there had to be more to her being here than just to visit him. If convincing him to return to Charleston was her mission, she'd soon learn that she couldn't have her way this time. He was more than up to the challenge of turning her right around and sending her back to Charleston after Jake's wedding.

Franklin cleared his throat, serious once again. "I came by to let you know that I am ready to go over your father's will with you and your brother."

"Good. I want to get things settled once and for all." He paused, considering. "But I thought you'd be going into town with them today."

"I've had enough of traveling for now. What did Jake say this morning? Ah, yes—the road to Bexar was a 'kidney-crusher.' It doesn't sound tolerable. Besides, I brought the things from Charleston that he wanted for the wedding."

"All right. I'll let him know when he gets back tonight. We'll go over the documents first thing tomorrow morning."

"I also left a small item for you on your desk."

Intrigued, Brandon started back to the house. Then Caroline stepped into view at the side of the cabin and he stopped. She held a tall mug for him. Of course she'd known what he'd been inside for. It didn't surprise him. She'd always been like that—able to anticipate his needs.

"I'll leave you two to talk," Franklin said, and then lowered his voice. "Clothe yourself, sir." He turned and headed down the path through the trees to the hacienda, but not before shooting Brandon another stern look.

Brandon straightened and leaned the hoe against the chopping block. Caroline wore a calico skirt and cream-colored blouse—much plainer when compared to her traveling suit. Probably cooler, too. A thin, deep red ribbon wove through the thick braid of blond hair which she had piled high on her head. Positively festive, Brandon thought, his mood turning surly.

With Franklin's words echoing in his head, he reached for the mug. Caroline's gaze flashed to his and then skittered off to contemplate the distant hills and oaks.

Perversely he enjoyed her flustered attempt not to ogle him. He *wanted* to make her uncomfortable—just like she made him feel by being here. Before she'd arrived, he had been successful at burying the life he'd had in Charleston. He didn't want to remember it. It was his past—part of his life that no longer existed. A life he could no longer return to. Not when the spells came upon him more and more.

And now he couldn't get the image of her holding a gun on Franklin out of his mind. She *was* impulsive—and daring—and…fun. Her unpredictability had been a source of excitement when they'd courted and once in a great while a source of embarrassment. All in good fun, though. With the exception of her braving the tree limb for that silly bit of cloth, he hadn't seen that side of her since her arrival.

"This is why you came inside in the first place, isn't it?" she asked. "For a drink?"

He snapped out of his reverie, gulped down the cool water and then handed the earthen mug back to her. He grabbed his shirt from the chopping block.

"You don't have to."

"Oh, but I do. Franklin made it clear to me I was in the wrong, presenting myself this way." He drew the cotton shirt over his head and shoved his arms into the sleeves. Glancing at her as he laced it up, he continued, "My only defense is that I didn't know you were here."

"It seems unnecessary…considering what has occurred between us."

At her words, a vision entered his mind that was not entirely innocent—her long, silky limbs, tangled in the boat's blanket and around him, her skin glowing in the slash of moonlight through the boathouse window. He shut the image from his mind and forced himself back to the present. "Maybe. But I don't want you compromised. Not in front of Franklin or anyone."

She stared at the ground where he worked as a blush stole over her cheeks and he wondered if she remembered that night as perfectly as he did. Her next words confirmed it.

"I believe in all honesty, I already am." She raised her green gaze to his. "Compromised."

She was right. Yet he didn't regret it. The memory of her had kept him alive, given him hope. Even if it all seemed pointless now. "I won't say I'm sorry for our one night together, Caroline. I can't be sorry."

Her lower lip trembled. "Nor I."

He swallowed hard and chucked his hoe into the hard earth. This line of talking had to stop. He'd clung to his anger like a shield, feeding it, making it grow. As long as he had believed she had betrayed him by marrying so soon after he'd left her, it had been possible to hate her and bury her memory.

But then she'd shown up.

"I wanted to speak to you about yesterday," she said.

He kept his head down, digging at the dirt, bracing himself. A fool would know what was bothering her.

"What made you hesitate with that longhorn?"

"I didn't," he lied. "I waited to see if the bull would turn. When I was sure shooting him was the only option left, I fired. You just happened to cry out at the same time."

Her brow furrowed. "That's not how it seemed to me."

"That's how it was." He straightened and held her gaze.

She seemed on the verge of saying more, but then surprised him by turning away. Walking the perimeter of his garden plot, she crouched to pull a small weed.

"I've wandered through the flower and vegetable gardens back home, but I've not seen the likes of some of these plants."

"They're herbs. For medicine."

She went still at his words.

"Some things I can gather wild—the onions for poultices, the foxglove for heart conditions, but there are others that are not readily available."

"Isn't it too late for planting?"

He shrugged.

A smile tilted the corner of her mouth. "Having a garden

is not something I would have expected of you. At least not in Charleston."

"Victoria is the one who started it. She badgered me about what kind of things I might need and then I found her out here one day, planting. She dared me to keep it going."

"That explains it, then. I guess there is a need."

"In Charleston all I had to do was stop at the apothecary. Here, there isn't one."

She shook her head. "Why would anyone want to live out here, Brandon? I really don't understand how Victoria manages. People lack the basic necessities and then to constantly worry about Indians and drought. It's all so scary—and so unnecessary when you can live somewhere like Charleston."

He took a deep breath. She'd very subtly turned the conversation and he had an idea where she was heading with it. "You wouldn't understand. You've had the life of a princess with a doting father and servants at your beck and call."

She frowned, defensively. "There's nothing wrong with the way I was raised."

"I didn't say there was. Only that you wouldn't make it in Texas. Life here is too harsh."

"And you haven't had difficulty? I realize that you weren't raised with a silver spoon in your mouth, but your family was quite comfortable."

"It's different for a man. We're tougher. We don't need the same trappings that women need. Women always make things complicated."

He didn't want any further complications in his life— no strings from the past to tie him down, no constant reminders of the life he could no longer have. She would leave and be none the wiser that he could no longer doctor.

He just had to keep his distance and make sure she understood things were over between them.

"I disagree." She motioned vaguely toward the cabin. "The addition of a rope bed and feather mattress rather than a straw mat on the ground seems like a complication most men would welcome. And a cookstove instead of a fireplace. Much more efficient. The same goes for medicinal supplies."

"You're entitled to your opinion. I won't argue with it."

She put a hand on her hip. "One of the things I have always admired about you is that you wanted to make the world a better place. You did it in a big way when you took off for this wilderness. Now you are doing it again, in a small way, with this garden."

"Don't deceive yourself, Caroline. Five months ago I might have felt that way. I was an idealistic fool, sure I could make a difference."

"But you ca—"

"Then I came up against Santa Anna's army and saw what happened when men had absolute power over others, or worse—when men were reduced to starving animals. The line vanishes between civilized and savage."

Her eyes were wide as she took in all he was saying.

"Trust, compassion and hope are luxuries a common man can't afford." Brandon remembered the moment the reality had shifted, become clearer—and much uglier. He'd seen it in his nightmares ever since.

"But Brandon…what of your plans?"

He could tell this was hard for her, but he couldn't back down. She had to know the truth. "What I do will have little effect on things. I can't fix the world's problems." Heck, he couldn't even fix his own problems.

Her green eyes clouded over.

"You're disappointed."

"It doesn't sound like you."

"I'm being realistic." His voice sounded harsh, even to his own ears. "It's better that way."

He turned his back on her and continued working, feeling the prickling sensation as she continued to stare at his back.

"Do you mind if I stay?"

Anyone else would have run away at the sourness of his mood. Not Caroline. "Suit yourself."

She brushed the wood shavings from the chopping block and settled herself there. After a while, she began speaking of their mutual friends—the cotillions, the weddings and the ones expecting babies. He thought about stopping her. He didn't want to hear any of it, but her soft, musical voice, the warmth of the sun on his back and the light breeze tickling his skin, converged to lull him into a peaceful rhythm as he chopped the hoe into the hard dirt.

When she began talking about the hospital and the new wing her father was building, Brandon stopped hoeing and straightened. "It's hard to reconcile that life with the one I have now."

"I suppose so, but when you return, it will seem like you never left. Father is looking forward to handing some of his responsibilities over to you. The west wing—just like you wanted."

He held her gaze. "I don't plan to work at the hospital."

"Whatever do you mean? You have your father's practice. His patients are asking for you."

He didn't answer.

"You can't have much opportunity to doctor here."

"I've patched up a few cuts, pulled a tooth or two."

"But I thought…once Jake's wedding is over you would be coming home. You are a brilliant surgeon. This can't be what you want. Not here. Not Texas."

When he didn't answer again, she stood.

Slowly comprehension filled her eyes. "Jake was right, then. You don't intend to return," she whispered. "You don't want to come home. Not to your work waiting for you. Not…not even to me."

The shattered look on her face nearly had him reaching for her. He clenched his fists tight at his sides. She'd come a long way to be disappointed, but there was no getting around it. Things were different now. "No."

She put her hand to her mouth, her eyes brimming with tears. "This is all because I kissed Jake, isn't it?"

He stared at her in surprise as she rushed on.

"It was foolish. I know that now. I should have refused to go through with it, but everyone was watching, expecting me to do something."

"I told you before that I don't have a problem with that." Which of course was a big, fat lie. The thought of that kiss had churned like acid in his stomach for months.

"It doesn't sound like you understand—or that you have forgiven me. How many ways must I say that I'm sorry?"

"Then why did you do it? I thought another girl was supposed to dole out the 'prize.'"

"Abigail Satterly was, but she hadn't told her parents. When they found out, they took her home."

"But why you?"

"It was my benefit—my responsibility. Practically everyone else there that day was married. How could I ask any of them? Besides, you were supposed to win the shooting match. You've always been the best shot."

He grimaced. "Until Jake showed up." He let out a long

breath. "I thought he had turned your head, like he had every other woman there that day. They were fascinated by him."

"I wasn't. Not ever."

He'd been angry with her for so long he found it hard to let go and believe her.

She pressed her fingers to her forehead. "You've obviously forgiven Jake. How is it you can forgive him and not me?"

Her question brought him up short. How could he indeed? "Jake proved a few things when he risked his life to save my hide and get me out of that Mexican prison."

"And I haven't proven anything. Is that what you're saying?"

"You're saying it."

A furrow formed between her brows.

He'd had enough. He wasn't going to examine something that happened so long ago any longer. "Drop it, Caroline. It's over now."

"Then is it someone else? Someone here?"

Lord save him from such a tenacious woman! The question was nearly laughable to him, but he didn't feel like laughing. Caroline had been the only woman for him since the moment they had been introduced on the beach. She'd been so enchanting and so out of reach that he'd wanted to impress her. Along with his friends, she'd teased him until he had swum the channel, surprising even himself, and arrived back half-drowned at her feet. Everyone there had deemed him crazy, but he was the one who had ended up taking her home.

She had changed over the past two years, in spite of what he'd told Franklin. Before she'd been pretty, but now she was beautiful and vibrant. With maturity her allure had deepened. He liked the way she looked, the honeyed hue of her skin, the sun-lightened gold of her hair. Despite what she might think, he liked being with her, liked hearing her voice and the excitement that always surrounded her.

He liked it too much.

He smoothed a crease in her collar. From there his finger brushed against the pale skin of her neck. Her pulse jumped under his touch. He dropped his hand away.

"You're not talking sense. Don't ever think that." His voice came out a growl. There had never been anyone but Caroline, but he couldn't say that. He couldn't give her that kind of power over him.

"Then why aren't you coming back with me?" She moved to stand in his path, forcing him to see her.

"Caroline…"

"Don't you feel anything anymore?" She placed her hand on his chest. "Your heart beats just as strong, just as steady as it once did. Do you feel nothing at all for me? What has become of the man I once knew?"

She stepped closer, circling his neck with her hand, drawing him to her. Her green eyes deepened to the color of the pines surrounding them. Mesmerized by the intensity of her gaze he stood rigid as she pressed her lips against his. They were warm and searching. And damn soft.

Unfortunately he'd been right. With her touch, he wanted more than a sweet kiss and he could feel himself going down for the count. He moved his hands to her waist and gripped her skirt, his fingers tangled in the material. He tried to remember his earlier resolve and restrain himself. He lasted about three seconds—a paltry attempt at resistance—and then gave in, wrapped his arms around her and pulled her close.

He deepened the kiss, sucking in her full lower lip before centering his mouth on hers. She molded her lips to his, soft and pliant, and tentatively touched her tongue to his. Heat flooded through him. He fisted his hand in her hair, destroying her fancy style and not caring one whit. Pins dropped to the dirt as her braid loosened and uncoiled down her back. Her touch ignited him beyond anything he'd been prepared for. His breathing came harder, faster.

"You'll come back with me, Brandon. I know you will."

Her words crashed through his mind, rocking him. He pushed her away. "You're playing with fire, Caroline."

He took a step back and raked his fingers through his hair feeling utterly disgusted with himself. His stomach churned. Acid washed up in his throat. He was tense with unsatisfied desire and the feelings she stirred up. He'd been successful at burying most of them and he'd promised himself he wouldn't allow them back to the surface no matter what she said to him.

"The man you once knew is gone. You can't bring him back."

She covered her swollen lips with her fingers.

"I just had to try," she mumbled.

He stared at her. He didn't like being manipulated. "Try? What are you trying to figure out?"

"It's foolish. I understand that now."

She had to understand once and for all that he wasn't ever going back. He gripped her upper arms, squaring her to him, forcing her to meet his gaze. "I won't be going home with you to Charleston. Believe me when I say there's nothing left for me there. Be satisfied with that." He took up his hoe for balance and strode into the cabin.

Standing there on the other side of the closed door, he waited for the tightness in his chest to ease and listened for the sound of her footsteps on the path to the hacienda. He looked around the small cabin—his makeshift office. It was all he could handle anymore. He'd told her he wouldn't be going back to the life waiting for him in Charleston. He snorted. That was a lie. The truth was he couldn't go back. The spells were getting worse. He couldn't stand to see his friends and his father's colleagues look on him with pity. With the shakes, the hallucinations, he didn't know how long he'd be able to practice—or even more importantly—how long he'd be of sound mind.

The thought of Caroline watching him while he came apart was unbearable. Just listening to her talk about the parties and cotillions—all the things that made life worth living to a woman like her—had embedded the realization even deeper. He couldn't give her any of that—didn't want any of that now. It was best for everyone concerned that he did not accompany her back to Charleston after Jake's wedding. If he were to go with her, sooner or later she'd come to hate him.

Chapter Seven

Long after Brandon had disappeared around the front corner of the cabin, Caroline stared at the path he'd taken. Now she covered her face with her hands as a strangled cry escaped. She'd ruined everything—in one impetuous moment. Her nerves on end, she drew in a shaky breath.

"That didn't go so good."

She spun around to see Jake leaning against a tree. "Wh—what are you doing here? I thought you'd gone to Bexar with the others?"

"I can see that," he drawled. "Just getting a late start. Kind of glad, though. Would have missed the show, otherwise. You do tend to do things in a big way, Miss Caroline."

She clenched her fists at her side, mortified at what he'd witnessed. "I had my reasons."

"You expecting to wrap him around your finger again? Is that your reason?" His voice lowered and she felt rather than heard the underlying tone of anger. "Can't you just accept the fact that he's his own man now and not someone you can push around?"

"You don't know what you are talking about," she said. She had wanted to do anything to shake Brandon out of the limbo he'd created for himself. Anything that might bring back the man she'd once known. "I had my reasons," she repeated.

"You always do," Jake said.

She inhaled sharply. It was true she had not gotten on well with him from the start but Jake obviously cared about his brother. Perhaps she could enlist his support despite his animosity toward her. "Please, for one moment, put aside your negative feelings for me and try to help."

"Why should I do that?"

"Because something isn't right, Jake. Something has happened to him."

He pushed off from the tree and sauntered toward her. "Of course something has happened to him. He survived a damn war. You don't go through something like that untouched. For all he's been through, he's doing fine."

"I don't think he is. I'm…I'm worried about him."

Jake's brows drew together. "Everything was great until you showed up."

"If you're saying that I'm the cause of his problems…"

His eyes were hard. "That's exactly what I'm saying. You're always wakin' snakes everywhere you go."

"I just wanted him to come back to Charleston. It's his home. All his friends are there. I thought he'd want to come back, too."

"He has friends here now."

Jake wasn't going to help. That much was obvious. He was as stubborn and opinionated as Brandon—even more so. "He has a much sought-after position waiting for him—working with my father."

"Texas needs doctors same as Charleston."

I need him, too, she wanted to say, but held her tongue. Jake studied her.

She plucked up her courage to try once more. "His talent is wasted here. He's a skilled surgeon, not a back-country rustic. He belongs where he can do the most good, take care of the most people."

"Which, of course, can only mean in Charleston." Jake snorted. "And with you. Lady you are one stubborn woman. *You* are the one beating him up."

"That has never been my intention. I want what's best for him. I…I care about him."

"Then you shouldn't have come—on both counts."

Hurt by his brash words, Caroline stared numbly at him, unable to formulate a sentence.

"Médico! Ayúdame!"

A Mexican woman rushed into the clearing, pulling a young boy behind her. One look at his tearstained face had Caroline putting aside her worries with Jake. "He's inside," she said quickly and led the way.

The boy held one hand gingerly as blood dripped from his thumb. A cactus needle? Snakebite? Caroline ran ahead to open the door, surprised when Jake scooped up the boy in his arms and followed her inside, depositing him on the exam table in the center of the room.

"Got a customer for you, Doc."

At the sudden commotion, Brandon rose from his seat at his desk. He knew the boy—Jaime—a son to one of the cowboys on the ranch. At ten years of age he was always getting himself into scrapes. What this time? He was about to ask what was wrong when he saw the hook protruding from the boy's thumb. His shoulders relaxed.

"Jaime, fish aren't interested in young boys for bait."

Jake grabbed up a canteen hanging on a peg in the

corner and headed for the door. "Looks like you can handle this on your own. I'll see you when I get back from town."

Brandon grunted, intent on examining Jaime's wound. He understood Jake's reasons for a quick departure. As much as his brother had been forced to doctor in the war, he'd only done it to stay alive. It wasn't something he wanted to do.

Brandon turned Jaime's thumb slightly, examining the type of hook and how large the size of the barb. The iron hook curled into the plump padding of the boy's thumb. Brandon trimmed off the piece of twine and then reached for his pliers. Jaime's dark eyes widened at the sight. A tremor ran through his thin body. "No! *Señor!* No!"

"It's the only way if you want it out," Brandon said to the boy, knowing he understood only half the words but probably the meaning was clear. To his mother, he said, "You'll have to hold him."

The woman moved in and did as he'd asked. It was then he noticed Caroline. She stood a few steps back, her eyes large, staring at the boy's wound. "You should go back to the house."

"P-perhaps I can help."

He took in her stance—her arms wrapped around her middle. She looked ready to bolt. "It won't be pleasant."

"I can, Brandon. I assisted my father on occasion. I'm not the least squeamish."

The pallor on her face said otherwise. He shook his head. He didn't need two patients. "I won't need any help. It's a simple extraction."

"But—"

"Don't argue with me on this, Caroline. I'll come up to the house soon. I promise. You're just making Jaime wait that much longer."

Her jaw clamped shut and her expression turned mutinous, but she headed for the door.

He relaxed slightly. Why had she even tried to stay? She didn't have the stomach for surgery—even something this mild. She was a society princess after all and certainly too delicate for this.

He was glad she had finally left. Such a small thing as an imbedded fishhook shouldn't fire up a spell, but he couldn't anticipate them anymore. They happened at the strangest times. It was just better all around if she wasn't here to see one.

He turned his attention back to Jaime and his injury. The tissue around the iron had already started to swell, the edges reddened. Blood dripped onto the floor. A wave of dizziness washed over him. The edges of his vision darkened. He couldn't let it happen. He dragged in a breath and steeled himself against the feeling, forcing himself to concentrate.

"Do you have a strong hold?" he asked the boy's mother.

She grasped the boy firmer in response, watching Brandon closely. A stoic resolve settled on her face. They both knew what was necessary.

Brandon gripped the pliers again. At his motion, every muscle in Jaime's small body tensed. Grasping the dull end of the iron hook with the pliers and working as carefully as possible, Brandon pushed the sharp, barbed end until it pierced through the skin and appeared again. Dizziness threatened as a vision came to him. Not the small stab of a fishhook breaking the skin, but the grotesque point of a bayonet emerging through flesh. He swallowed hard. He had to concentrate, had to finish this. His hands began to shake.

Jaime screamed and jerked his hand, his body stiffening. Tears streamed down his face.

Brandon shut out the sound, focusing on his work.

Using clippers to remove the barb, he withdrew the hook rapidly, then staunched the trickle of blood with a fresh cloth and applied pressure. Great hiccup-sobs racked the boy's small frame. Brandon waited, letting the pain ease, giving Jaime a chance to calm down. Giving himself a chance to calm down. He looked up and saw tears in the mother's brown eyes.

Abruptly he turned away, unable to bear her emotions on top of his own. She shouldn't share in her son's pain like that. It didn't serve a purpose. It didn't absorb and lessen the boy's pain. It only made her hurt, too—and ache all the more. He wondered if she would have nightmares like him. Maybe not over something this small, but then it was worse when you loved someone. Worse all around.

He took a deep breath and walked to the stove. Dipping a finger into the pan of bacon fat, he slathered it over Jaime's wound and then wrapped the thumb snugly with cloth. He took the piece of twine he'd cut from the hook and tied it around the bandage to secure it.

The boy's crying slowly subsided. "It'll be sore, but should heal in the next few days," Brandon said. He wasn't sure how much the boy or his mother understood.

"*Gracias,* Señor Doctor." Jaime's mother squeezed his hand gratefully as she dropped a leather pouch into his grasp. He murmured something—unsure what exactly it was—and waited until they left.

Only then did he toss the pouch on his desk and sink into his chair.

The shaking had started sooner than before—in the middle of the operation. He had suppressed it a small amount, but now he could feel a tingling sensation overtaking him. He tried to ignore it and busied himself, loosening the cinched top of the pouch to find it filled with ground corn. Still the tremors came. He pressed his palms to the desktop, trying by sheer will to make them stop. When they didn't, he watched his hands vibrate, half in medical fascination and half in horror. "No!" he ground out. Unable to control them, he linked his fingers and dropped his head in his hands.

How long would he be able to practice? The spells worsened each time he did anything that involved blood. With Jaime's wound, the amount of bleeding had been minimal, almost nonexistent compared to the soldiers he'd doctored and still he'd had a reaction. Soon he wouldn't be able to hide the spells. When that happened, no one would trust him to care for them or their loved ones. He'd be a laughingstock, the butt of jokes, the doctor who couldn't stand the sight of blood. What the hell would he do then?

A shadow fell across his desk and blocked the sunlight streaming through the window. Immediately he shoved his hands under the table. He knew without moving it was Caroline.

What was she doing still here? How much had she witnessed? he wondered. How much would her face and her eyes reveal when he looked up? "I thought you'd gone."

"What just happened, Brandon?" Her voice was low, cautious—curious.

She stood in front of the desk now. Instead of the disgust he'd anticipated, concern filled her eyes. Well, he didn't want pity, either. Especially from her. He shoved the sack of cornmeal aside. "Pay isn't much here. As you can see, not like in the city."

"That's not what I mean." She stepped closer. "It was the same as with the bull yesterday, wasn't it?"

"The injury? Of course not. It was a simple operation. I'm sure if the boy's father had been nearby he would have pulled out the hook. Women are easily sickened by such things. That is why I asked you to leave."

"You forget that I am the daughter of a surgeon," she said, frowning. "Although, I'll admit my stomach has been squeamish of late. You did a fine job removing the hook."

"So glad you approve." The moment the words were out he realized how petty they sounded. It wasn't like him to hide behind sarcasm. He'd like to say she was making him crazy, but it wouldn't be true. It was the spells and the nightmares that were pulling him toward insanity.

Her eyes clouded.

"My apologies. That was unfair. I learned a lot from your father, as I'm sure, growing up at his side, you must have, too."

"No, Brandon. You are purposely avoiding my question. Why?"

He didn't answer. Why couldn't she just let it go?

"I want to know what happened to you just now. Why were you shaking?"

He'd always respected her tenacity in the past, but then, it hadn't been directed at him. "Reaction to an empty stomach I suspect. I ate at daybreak and then worked all morning in the garden."

He stood and, leaning on his cane, made his way to the pantry. "I'd offer you something, but I'm sure you've eaten at the hacienda. What I have here is not adequate fare for you."

He felt her staring at his back as he cut a thick wedge of cheese from a half-eaten wheel. He was being a lousy host, but at this point he didn't care. He just wanted her gone. Now.

"Before the boy and his mother interrupted…"

"You misunderstood," he lashed at her. "The boy and the mother were not an interruption. They are my job—such as it is," he said harshly. "I don't have the luxury of scheduling my patients like your father does. This is Texas. I take what walks through that door."

She recoiled as if he'd hit her.

"I have some things to attend to today." He turned away from her and shuffled through the few papers on his desk. He didn't know what he looked at, didn't know what the papers said, he just couldn't look at her anymore. He felt her gaze on him, felt her censure with every movement he made. A cold, unfriendly silence stretched through the room.

"I'll just leave you to your meal, then." She plucked her fancy straw hat from the wall peg. "I'm sorry to have intruded."

Always the perfect response, he grumbled to himself as she left. His stomach churned with acid. Anger swelled inside—anger at her for intruding when he didn't want her to, anger at the betrayal of his body and the spells and hallucinations he couldn't control, and anger at himself for wanting beyond anything else the life he had once had with Caroline and knowing it was forever out of reach.

What vile things was she calling him now? he wondered. She couldn't get away fast enough. And wasn't that precisely what he'd been seeking? To have her leave?

Then why did he feel like such an ass?

Because he was one.

He picked up the cheese, stared at it and then threw it at the closing door.

Frustrated beyond rational thought, Caroline couldn't stand the idea of returning to the hacienda and facing Franklin or Juan. She entered the stable. Of the few horses left in the stable, the piebald from her ride yesterday stood waiting. She saddled her, anxious to get away. She had to leave this place and go somewhere to think. Thankfully the rest of the family had left for town. She wanted to avoid running into Jake or Victoria right now. She didn't feel like talking to anyone.

Something was wrong with Brandon. Something he didn't want her to know—maybe didn't want anyone knowing. He had frozen again while examining the boy's injury. It was barely discernible unless one watched closely. The episode was similar to the one he had with the bull, but at least this time it wasn't as dangerous—he didn't have a beast bearing down on him—and it didn't last as long. Was she the only one who saw it?

Jake's cruel words came back to her. If he knew anything about what Brandon was feeling or going through, he wasn't going to share it with her. Neither brother wanted her around. She upset their routine—challenged the areas they wanted left alone. And she was an outsider. Perhaps Jake was right. Perhaps the best thing for her to do was to leave.

Why, then, did she feel like she was deserting Brandon? At the errant thought, she sank down on a low bench. What was wrong with her? She shouldn't care anymore. But plain as day she'd argued with Jake and told him she did care. Was it just as a concerned friend?

Berating herself under her breath, she fixed her hair, haphazardly combing through the strands with her fingers and then plaiting it in one long, loose braid.

Although she'd acted on instinct and impulse, the reason for the kiss had been twofold. First, she'd wanted to shake Brandon up. She thought he'd lost all ability to feel anything for anyone. How wrong he'd proved her! Underneath his diffident attitude lay a sleeping cougar. She touched her swollen mouth. Her lips ached from his kiss. And, heaven help her, she had wanted more. Remembering the strength in his arms, the flare of desire in his eyes… Why, if he hadn't held her, she'd have swooned. Which wasn't like her at all. She blamed her heightened senses on the child she carried. His child. Her reaction couldn't be because she still loved him, could it?

Which brought her to the other reason she'd kissed him. She had wanted to know if a spark for him still existed. She had been so angry when he had headed off to help the Texians, and then again when he hadn't returned after the battle. She didn't *want* to care for him, didn't want to worry about him. He'd left her carrying his baby with nary a care for her. How could she even think or worry about him now when it was her own life that was in such turmoil? Her attention must be toward her own future and that of her baby. Brandon didn't deserve it and yet…and yet he was her baby's father, the man she had loved. How could she ignore what had changed him so?

She flipped her long braid back over her shoulder and stood. Leading the mare outside to the corral fencing, she found comfort in the beast's gentle plod, the sound of hooves against straw and dirt, the steady puff of warm breath on her shoulder. A ride would do her good. An hour or so at most and she'd feel better—perhaps then she could muddle through this situation more clearly. Using the low railing as a step, she mounted. With a last look at the path through the pines toward Brandon's cabin, she reined the horse away from the hacienda and urged it into a gentle lope.

Chapter Eight

Jake strode purposely into the cabin and came to a standstill at the sight of his brother holding a new physician's bag and stethoscope. "Where'd that come from?"

"Franklin brought it from Charleston."

With a grunt, Jake acknowledged he'd heard while at the same time surveying the room. "Is Caroline here?"

"She's at the house."

"No, she's not."

His brother's tone caught Brandon's attention. He stored the stethoscope in the bag. "Why? What's going on? And what are you doing back? I thought you were going to Bexar."

"We got as far as the Svendsons'. Their barn was burned last night. We thought it best to get back here and warn Juan, especially in light of the things you saw yesterday."

"Any signs of who it was? Comanche or the renegades?" He sucked in his breath at the thought. If Comanche were causing trouble, nothing would be left of Lars, and Ilse and the boys would be gone—taken.

"Renegades. There were signs of a struggle at the house."

"Lars?"

"Everyone is all right."

Brandon exhaled and followed as Jake headed to his sleeping pallet. Haphazardly Jake began stuffing his few belongings into his canvas duffel bag.

"What are you doing? You think they're headed this way?"

"Don't know. But you did say you saw something at the river."

"Near the crossing."

Jake rolled his straight razor, soap and comb in a cloth. "I'm staying at the house from now on. I don't care if I have to sleep in the pantry, I'm not leaving Victoria's side."

Brandon thought about Caroline in the house and whether he should do the same. Then he remembered their kiss. She was safer with him *out* of the house if that kiss was an indication of his self-control.

"We need to alert the neighbors," Jake continued. "Let them know the situation. Diego has already headed south. Damn! I shouldn't have let Victoria talk me into going to town. I hate going there. My gut has bothered me since I woke up and now this."

"At least you found out about the Svendsons. If trouble comes, we'll be prepared."

Jake rose and slung his duffel over his back. "They lost a horse and were scared pretty bad. Lars is taking his sons and Ilse into town to her sister's house for a few days while he cleans up the place."

Brandon only half listened as a new urgency came over him. "But you said Caroline isn't at the house?"

"No. How come she isn't here with you?"

He groaned. "Because I was an ass."

Jake pressed his lips together. "Well, you better find her. She shouldn't be on her own."

Brandon barely heard his words. He'd already grabbed

his cane and hat and was out the door, striding toward the hacienda. Of course she was there. She was probably burrowed in the library or in her room, nursing the cruel remarks he'd thrown at her. He'd been rough on her. The more insistent she'd gotten that he answer her questions, the deeper he'd dug his heels in and refused.

At the house he came no closer to finding her. She wasn't where he'd thought she'd be. No one knew where she'd gone. He strode back outside and surveyed the surrounding woods and the meadow. She couldn't have gone far. She had a lousy sense of direction. It was something he'd teased her about in the past, but she was smart enough to know not to wander off. Then again, in retaliation to her pressing his sore points, he'd made her as frustrated as he'd felt. It would be just his luck that he'd riled her until she took off without concern for her own well-being.

If anything happened to her, because of him…he'd never forgive himself.

In the stable, one of the horses was missing—as well as Victoria's saddle. All right, he'd have to track her. He'd learned a few tricks from Jake. Unfortunately if he could track her, so could the renegades. Moving faster, he bridled his mount.

"Señor Médico!"

He turned from cinching the saddle. The cook ran up wringing her hands on her apron.

"I don't have time, Maria. What is it?"

"You ask for Señorita Caroline? She take horse. Go." Maria pointed toward the foothills in the west.

"When?"

"A mediodía."

"At noon!"

"Si, señor."

She'd been gone two hours! His heart pounding, he mounted his horse and kicking him swiftly in the flanks, set him galloping from the stable.

He tried to second-guess where Caroline would venture, keeping his eyes open for newly trampled grass and hoof-prints. Across the meadow and just before the mud pit he veered north and headed toward the river. She'd been angry enough and frustrated enough that she just might try getting that rag from the water again. He came to the tree she'd shimmied. The cloth was still caught against the rock in the middle of the river. There was no sign of Caroline. No hoofprints. No sound but the water rushing over the rocks.

The scent of wildflowers and Mesquite brush permeated the blistering-hot afternoon. A barely nonexistent breeze stirred the leaves on the trees. He removed his neckerchief and mopped the sweat from his forehead, wishing he had time for quick dip in the river.

Suddenly he knew where he'd find her. The thought paralyzed him. She'd be at the pool. He turned his horse toward the hill country. What he would say when he found her, he didn't know. He'd treated her arrogantly in his hurry to avoid talking about his spells. She could be exasperating in her drive to get to the truth of all things and he hadn't been in the mood for her questions. Yet as short-tempered and condescending as he'd been, she hadn't backed down. She'd simply left, picking up that fancy bonnet of hers and sweeping out the door with a graceful flourish like she was some grand dame in a gentleman's supper club and being asked politely to leave. He had to admit, he did enjoy the color that had flushed across her cheeks when she got in such a state. The sooner he found her, the safer she'd be.

He dug his heels into the sorrel's flanks, spurring him into a gallop across the open grassland.

The scrub oaks thickened interspersed with cottonwoods and a pine or two. Rocks and boulders lay hidden in the tall grass. He broke through the oaks that lined the clear water pool. Across the water, he spotted something white against the backdrop of the green foliage. He reined toward it, urging his horse into a gentle lope. Another flutter—blues and reds and yellows—material, he realized, and then recognized Caroline's skirt and blouse draped over a low bush.

He surveyed the perimeter. The trees crowded close, but there was no sign of her.

Flat limestone banked the pool on three sides. He walked his horse to the edge. The water was so clear it was possible to see fifteen feet down to where the large rock slabs dovetailed together. A few contented trout circled lazily along the bottom.

He pulled away from the edge, telling himself he hadn't worried about her drowning even though his chest was tight for some reason. Like she had said—she was a strong swimmer. It just eased his mind to know she wasn't down there.

"Caroline!"

She couldn't have gone far—unless the marauders had already come across her. The thought of what could happen to her in a situation like that made his gut twist. He had to find her!

"Brandon? What is it?"

At the sound of her voice, he reined his horse back around. Fifty feet away, she rose up on one elbow from lying on a white slab of rock. She'd been so still, so pale against the stone formation, that he must have missed her the first time he looked.

His heartbeat settled into a quieter rhythm. She was obviously all right, obviously safe. Thank God. Dismounting, he strode to her and dropped to one knee.

She'd stripped to her cream-colored chemise which was still damp from a dip in the pool. Her eyelids were heavy with sleep. The nearby water seemed to sparkle in the depths of her green eyes. Blond hair hung in damp, wavy tendrils to her waist. Did she have any idea how beautiful she looked? He shook that thought from his mind. The important thing was that she was safe.

"What is it?" she repeated softly. "What are you doing here?"

I was worried about you, he thought to say and then didn't.

"It's you." His tongue stumbled over the simple words. He removed his hat, fingering the brim as he sent up a prayer of thanks that he'd found her and she was unharmed. He tried again. "You've been swimming."

"I didn't mean to fall asleep—it was just so peaceful here. So peaceful and warm."

He hadn't seen her this content and relaxed since she arrived. Maybe he should have brought her here sooner. His mind balked at the idea. Since her arrival, he hadn't been much in tune with her needs, only his own and the need to keep her as far away from him as possible. "You do know that snakes like to sun themselves on big warm rocks."

"Are you trying to scare me? Or are you calling me a snake?" Her lips curved upward. "Or yourself?"

He fingered the damp material on her shoulder. His knuckles brushed her soft skin. A shiver went through her. Could it be from the light breeze or was it his touch? It used to be his touch. "Myself," he murmured, remembering.

"I didn't mean to cause any worry. I was upset about this morning, about what happened. I just needed time alone. Away from the hacienda."

Away from me, he realized dismally. He'd succeeded, then.

A slow smile lit her face. "Can you believe that I lost my way only twice?"

"Proud of yourself?" he teased, again remembering how easily she could get turned around in a new area of Charleston. The fact that that deficiency hadn't stopped her from traveling across the country registered. Maybe she was braver than he'd given her credit for.

"Franklin told me about the rivers here."

"Did it help?"

"Not really. I'm still dismally inadequate without familiar streets."

"You shouldn't have ridden so far from the big house without me." His fingers brushed her skin once more. "How would you have found your way back on your own?"

"At the time, I didn't want to think of that."

"Irresponsible of you." His voice was gruff, but even he heard the touch of fond exasperation in it.

"I know. Chide me if you must, but I had to think. There is something I must tell you, Brandon, and I'm not sure how to go about it."

She looked vulnerable all of a sudden and unsure. How unlike the woman he was used to. It made him want to reassure her—comfort her. What was she doing to him? If he followed the tug he felt inside, it could only lead to problems. He drew his hand back. "Go on."

"I wanted to hate you," she whispered. "You have no idea what happened when you left."

She was talking about Charleston, he realized.

"You abandoned me when I needed you most. I—I do hate you."

"I can't change what happened."

She caught his fingers and drew them back to her, pressing his palm against her slender neck, holding his hand there and acting as though his touch was the most precious of things to her.

She didn't know, she couldn't know, what his hands had done. She wouldn't want them on her if she knew. Still, he couldn't drum up the strength of will to pull away again.

Her eyes held tears when she looked at him again. "What was so important that you had to leave?"

He studied her face. "I had to prove myself."

"To whom? Me? Jake?"

He shook his head, thinking back to that time when he'd left for Texas. "To myself."

"You? I don't understand."

Brandon sighed and sat down beside her. "Jake came home, strong and tough from living off the land for so long. Next to him, I felt like a green schoolboy. In spite of all my book knowledge and position as a surgeon, I couldn't measure up in his eyes. I saw the way women looked at him, like he was the answer to their dull lives. Everywhere we went, they vied for his attention. I guess I was jealous."

"Have you then? Proved yourself?"

He thought about that. Proving himself in battle had quickly changed with the need to survive. "Yes, but it's behind me. I don't want to talk about it. Not here. Not now."

She dipped her head and rubbed her cheek against his wrist. "I never looked at Jake that way."

Silvery tingles raced up his arm.

"Caroline…" he breathed. "Don't…"

But he couldn't finish his thought. His body thrummed

with feelings he'd long thought dead—feelings she'd awakened with her kiss. He moved his hand down, sliding his fingers slowly under the fabric's edge to the sloping curve of her breast.

Her breathing hitched. She leaned toward him and imperceptibly her breasts strained against the cotton fabric—a silent invitation for him to continue.

He was trespassing. He didn't deserve this. Yet he closed his eyes, concentrating on the feel of her smooth skin. He had always wanted her, would always want her. There was the crux of it. The battle between what he wanted and what he should do kept him from going any further, kept his hand poised there, at the soft rise of her breast.

She trembled, and this time he knew he'd caused it. A feeling of power surged through him, a power that wasn't right for him to use with her. He had to get control of himself, of the situation. He'd come here to make sure she was safe, not maul her like some randy cowboy that didn't know hay from locoweed. He closed his hand into a fist.

"Caroline, we need to talk."

She froze for a second, and then turned from him, batting his hand away. Sitting up, she drew her knees to her chest and pulled the hem of her chemise down to cover her ankles.

"We need to clear some things up between us."

Her lips pressed into a solid line. "I know, but I thought…I hoped you came to apologize for this morning's behavior."

He chose to ignore that. He wasn't going to apologize for what he'd had to do at the time.

"Fine, then." She scrambled to her feet. With her hands on her hips, she continued. "What is it you want now? Only three hours ago you shouted at me to go away."

He rose. "I didn't shout."

"You did! Why were you so angry?"

He knew what she was asking but he wasn't going to talk about it. He never wanted her to find out. "It's not safe for you to go off alone like this."

Her gaze narrowed. "No one has bothered me—except you. I feel perfectly safe. You may return to the hacienda reassured. Eventually I will find my way back." She turned her back on him and strode to where her skirt and blouse lay on the bush and gathered them up.

"Someone set fire to the Svendsons' barn."

She turned back to him, holding her clothes before her like a shield.

"It's in the valley just beyond the hacienda."

"Is everyone all right?"

"They're shook up. Mrs. Svendson and the boys especially." A honey bee buzzed around her head which he swatted away with his hat.

Her brows knit together. "What is going on, Brandon?"

"Things aren't settled here—haven't been since the rebellion. That's what I meant when I said it was too dangerous for you to be here, why I didn't want you to come. Mexican renegades, Comanche—they don't make friendly neighbors."

"I understood the risks, Brandon. They are the same for Franklin as they are for me."

"No, Caroline. They're not." He glanced down at her creamy exposed shoulders—the skin turning slightly pink. He wished she'd cover up a little. She was enticing enough with clothes on, let alone a thin cotton shift. "If you'll get dressed, we'll head back. It's safer for now if we both stay close to the ranch."

A stubborn look tilted her chin. "I'll return with you, but only after you explain what happened this morning at your cabin."

He swiped a hand through his hair. "Just leave it be, Caroline. I don't want to discuss it."

She met his gaze, studying him quietly. Then, rather than being upset, to his surprise she rose up on her tiptoes and kissed him lightly on the jaw.

"What's that for?" he said suspiciously.

"Apology accepted."

"I don't remember apologizing," he countered.

"Oh? You came after me, didn't you? And at least now you are not denying that something happened with the boy. It did. I saw it, and you know I did. I won't press you about it further. Just know that I'm here when you are ready to talk about what's going on. And…that I care."

The jut of her chin, the challenge in her eyes—she knew him better than he knew himself. She always had. He let out a long, slow breath. "I've always had feelings for you—since the first day your father introduced us."

"But?"

"But those feelings serve no purpose now. I can't go back with you, Caroline."

She paced the distance between him and the chaparral. "For two years I waited for you through your apprenticeship and I wasn't exactly idle. I did help out at the hospital. Remember?"

"Much to your father's chagrin. It's a wonder he approved our engagement after you started doing that."

"Well, when I learned of the conditions there, it was obvious something had to be done. Someone had to do it, so I did."

"I remember," he murmured. Once Caroline had made the poor conditions known to her friends, they'd taken it upon themselves to start the charity group in order to raise money for the hospital. She'd been instrumental in organizing it and seeing it through.

"While there at the hospital I saw things, learned things. What I'm saying is...perhaps I can help, if you'll only open up to me."

He didn't answer. He couldn't.

She waited. One minute stretched to two. She sighed then, and made a motion, indicating he should turn around while she dressed. Reluctantly he turned toward the water. Two bees buzzed across the surface while Caroline continued speaking.

"Whether you like it or not, Brandon, we are joined— by our regard for each other more than anything. You do remember our night together, don't you?"

"How could I forget? That was the one bright spot, the one thing that saw me through the blasted war. I'll always be thankful for that."

"I need more than for you to be thankful. I need you to understand something. That night—" she took a deep breath "—that night changed my life."

He turned back to her, understanding flooding him. "You were a virgin."

"Yes, of course, but not just because of that. Because— Ouch!"

"What wrong?"

"I just got stung!" She squeezed her forearm.

"Where? Let me see."

"Oh, it smarts!" Tears brimmed in her eyes as she brought her arm up for his inspection.

The reddened area near her elbow transformed into a welt the size of a cow's eye before his eyes. The offending stinger protruded, which he quickly pulled out. "We're near their hive. You must have disturbed them with all of your caterwauling."

"Me!" She glared at him.

He couldn't help chuckling—or touching her. He swept a lock of golden hair away from her cheek and tucked it behind her ear. "Knew that would rile you. I'll get some mud."

Before he'd gone two steps, a low drone invaded the quiet space.

He glanced toward the sound. A small, dark cloud quickly approached. Bees! Before he could react they swarmed him. He swatted two away from his neck only to get stung. "Caroline! Into the water! Now!"

Immediately, Caroline dropped the clothes she held. "You, too!"

"I'm right with you!" He pulled his gun from its holster and threw it into the brush. Then grabbing her hand, they jumped off the rock into the clear pool.

The water closed over his head in a whoosh, fresh and cold. The trout at the bottom raced away to a cranny in the rocks. The water was so clear that, looking up, he could see the swarm hovering just above the surface. Caroline had noticed them, too, for she didn't object when he continued to grasp her hand and hold her firmly under the water.

Her shift wrapped around her torso and clung, bulky, at her waist. She struggled to push it down, but it floated immediately back up, revealing her long legs. As she struggled with the material once more, Brandon couldn't help grinning, even though he lost some air in the process. He pulled her close, close enough to feel the tingle of arousal starting within him. Good Lord! Even in the water she could get to him.

Trying to ignore the sensation, he helped her push the fabric down, but then couldn't resist skating his palm down the curve of her derriere. Her muscles tightened firm and

For Busy Women Only!

You deserve it!

Mail this card for your:

- ✓ FREE BOOKS & GIFTS
- ✓ Time-saving quick reads
- ✓ Step-saving home delivery
- ✓ Sanity-saving "just for me" treats

Scratch off the gold circle to see the value of your 2 FREE BOOKS and 2 FREE GIFTS. We will send them to you with no obligation to purchase any books, as explained on the back of this card.

We want to make sure we offer you the best service suited to your needs. Please answer the following question:

About how many NEW paperback fiction books have you purchased in the past 3 months?

❏ 0-2   ❏ 3-6   ❏ 7 or more

349 HDL EZUW   246 HDL EZU9

FIRST NAME	LAST NAME

ADDRESS

APT.   CITY

STATE / PROV.   ZIP/POSTAL CODE

Visit us online at www.ReaderService.com

The Reader Service - Here's How It Works:

Accepting your 2 free books and 2 free mystery gifts (gifts are worth about $10.00) places you under no obligation to buy anything. You may keep the books and gifts and return the shipping statement marked "cancel." If you do not cancel, about a month later we'll send you 6 additional books and bill you just $4.94 each in the U.S. or $5.49 each in Canada. That is a savings of 18% off the cover price. It's quite a bargain! Shipping and handling is just 50¢ per book.* You may cancel at any time, but if you choose to continue, every month we'll send you 6 more books, which you may either purchase at the discount price or return to us and cancel your subscription.

*Terms and prices subject to change without notice. Prices do not include applicable taxes. Sales tax applicable in N.Y. Canadian residents will be charged applicable provincial taxes and GST. Offer not valid in Quebec. All orders subject to approval. Credit or debit balances in a customer's account(s) may be offset by any other outstanding balance owed by or to the customer. Please allow 4 to 6 weeks for delivery. Offer available while quantities last.

strong beneath his hand. She moved away slightly and looked at him, her eyes searching his face in confusion.

Her long blond hair floated around her head and everywhere the filtered sunlight touched, the strands gleamed silver. She became a water sprite, sleek and infinitely alluring. He kneaded his fingers in her flesh, gently at first, then as an answering tension in his gut strung taut, with more force.

He shouldn't be doing this. He knew that. But ever since she'd arrived, it was all he thought about—touching her, his skin on hers. He'd struggled against the urge but she had bewitched him all over again the same way she had that first summer they'd met.

Somewhere in the back of his mind, a voice told him to stop, that he didn't deserve her anymore. But he was tired of listening to his conscience, tired of doing what was right, what was expected. He wanted to feel alive again. Wanted to feel loved and desired in return. For this one moment, he wanted her. Selfishly. Completely.

Releasing her hand, he inched his palm slowly down to cup her bottom with his other hand. He pulled her flush against him and she ceased battling with her shift as it wrapped once more around her waist. She stilled against him.

Here in this strange sanctuary of quiet, where only the two of them existed, he felt whole again. He felt strong. And he wanted her with a desperate, burgeoning passion. He had denied it over and over again, succumbing only once before. He couldn't deny it any longer.

His heart hammered in his chest. Unable to resist, he nuzzled her jaw, her cheek. And then found her lips.

Chapter Nine

Heavens, but she needed to breathe! Her lungs burned, her muscles ached, and her heart thumped wildly in her chest. Brandon's touch was like liquid fire, making her senses come alive, pushing her body's need for air to the limit. She broke off the kiss and stretched for the surface.

Brandon understood immediately. Keeping a tight hold on her, he pushed off the bottom boulder and jettisoned them toward the sunlight. Breaking out into the warmth, they both gulped in huge amounts of air. A lone bee buzzed between them. She gasped and pulled back, preparing to duck under the water again when his lips found hers.

They slanted across her mouth, pressing, demanding. He adjusted the angle and his tongue touched hers, sending desire spiraling, crashing, through her. She grabbed his shirt and hung on, letting him keep them both afloat.

Slowly he drew back. Water drops sprinkled his tanned face and plastered his dark hair to his forehead and cheeks. The look on his face was that of a man determined to have his way, yet controlled enough to make sure it was what she wanted.

She inhaled. It was all wrong according to her upbringing, but she was already a fallen woman. She had transgressed and would forever pay the price. Blind love had been the reason the first time. This time it was different. She knew exactly what she was doing and love again had everything to do with it. With Brandon's first touch, he'd started a yearning inside that she couldn't control—didn't want to control.

It must have been the desire banked in his blue eyes that made her a bit reckless, a bit daring. "You'd better remove your boots then, cowboy." Even she was surprised at how husky her voice sounded.

A smile broke slowly across his face, spreading warmth all the way through her to the far corners of her soul. She'd not seen that smile since Charleston, since *before*. Her heart skipped a beat. He smiled at her as though she were the most treasured thing on earth.

"Don't disappear on me, woman," he growled, kissing her nose lightly.

Releasing her, he took four powerful strokes to the closest bank. Standing in waist-high water, one at a time he pulled off his boots and tossed them over his shoulder on the grassy mound by his gun. Next, he unbuttoned his shirt, flinging it after his boots.

She drifted on her back, treading water, as anticipation built inside. A niggling thought occurred. She should tell him about the baby. She should, but it would ruin that look in his eyes—that soft, hooded look that said at this moment he thought she was the sun and moon and stars.

He lowered himself until the water lapped against his chin and then moved across the pool, barely disturbing the surface. Like a stealthy alligator, he floated toward her.

Ensnared by his steady blue gaze, the arguments they'd had melted to bits of nothing in her memory.

She glided her hands onto his strong shoulders as she felt his arms surround her waist and pull her close. The water lapped against his chest, straightening the dark curled hair.

"This isn't smart," he murmured.

She stopped his words with her palm. "Neither was traveling fifteen hundred miles to see you. I know how you are, Brandon. You can think yourself into or out of anything. You're clever that way. For once, please don't think."

She searched his eyes, feeling the need running through both of them. Her heart drummed a deep, abiding love for this man. She pressed her body against his—an invitation.

He groaned and finally gave in to his desire, dipping his head down to meet her mouth-to-mouth. He sucked her lower lip and then broke away to kiss her cheek, her neck and then behind her ear. She trembled, and felt his lips curve into a smile against her skin. So he remembered! A giddy feeling raced through her.

Whatever dark thoughts he'd been wrestling had departed, because now there was no hesitancy, no awkwardness in his movements. He came back to her mouth and, insistent, ran his tongue along the seam of her lips.

She welcomed him without hesitation, opening her mouth and accepting his thorough kiss. This was the Brandon she remembered—dogged, determined, his only thoughts on the goal ahead. And for this moment, that goal was her. Longing coiled deep in her center at the thought.

"I want you, too," she murmured in his ear. She brought her legs up to encircle his waist, her softness riding against his hardness. White-hot heat streaked to her core despite the cool water.

His nostrils flared. "You've grown bold. Not that I mind. With my weak leg, this position would be awkward for me were it not for the fact we are both in the water."

"Only for you, Brandon. Bold only for you," she said. It was the first time he'd mentioned his injury without the surliness he usually attached to it. She smoothed her fingers over his chest, rubbing over his nipples which were already hardened from the cool water.

He sucked in a gulp of air. "Glad to hear it."

With a firm grasp on her wrist, he lowered her hand. But he didn't touch her breast—at least not with his hand. Through her chemise, he took her hardened nipple into his hot mouth and desire streaked through her. Combined with the cold water she was completely lost in the sensations racing through her body. Her head lolled back and her breath came in short gasps as she wiggled against him.

He groaned again. "Caroline. Don't move."

She paused. Did he wish to stop? Now, when every part of her yearned for him? For his touch? "Why?"

"Because you make it impossible to go slowly."

"Then don't," she said, before kissing his chest. "I don't think I can bear it if you wait."

He moved with her toward the grassy bank. She lowered her feet, finding solid rock beneath her. If she'd allowed herself to dream of their reunion, here in the still waters of the pool is not where she would have ever imagined it, but she found the place suited him. Perhaps Texas suited him. Maybe this is where he truly belonged.

He spread his shirt over the sun-bleached bank and laid her down with her body still half-submerged in the water, her shift floating on the surface. Keeping one hand to her lower back, supporting her, he slid into her.

And, with his sigh mingling with hers, brought her home.

* * *

Later, much later, Caroline stirred in his arms, rubbing her bottom against him. Brandon woke instantly and tightened his arms around her. The sun had moved to the western sky, and cottonwoods shaded them now. They'd have to get back to the hacienda soon or a scouting party would be out looking for them. But for right now, he wanted to hold on to this moment.

He loved her. He hadn't told her, not since he'd asked for her hand months ago. He'd tried to deny it to himself—tried to stop from feeling anything. It was easier that way—and better for her not to know what was happening. He hadn't wanted to be there when the love he'd always seen in her eyes turned to fear, or worse—pity. When he could no longer keep the monsters at bay and the dreams and the visions took over—when he was no longer sane.

But he'd loved her just the same and always would.

Her hair was nearly dry, and hung tangled and wild down her back. The slope of her neck called to him and he rose on one elbow and kissed the silky, sensitive skin there. A shiver coursed through her as he'd known it would. Rising on one elbow, he realized she had goose bumps on her arm.

He squeezed her shoulder and watched her eyelids flutter open. "You're cold. We should get back."

A sigh made her breast rise and fall. "Can we come here again?"

The innocent question from her half-asleep lips made him smile. He kissed her neck once more, rolled to his back and stood. His pants from the knees down were still soaked through, and the skin on his toes were wrinkled from the water. "Come on, darlin'. Get moving." He walked across the slab of rock and gathered her clothes.

By the time he'd returned, she had repositioned herself

onto her back. He stopped for a moment to feast his eyes on her. Once she clothed herself, he'd have to rely on his memory. Her cotton shift, still damp, clung to her skin from her knees to her breasts.

It was the small rise to her midriff that suddenly caught his eye. The air evaporated in his lungs. What exactly was going on?

He glanced from her waist to her face and then back again. It couldn't be… "Caroline?" Her name came out on a choke.

Her eyes flew open and she sat up. Her face flooded with worry. "I wanted to tell you. Truly I did. But I didn't know how."

A baby! Good God! A baby! Stunned, he dropped her clothes, stumbling back a step. Slack-jawed, he stared at her, his mind racing over the events of the past months.

"When?" he finally managed to ground out.

She cupped her hand over her abdomen, as if that would protect the child from him, as if he would ever hurt her. "Autumn. Late October, I think."

A slow, deep anger began to churn in his gut. She'd deceived him! She'd lied to him!

"No need to hide it now." His tone was harsh.

Her shocked expression let him know his arrow had hit home. Well, so had hers.

He strode over and sat down to yank on his boot.

"Brandon, we should talk about this."

"Why now?" he said. "It wasn't important enough to tell me before."

"I just needed it to be the right time."

"Well, that time has come and gone. That time was before I left Charleston."

"I didn't know then. I only learned of the baby after you'd already gone."

He pulled on his other boot, his thoughts in too much of a jumble to think coherently. What the hell was he going to do with a baby?

"Look," she said. "I understand you're angry. I know this is a shock."

"Damn right it's a shock. You'll excuse me if I'm not playing the pleased father." He gripped the saddle to mount, but then paused. "That is the reason you came all this way."

She nodded. "Yes."

"Did you refuse Graham before or after you knew you were in a family way?"

"Both times."

That stopped him. "He asked you a second time? Even after your first refusal? A glutton for punishment."

"You're not being fair," she said, the volume of her voice rising in frustration.

He held up his hand, blocking her words, blocking the sight of her. "It's really none of my business."

"Of course it's your business. Otherwise, I wouldn't have come. I thought you should know."

He scowled. "Eventually."

Caroline glared at him.

He pressed his forehead against the smooth saddle in front of him, breathing in the familiar scent of leather. He should be happy but all he could think about was that she'd lied to him. And for the moment, he couldn't get past that. He dragged a hand through his hair and stared at the pool where they'd made love. How had he not noticed it earlier?

The answer was embarrassing. He'd been so consumed with passion, so aroused that nothing else had mattered. Had he been rough? He tried to remember, hoping he hadn't hurt her or the baby. Her breasts had seemed fuller, perhaps more sensitive. But then they'd both been overly sensitive to every nuance, every touch, every kiss. Even now, thinking of it again, his traitorous body pulsed with renewed wanting.

He grabbed his hat from the ground and settled it on his head. "Get dressed," he grumbled.

"Brandon…"

He turned his back on her. The cotton material of her shift rustled. He glanced back to see her rising awkwardly. Again he asked himself how he could not have noticed before. He took her arm and helped her to her feet.

"Thank you," she said, but jerked away as soon as she steadied herself. Her eyes flashed with banked anger.

He waited for her to finish dressing and then helped her mount her mare.

"Can we talk about this before we go back?" she asked.

He handed her the reins. "Not now, Caroline. You've given me a hell of a lot to think about." He mounted his horse without glancing at her again.

Good Lord. A baby.

Brandon maneuvered his horse down the steep hill and through the trees. The tightness in his jaw and the rigid set to his shoulders kept Caroline from trying again to speak to him. He helped her down at the corral, his eyes averted from her face, and led both horses into the stable.

She followed him. "We really must talk about this, Brandon. I don't want to part like this."

He turned from hanging the tack on the wall peg. "I take it Franklin knows." At her nod, he continued. "No wonder you have him in your pocket. He's always been a pushover for a woman in distress. My mother made good use of it."

He'd never spoken of his mother that way. Although curious, she was uneasy at his mood and held her tongue.

He removed the saddle and blanket from the piebald mare and set them on a bench outside the stall. "Who else is aware? Hopefully I am not the last to know."

"I think Victoria's mother suspects, but she hasn't said anything."

"Her mother? How would she know?"

"At dinner, I saw the look on her face when I could not tolerate the spicy food."

He snorted. "My power of observation, which as a physician should be razor-sharp, has failed." With his face set in stone, Brandon moved back to his horse and removed the saddle.

"No one else knows, Brandon. Truly."

He turned to face her, his eyes unreadable and shadowed beneath the brim of his black hat. "Other than having trouble with your digestion are you well?"

The question took her by surprise. He sounded more like a doctor than a worried father. She didn't know whether to smile or be angry and so she simply answered. "I'm sleepy all the time, but…yes. I'm well."

He nodded slowly, set the saddle on the bench and then walked out.

Chapter Ten

Brandon didn't join them for supper that evening. Curious glances came her way but no one treated her any differently so she was sure Brandon hadn't said anything to them. Soon they would know the true reason for her visit here and then she would have to bear their scrutiny in another, less pleasant way. But for now, talk at the table centered on helping the Svendsons.

Afterward, she didn't seek Brandon out. It wasn't every day a man learned he was going to be a father. He needed time to adjust. After all, she'd had months to consider the change along with the movement going on inside her body that confirmed a new life there.

As she headed to her room, Victoria called her from the open door of the library.

"Would you do a favor for me?" she asked. At Caroline's nod, Victoria continued. "Your trip today to the clear spring reminded me that we are low on honey. Would you ask Diego to go gather some? I need enough for the wedding guests and perhaps some for the Svendsons. He should be at the stable."

Caroline left the hacienda and walked across the expanse of packed ground to the corral. She stood at the gate waiting for a break in Diego's routine with the new horse. He wore a loose white shirt and buckskin pants. Instead of boots, he wore soft moccasins. With his long black hair tied back in a wide leather strip, he looked more Indian than Tejano. Standing in the center of the corral, he flicked a long whip that landed lightly on the filly's rump as it loped along the perimeter of the pen. At the same time he spoke softly, soothingly, letting the horse get used to his voice and his verbal commands.

When he noticed her, he slowed the horse to a walk and lowered his whip.

"Señorita Caroline. You wished to see me?"

"Yes. Victoria, uh, Señorita Torrez, has a request."

He smiled. "She has been Victoria to me since we were young. She is my cousin, so it is allowed."

"Oh. She would like you to gather honey up at the spring. She needs more for her wedding guests and some for the Svendsons."

"When the bees quiet. At dusk."

"That is nearly upon us. Do you need help?"

Diego's smile challenged her. "With the honey? Or with this filly?"

His teasing took her by surprise.

When she didn't answer he grinned good-naturedly and opened the gate. "Come in—the horse will not hurt you. She is nearly tame."

Caroline stepped tentatively inside the corral. The sleek, black animal pranced away from them, then put her nose up, sniffing the air for Caroline without coming too near.

"I think you are both nervous of each other," Diego said.

"I haven't been around unbroken horses. Father has a

horse for his patient visits but it is old and plodding." Caroline held out her hand to show the horse she had nothing to fear of her. "She is beautiful."

"She is to be bred to Juan's stallion. Victoria is very good with bloodlines and she and Jake are to have the first foal as a wedding present."

"I'd heard that. Tell me about this horse," she said, studying the animal. "What makes her better than the others?"

With a look of approval, Diego turned to whistle to the filly. She inched closer a few steps, and then skittish, she dashed away.

"Rosa!" Diego called softly, his voice calm and entreating. "Is that how you treat a guest? Come say hello." He walked toward the horse, which now shied away from him and circled the railing slowly, cautiously. Diego paused. "She is acting strange. Perhaps you had better—"

He stopped talking and, narrowing his gaze, peered into the stand of pines on the far side of the stable.

"What is it?" Caroline asked. Then a noise behind her made her turn.

Brandon stepped from the stable door and started toward them. He wouldn't be the reason for Rosa's nervousness.

Caroline looked back to Diego. With a brief shake of his head, he placed a finger to his lips. "Shh." Slowly, still watching the trees, he moved between her and the animal.

Suddenly the horse bucked, tossing its head, and then raced along the perimeter of the corral.

"Caroline!" Brandon yelled. "Get the hell out of there!"

She grabbed up her skirt and ran for the fence. Brandon raced toward her, his pace surprisingly fast despite his injury. He slipped through the wooden rails and rushed at the horse, waving his arms at the animal. "Ha! Ha!"

The filly skidded to a stop and reared, pranced backward a few steps and then dashed to the far side of the corral. With a knot in her throat, Caroline climbed through to safety on the other side of the fence, her chest heaving and her heart pounding.

Brandon strode toward her, his limp more pronounced than usual, his brows drawn together in a fierce frown. Once he'd slipped back through to the outside of the corral he turned to her. "What do you think you were doing?"

Caroline backed up. She'd never seen him so angry. Crystal sparks seemed to fly from his blue eyes.

"That horse is unpredictable. Didn't Diego tell you that? You could have been killed."

He'd gotten it all wrong. "It wasn't Diego's fault, Brandon. Something set her off."

"You shouldn't have been in there."

Diego climbed through the fence rails and looked from Brandon to her. "Are you all right, *señorita?* I am sorry for your scare."

"You ought to be," Brandon said, giving her no chance to answer. Caroline had never heard his voice so ugly.

Diego's eyes narrowed on him. "There was something in the woods making the filly nervous."

"I just came that way from the cabin. Nothing is there." Tension radiated off him in waves.

"You are calling me a liar?" Diego said with a sudden calm to his voice.

"Sounds like it." Brandon clenched his fists at his sides.

This wasn't the Brandon Caroline knew—a man spoiling for a fight. She put her hand on his shoulder.

He flinched and shook her off. "Back away. This is between Diego and me."

"Brandon, what are you doing?" she asked.

"Do as he says, *señorita*." Diego kept his gaze trained on Brandon.

Alarmed, she stepped backward.

"You will recall your accusation now, *hombre*."

"I'll do better than that!" Brandon swung his fist into Diego's jaw.

Shocked, Caroline screamed. "Brandon! No!"

Similarly stunned, Diego rubbed his chin. "You should not have done that, *amigo*." His eyes blazed as he rushed at Brandon, his head low, and slammed his fist into his opponent's gut. Air rushed from Brandon in a whoosh. He lost his balance and stumbled backward.

Diego rushed at him again, ready to plant another hard knock.

This time Brandon had the presence of mind to grip Diego's fist as it sailed toward his face. He grabbed onto the boy's arm, grappled with him and they both went down, dust flying.

On his back, with Diego on top of him, Brandon pushed and twisted until he straddled him and took the upper hand. He was the heavier of the two and Caroline cringed at what he might do to the boy. Then suddenly, Diego used leverage to knee Brandon in the back and push him over his head. Brandon landed with a thud, sprawled face-first in the dirt. He spit dust from his mouth, flipped over and found Diego's foot on his chest.

"Stop!" she cried out. "Stop!"

They didn't hear her—or more likely, they didn't care. Brandon grasped Diego's foot and pushed up, at the same time twisting it. Diego, the lighter of the two, dropped in a heap at his side.

She looked about the yard, hoping to find help on the way. No one was in sight. Her anger growing, she searched for a way to make them stop fighting. Spying the bucket at the well, she marched over, dropped it down to collect water and brought it back up, full. She stomped over to the two and dumped the water on them.

They barely noticed the splash. Blood dripped from Brandon's nose as he straddled Diego, rearing back with his arm, preparing to throw the next punch.

"I'll take over," Jake said, appearing at Caroline's side with Victoria just behind him. Victoria took her hand and pulled her out of the way.

Jake gripped Brandon's collar and hauled him backward, then let him drop, off balance, into the mud. Brandon lay there, stunned and breathing hard.

"I didn't save both your asses in battle just so you could kill each other here," Jake said, glowering over them. He turned to Brandon. "What are you trying to do? Knock him into a cocked hat? What's this all about?"

With a wary eye on Brandon, Diego stood. He fingered the cut on his lower lip gingerly, then turned his head and spat bloody saliva into the dirt.

"Well?" Jake waited.

Brandon sat up and dragged a hand through his hair. He'd have an awkward time getting up, Caroline realized, but she didn't move to help him. He deserved whatever he'd brought on himself this time. With a grunt, he slowly got to his feet. Still he didn't move to answer his brother.

"The horse spooked," Caroline said.

Jake raised a brow. "And that caused a fight?"

"No," Diego said. "He accused me of lying."

"You had no right to have her in there," Brandon ground out. "She could have been killed."

"I would not have let that happen," Diego countered.

"You know me well enough to know that. Something else has got you tied in knots."

Caroline had a suspicion she knew—it was about the baby. But please, he wouldn't announce it here, would he?

"You two," Diego said, looking from Brandon to her. "Settle your quarrel and leave me out of your troubles. I've got work to do." He stepped back into the corral to calm Rosa.

Numbly Caroline picked up the bucket and walked over to the well to set it down. She could feel Brandon staring at her, feel his stubborn glare burning into her back. Her heart constricted in her chest.

"I'm going to the house," she managed to say. She walked away but once she reached the gate, she glanced back. Jake and Brandon were headed toward the cabin, neither talking. Brandon held himself stiff, leaning once again on his cane, and kept his distance from his brother. Would he tell Jake about the baby now? Jake—who despised her? He would warn Brandon away from her.

Well, what had she expected? A declaration of love from Brandon? She wasn't foolish enough to think everything would magically be all right when he learned of the baby. He wasn't the same man she'd known in Charleston, but she had hoped he would want to help her, hoped he would eventually accept the baby.

She could almost convince herself leaving would be a relief. Franklin would take her to her aunt's house in Virginia where she'd stay until her confinement was over, and then…what then? She couldn't return home with the baby. Her parents had said as much. And she didn't think she could be separated from the child—Brandon's own flesh and blood. She placed her hand on her abdomen, unsure what she was going to do if he wouldn't help her, but she'd figure it out.

Yes, leaving this place would be a relief. The only problem was…she didn't believe it anymore.

Chapter Eleven

Goliad

Brandon opened his eyes and stared through the window of his prison. A thick, early-morning fog hung in the air. Ice crystals sparkled on the new sycamore leaves beside the small house. His stomach growled, still hungry even after the meal he'd had late last night before the guard had shoved him into this room. It had been dark then and he had stumbled over the men sleeping on the floor.

He could see them now in the gray light of dawn—wounded Mexican soldiers lying any way that would keep them comfortable. Soldiers he was expected to heal with a miraculous wave of his hand—without enough bandages, without instruments, without hope. Hope being the main ingredient of survival. The one ingredient no one in the room possessed.

Paradoxically he'd made a name for himself among them. He was fast, which meant *less painful* when it came to the necessary amputations of his trade. An ironic way to heal a man—cut off what bothered him. If he was bitter, so be it. He'd seen too much of mangled arms and legs from shrapnel and bullets. A man couldn't see so much horror and come out unscathed. His mind would never be free of it again.

His personal guard saw him stir—a man of forty years, short and squat. The guard stepped near and booted him in the ribs. Brandon rolled away from the insult, finding small relief in the fact that yesterday's kick had been on the opposite side. At least his bruises were spread out over his body and not concentrated in one horrible spot. It was a normal beginning for the day and a repeat of the past twenty-five days he'd been in Goliad.

At least for now he still had his boots. Many of the Mexican soldiers had worn through theirs and had to wrap their feet in rags just to walk. He stood, his body aching in places he'd not known existed before his capture. With his movement the ropes that bound his ankles chafed against the raw skin there. He hissed in sharply.

At the sound, a slow, ugly grin came on the guard's face. He pointed to a wooden bucket in the corner used by the men for defecation. Brandon picked it up, nearly gagging as the contents sloshed and emitted the strong odor of urine and ammonia. He followed the guard to a pit behind the livery and threw out the contents of the bucket.

He took a moment to relieve himself in the pit, clinically amazed that his body could continue to make water when he seldom received any to drink. Perhaps when he returned to Charleston he would write a report on it and submit it to the medical group. The errant thought—one of many he had daily—only advanced the probability that he was losing his grip on reality. The truth was he'd never be free of this place alive, never go back to Charleston. Never see Caroline again.

The guard nudged him with his rifle, jostling him out of his reverie. Brandon buttoned his pants and followed the guard to the river where he rinsed out the bucket in the water.

On the far bank, a door opened in the tall stone fort. A line of ten men emerged, blinking and squinting into the bright sunlight. By their looks, they were Texians, not that he could tell by their clothes which hung in rags. One had red hair and appeared young—still just a boy. Another had dirty blond hair streaked with gray. The man glanced across the water, meeting Brandon's gaze. Brandon was shocked at the bleakness in his face. A few of the men were Tejano with dark hair and eyes. Half of them carried makeshift shovels. Prodded by the bayonets and rifle butts of their guards, the Texians marched away from the river and up over a knoll, moving from his line of sight.

The guard handed him a second bucket and they walked upstream a hundred yards through the grass. As they did every morning, the birds in the trees along the water called out to each other, creating a cacophony. Brandon stopped at his usual place and collected fresh water in the second bucket. Curious about the men he'd seen, he took his time, kneeling at the bank and splashing water on his face to help him wake up.

Suddenly shouts arose from beyond the hill—Spanish and then English alike. The swift, rapid cadence of gunfire split the morning silence. Then even the birds were quiet.

Something went berserk inside him. He had to see what had just happened, although he was terrified he knew. He lunged into the river and swam to the other side. On a subconscious level he felt the icy water and the drag of the current, but refused to consider it. All he felt was rage. Rage at the soldiers who'd kill unarmed men like dogs.

Rage at General López de Santa Anna who had most likely given the order. And rage at the inhumane carnage of war.

A rifle fired and his guard shouted at him to stop—then followed with a stream of obscenities in Spanish. Brandon didn't care and it didn't stop him. He reached the opposite bank and then half ran, half crawled up the grassy knoll to view what had happened. Some mad impulse urged him on to see it with his own eyes. Would there be any he could save—any he could help?

When he reached the top, he froze in horror at the sight. The Texians had been slaughtered, lying this way and that, their arms and legs bent at odd angles in grotesque shapes in a shallow mass grave. The men stared at the sky, their eyes unseeing, with blood splattered everywhere.

He doubled over and retched.

Suddenly white-hot fire cracked his right ankle and he collapsed to his knees, too startled to cry out. He twisted, falling further, and sprawled on the grass. His guard strode toward him, the musket in his hand still emitting smoke from the barrel. Pain would come soon. Brandon braced himself as daylight faltered and the edges of his vision grew dark.

"Now you will not try to escape, *Médico*." The guard's voice rasped through his mind, harsh and guttural.

Escaping had been in his thoughts constantly since he'd been captured, but oddly, not at that moment. All he'd wanted was to know for sure what had happened. In a way, to witness it so that those men would not die in vain.

Pain pulsed through his leg and up to his knee. He turned over slowly, fighting the dizziness, and sat up to examine his leg. The ankle bone protruded through the skin. For now the bleeding was minimal. Apparently the plug remained inside, providing pressure to the small bleeders.

"I didn't intend to escape," he growled, tense, expecting a kick in the ribs or a musket jabbed into his back.

Why hadn't the guard finished him off? Seemed like the easiest thing to do now. He wouldn't be much good for doctoring the Mexican troops if he couldn't walk.

The man's musket suddenly landed on the ground beside Brandon. Since the one bullet had been spent and it did not sport a bayonet, the weapon was useless to Brandon, but it was odd the guard had dropped it—and within Brandon's reach. He glanced up. The guard's face had paled, immobilized into a horrified expression as he stared on the massacre below.

"No!" he cried out and then ran wildly down the hill toward a gathering of Mexican soldiers. Once there, he didn't stop but pushed the men aside to gain access to the one they surrounded—someone lying on the ground.

He'd lost someone special, then. Brandon couldn't dredge up the energy to care. He'd seen too much of death.

Alone for the moment, Brandon took the opportunity to withdraw the small, ivory-handled knife hidden in the lining of his boot. Gritting his teeth, he probed for the bullet. He felt strange, erratically hot and cold at the same time and knew he must be going into shock. Sweat poured from him as he struggled to wedge out the plug. It'd be so much easier with forceps, he thought, grimacing further as he moved the plug with the tip of his knife. The pain intensified. Finally he dislodged the bullet and popped it out onto the grass. Working quickly, he ripped off a portion of his sleeve and bound his ankle tight with the cloth.

He glanced down the hill once more. The guard had gathered his comrade in his arms and with the help of another soldier, they started back toward Brandon. He tried to stow the knife in his boot once more, but his vision blurred. No! He needed the weapon if he was ever going to escape. He had to hide it. He swallowed hard. He needed the weapon. He needed the…

Blinding pain at the side of his head shut out all thought and the ground swirled around him before going dark.

Light filtered through the dirty cabin windows and splashed across Brandon's eyelids. Morning! Disoriented, unsure for a moment where he was, the nightmare of Goliad slowly receded.

He opened his eyes and whipped the covers off, sitting up in one motion. Pain exploded through his head. His skull was going to split wide-open. He pressed against his ears with his hands, willing the pounding to stop. Dry mouth, scratchy throat, headache—all symptoms of drinking too much mescal last night.

The fight with Diego had ended the strangest day of his life. Jake had demanded to know what was going on but Brandon hadn't been ready to talk about it. Frustrated, Jake had stormed out of the cabin muttering something about Brandon being stupid and bullheaded.

There was that pounding again. A light breeze touched his chest as the front door opened. "Brandon?"

Caroline. No difficulty knowing what she was doing here. "I'm not good company this morning."

There was a pause. "It's noon."

"Same thing."

"Brandon. You can't continue to ignore me. I want to know how you feel about…things."

Me, too, he thought to himself. His thoughts went from one extreme to the other—one minute excited and amazed at knowing he and Caroline had started a new life, and the next minute scared to the point of incapacity that he would let her and the baby down. What the hell was he going to do?

"I'll be out in a moment."

He was glad that he'd closed the curtain to his small sleeping quarter when he'd fallen in bed. It gave him a moment now to gather his wits. He shoved his stocking feet in his boots and stood.

Too fast. His head swam. His vision blurred. Oh, yeah. This was going to be quite a day.

Yesterday, he'd hurt Caroline. He'd been rough, wanting to lash out at her because she'd deceived him—about the baby, about coming to Texas, about everything. He understood on one level that she'd been afraid of how he would react, but that didn't excuse her deception. Did she think he could walk away now? Is that what had her worried?

When he'd gotten himself pulled back together he shoved his straw pallet into the corner and peeked out through the curtain. Caroline had tied a kerchief over her hair and a white apron around her waist covered her calico skirt. He took a moment to study her. Now that he knew she carried a baby, he saw that her waist did appear slightly larger. Funny he hadn't noticed it before—like when he'd first carried her from the river. He'd chalk that up to his total shock at seeing her in Texas territory.

He pushed aside the curtains and stepped into the large room. "What are you doing?"

She whirled around. "Goodness, you're a mess! You look like a big, grouchy bear."

He glared and rubbed his day's growth of beard. "Good day to you, too."

She frowned at him in response and then continued searching through the cupboards and behind doors.

Methodically he tucked in his cotton shirt and looped his suspenders over his shoulders. "I asked what you are doing here?"

"I'm looking for a bucket." She opened a tall wooden cabinet behind his desk and rummaged through its contents. "I never knew you to be lazy. The day is half-gone and you are just waking?"

"If you must know—yes," he grumbled. He worked his leg, easing his weight down on his injured ankle. It was sore every morning before he stretched it out. He looked up to find she had ceased her search and instead, studied his movements.

"When you are ready to eat, I brought breakfast from the hacienda."

He stopped exercising abruptly. Just what was she up to? "Maria made it?"

She put her hands on her hips and faced him. "No. I can make a simple breakfast, Brandon."

He rubbed a hand over his face, eyeing her, and then walked across the room to the other side of his desk where he picked up the bucket from the space between the wall and the desk. "I'll go with you."

"I am capable of fetching water."

"That I know. Your aim was true when you doused me last evening."

"As I recall, it didn't help much. You must think I can't do anything on my own."

"I never thought that at all. I just figured I'd get a little water to wash my face while I'm at it." And he didn't want her carrying a full bucket anywhere in her condition.

"Why were you fighting Diego? I was safe."

"He shouldn't have put you at risk. It was unnecessary. It was stupid."

"But to *fight* about it? Sometimes I don't know you at all, Brandon. You were never one to resort to fisticuffs."

"Sorry to disappoint you, but you're talking about when I was back in Charleston—where it's civilized."

"You always said man should use his reasoning rather than to fight about something. I thought you believed it."

He snorted. "And I remember you telling me yesterday that I think too much. Some things just can't be talked away. Sometimes it takes action. And sometimes the lowest common denominator—passions and emotions—rule." He looked at her stomach as he said the last. "Your condition being a case in point."

She slid her hand over the small bulge. When she looked up at him, her eyes were glassy with unshed tears. "I would not call this baby conceived by the lowest common denominator. This baby—our child—is the result of mutual caring and love, not fighting."

"Are you so sure it was love, Caroline? Not just passion? The heat of the moment?"

Her lips pressed together. "At the time, it was both for me."

He was baiting her, purposely holding her at arm's length and saying things to hurt her and he didn't know why. Perhaps because she'd turned his world upside down in the past twenty-four hours.

"You came to this conclusion because of the rebellion," she accused him.

"Fighting for a free Texas fixed that in my mind, I won't deny it. It's human nature—something I've come to know more in the past five months than in all the years before."

"It has hardened you."

He didn't have anything to say to that. It was true. But he had to be hard. If he let down his guard, the memories came crashing back in to suffocate him. The ghosts of men he'd fought beside hovered just beyond his waking consciousness, calling to him in his sleep and when he was too tired to keep them away.

"Tell me about the war, Brandon. What happened? How did you get hurt?"

The question didn't take him by surprise. He'd expected it eventually. But she had no idea of what he'd seen, and he didn't want her knowing. No one should get that close.

He held out the bucket. "Let's get the water."

Sighing in disappointment, she reached for the handle. Too late he realized he stood too close to her.

She sniffed, her pert little nose wrinkling. "Brandon...?"

"Caroline?" he said mockingly.

"Are you liquor..."

"Liquored up?" he finished for her. Drinking wasn't a crime and he didn't need a lecture first thing on waking. What he needed were answers to the mess he suddenly found himself in.

She stepped back, her face registering dismay. "Does your leg hurt that much?"

He'd quit using alcohol—and laudanum—for the pain over a month ago. That's not why he'd been drinking last night. It had everything to do with him finding out he was going to be a father. "I'm fine as frog's hair," he said sarcastically.

That quieted her. Clamping her jaws tight together, she headed outside, taking the path through the trees to the well. He followed, letting her rinse out the bucket before he took it from her hands. "I'll get it now," he said and filled the bucket with fresh water. "You shouldn't be lifting it."

Once back in the office, Brandon divvied up the water—some in a basin for his morning ablutions and some for breakfast. It was colder than snowmelt, but he figured it would wake him up, especially after all he'd imbibed last night. He poured the remaining water in a large kettle which hung on an iron hook in the fireplace.

"Are you sure you can cook this way?"

"It can't be too difficult." She grabbed the flint stone that sat on the mantel.

Leaving her to the task, he moved to the small mirror that hung on the wall of his "room" and proceeded to shave his morning growth of beard. He took his time, wondering if she really knew what she was doing fixing breakfast. As far as he knew, she'd never prepared a meal in her life. She'd always had kitchen maids and cooks growing up—and a stove instead of an open fireplace. Through the angle of the glass, he saw her glance his way a time or two—when she thought he wasn't looking. He finished up with the razor and walked over to her.

"You don't cook for yourself much," she said. "The grime is thick here."

"Most days I go to the hacienda." He watched as she turned the flint over in her hand and then hesitated. "Sure you don't want any help?"

"I'm sure." The hearth had been prepared for a fire with kindling and dried pine needles the day he'd moved in, compliments of Juan's wife, Gertrudis. Warm as it was, he and Jake had never used it. Like he'd told Caroline, he took his meals at the big house.

She struck the flint, trying to gain a spark. It didn't work. She tried again without any more success than her first attempt.

He was careful not to ask if she wanted help again. This could take a while if her fumbling attempts were any indication. She seemed determined to do this on her own, so he pulled up his chair and sat down.

She studied the piece of flint as though it held some magic answer, and then, squatting down next to the kindling, tried again.

Nothing happened.

Brandon leaned near her left shoulder to watch and unconsciously breathed her in. Warmth radiated from her body and with it the honey perfume of her skin. He closed his eyes, wanting to hold in the scent and not let it go. Here she was, fixing him breakfast as intimate as any husband and wife. Her fumbling attempts at starting the fire only endeared her to him all the more. She was good at so many things—entertaining, organizing fundraisers, dancing—but none were of any use in Texas.

If only things could be different. If only they could try again. But it wouldn't work. She was right. He had changed and he couldn't go back to what he used to be. It was impossible. Still, he took another deep breath, dragging in that light, sweet scent that was hers alone. When he opened his eyes, she still hadn't set fire to the kindling.

"Let me," he said and gently took the flint from her hands. At his swift strike, a spark jumped from the stone and the needles began to smoke. He blew lightly on the kindling and slowly the red glow turned into a flame. "Just takes practice."

Her lashes fluttered down, but she didn't move away from him. He stared at her a moment, feeling the pull between them, wanting to close the gap and taste her lips. He didn't act on the impulse. Instead he sat back in the chair.

She rose and took the coffeepot from the mantel, scooping out enough water from the large pot to fill it. "Thank you. Franklin lit the fire most evenings. That is, the times we didn't stop at an inn." She threw a handful of coffee grounds into the pot.

Brandon watched every movement, noticing for the first time that her hands were dry and chapped. What else had she been doing on her journey? "You must have found sleeping on the ground uncomfortable."

"I usually slept in the coach and he took the ground. There was one night—" She hesitated.

"Yes?" He had a feeling he knew what she was going to say.

"One night that it rained and he stayed in the coach with me."

"That would have been the sensible thing to do."

The tension in her shoulders eased.

"Yes. I thought so, too. He was a gentleman the entire trip. Although—" she wrinkled her nose "—he did snore."

He felt the hint of a smile come to his lips. He trusted Franklin. What's more, he realized he trusted Caroline. She really hadn't deceived him; she'd just been afraid to tell him about the baby. Now that things were out in the open, perhaps they could deal with the situation.

"You mentioned that you stopped in New Orleans to stay with his family."

"Yes, we did."

"He used to talk about them a lot when I was young. I've never met them."

"We stayed two nights. I…I needed the rest."

"You don't need to explain, Caroline. I don't begrudge you the two days. Considering the bone-jarring roads and your condition, the trip must have been exhausting for you."

"It…it was. I believe Franklin is looking forward to stopping there again on our return to Charleston."

Silence followed her words, the weight of it heavy with unsaid words.

"I'm not going back, Caroline," he said. "We've already discussed that."

Her gaze held his. "I'm not asking you to. Not anymore. I only wanted to tell you about the baby."

Her cheeks flushed as she moved quickly back to the hearth and threw a slice of ham into the three-legged skillet. It sizzled and popped, the aroma making his stomach churn with hunger.

"You can turn it now." He looked up to see why she didn't move. She held her hand to her nose, her face pale.

"Are you all right?"

She swallowed convulsively. "Never better."

He grabbed the utensil from her hand. "I'll do it." He forked the ham and flipped it over. His eyes narrowed on her. "You sure you're all right? You look a little green."

"Yes. Of course. How will you take your eggs?"

"Any way you want to fix them." Slowly he sank down to a chair. She seemed determined to do this.

Removing the ham to a side plate, she cracked the eggs into the skillet.

Suddenly the coffee boiled up and over the side of the pot. She reached…

"Caroline! No!"

His warning came too late. She gripped the hot tin handle with her bare hand.

"Stars and garters!" She jumped back holding her hand. He started to rise…

"No. I'm all right. Stay there." She grabbed the spatula and flipped the eggs, only to have both the soft yolks break at the last second. "Now I've ruined them!"

"They'll taste the same."

"But I wanted them to be perfect. I wanted it all to be perfect."

"Nothing is."

She pressed her lips together at his words. Moving the eggs to his plate, she set it in front of him.

He paused in bringing the first bite to his mouth, his gaze narrowing on her fingers. "Let me see your hand."

"I can take care of a burn." She whipped her hand behind her back and rummaged through the few canisters in the cupboard. "How can a doctor not have something for a burn?" she asked crossly. "It is a basic remedy."

"Caroline," he said again, standing. "Give me your hand."

She sniffed. "Not on your life. You're unfit. You've been drinking." She backed away, and continued her search.

"That doesn't make me incapable of administering first aid. In spite of this blasted headache, I do remember something about burns."

"I don't want your help." She found a length of cloth, ripped it lengthwise and began wrapping her hand, her movements jerky. "I don't want your help," she repeated.

He gripped her wrist to stop her and force her to look him in the face. "Are we talking about the same thing?"

"It's obvious, isn't it? You don't want to help, you don't want a baby, you don't want me—"

He could barely keep up with her mercurial mood swings. "I think what happened yesterday makes a lie of that. Hold still. You are going to get my help. On both counts."

"You don't have any butter."

Irrational! She was being ridiculously irrational. Carefully he unwrapped the cloth. She hissed when the air hit the ravaged skin.

He examined her reddened palm and the blisters, his anger growing. "This is worse than you let on," he accused.

Pulling her away from the stove, he plunged her hand into the remaining cool water in the bucket. "Keep it there."

He held his hand over the frying pan, testing the temperature. When he was reassured that it had cooled sufficiently, he scooped up a dollop of grease from the ham and applied it to the blistered and reddened areas of her palm. Then, wrapping the cloth snuggly about her hand, he tied it off efficiently.

"Don't ever be afraid to ask me for what you need," he said, holding her gaze. "I can't always give you what you want, but if you need something, you know I'd do what I could." He'd been thinking of her burn, but hearing the words come from his mouth, he realized he meant much more.

He released her hand and turned away, unwilling to delve deeper into the feelings that had surfaced. "I should eat this before it gets cold. You went to a lot of work and pain to make it." He sat and took a long slug of his coffee.

"Brandon," she said, her back to him, "I never came here to coerce you back to Charleston. I thought you'd want to go—that perhaps you just needed a reminder of what waited for you there. I can tell now that I was wrong."

He heard the squeal of the iron hook as she positioned it away from the fire. This time she used a long poker to do the work, rather than her tender fingers.

"Tell me one thing," Brandon said.

"Yes?"

"Did Franklin know about the baby before you came? Is that why he brought you with him?"

"Not at first, but he fished it out of me soon enough. He didn't want to believe it. You know how he felt about me. But after I lost my breakfast a few times he realized I was telling the truth. Then he made it a point not to eat so early, but to wait until we'd traveled for a few hours."

"And your parents? They couldn't have gone along with this."

"No. As you remember they wished me to marry Graham—as quickly and as quietly as possible to prevent any gossip or counting of months when the baby came."

"What did you tell them about coming here?"

"They don't know. They sent me to Virginia to finish my confinement with my aunt. That's when I stopped Franklin and came here instead."

"In Virginia," he repeated slowly.

"Aunt Beth expected me weeks ago. I sent her a note explaining that I was coming here first and that I would arrive late at her place. Franklin has promised to take me there when we leave," she added softly.

His breathing slowed to nonexistent in his chest. She'd planned everything out without a thought to staying. He sat back in the chair. Where did that leave him?

"What is it you want from me?"

"Well, of course, at first I'd hoped you would return to Charleston with me. I can see that will not happen now." She spoke softly, carefully. "After the baby comes, my parents have arranged for Aunt Beth to raise it. They won't let me bring the baby home."

If he knew her at all, he knew that wouldn't sit well with her. "How do you feel about that?"

She met his gaze. "I can't leave my own child into someone else's keeping. I feel it moving inside me. I want to raise it. I had hoped you would be able to help me."

She needed his help. He dragged a hand through his hair as he weighed the possibilities.

A hesitant smile crossed her lips. "I mean, you were so honorable that you would fight for Texas. I hoped you would also honor this life you have started."

She turned back to her task of cleaning up the dishes she'd just used. Watching quietly, he mentally searched for an answer to her dilemma, trying for once to think beyond his own needs. There had to be an answer for her. When she untied the apron from her waist and hung it on the peg with her hat, he rose to his feet.

"Walk with me." He raised his hand, palm up, and waited for her to take it.

He led her through the grove of pines and then further on through the meadow without saying a word, using his cane over the uneven ground. She followed silently, afraid to break the strange truce that pulsed between them. His steps slowed as he neared a smattering of boulders under three ancient oaks.

"Would you rest?" she asked. They'd come a far distance from the cabin with the sun beating down. The shade felt wonderful.

He didn't answer.

"Then might I rest? It's hot." Without waiting for his approval, she sat on one of the shorter granite boulders and removed her hat, fanning herself with the brim. "I can tell when the wound aches, Brandon. There's no point in denying it."

"I didn't come here to talk about my leg. What's done is done on that account."

She stiffened at his tone but kept her voice pleasant. "I'm sorry if my asking annoys you. I happen to care."

He sat on a nearby boulder, stretching his leg out before him to work the ankle within his leather boot.

"We've walked over a mile and you haven't uttered a word. What is it you wanted to talk about that couldn't have been said at the cabin?"

"Just wanted some fresh air. Bear with me, Caroline. I'm sorting all this out."

At last. Perhaps now they would come to an understanding. Perhaps he would help her so that she could keep the baby. A light breeze rustled the leaves overhead. As much as she wanted to press him, she kept quiet, giving him the space to think. Whatever he decided would affect her future, and that of their child.

"Your parents knew you were with child," he said slowly. "That's why they were so eager to marry you off."

"Yes." She'd thought that much was obvious. Apparently he'd just figured it out.

"Did Graham know?"

"Not at first. When he proposed, my answer at that time was no. That I was waiting for you to return."

"But I didn't—return."

"No," she said, remembering the hurt, the overwhelming worry for him when he'd left her. And then to hear that he'd *chosen* to stay in Texas. She felt humiliated all over again when she thought of that.

"I can see how you would feel that I deserted you. I did."

She stared at him in surprise. His admission took the edginess out of her in one breath. "You didn't know. You…you thought I had married."

"I should have returned—at least to straighten things out."

"You were injured. You had no idea about the baby. And then Jake wanted you to stay for his wedding."

"You're trying to absolve me?"

"Not really. Just trying to be honest about things. You understand then how things were for me—at least a little."

"It couldn't have been easy. I'm sorry for that, Caroline."

An apology! That was more than she'd expected. He began to sound almost like the man she once knew—almost.

He took a deep breath, removed his hat and raked his hair back from his forehead. "So what happened after you refused Graham?"

"He thought giving me time would change my mind. That the longer you stayed away, I'd come to see what a 'catch' he was. When he proposed a second time, I nearly said yes but I couldn't deceive him like that. I couldn't bring a baby into this world in such a false situation. By that time, I was sure you weren't returning from Texas and I was so scared. Scared of what would become of me. Scared of what would become of the baby. But more than anything, scared that you'd been killed and if so, my life was over already."

At her raw admission, Brandon looked away. His throat worked as he swallowed hard before he turned back to her. "I wouldn't have blamed you for marrying him."

Unbelievable! Here she'd just poured out her heart to him, and he thought she should have made a different choice! "Wonderful! I'll just return now and see if he'll take me back!"

Brandon scowled. "I didn't mean it like that."

"Well, that's how it sounded."

"You were in a fix, with few choices." He stood and grasped her upper arms, forcing her to look at him. "Caroline. Listen. What I'm saying is I'm glad you waited for me—as difficult as that was for you. I'm glad you didn't marry Graham."

"Why, Brandon? You obviously are not ready to have a family."

"For three good reasons. If you had said yes, you wouldn't be here now. I'd still be angry with you for backing out on your promise to me. I'd have no idea about the baby. And I'd have no idea how much you really do love me."

She tensed, her thoughts frustrated and mutinous. "That's four."

"So it is." The soft hint of a smile played about his lips. "Caroline, give in. Give me this."

"I…I'm afraid to," she whispered. To let down her guard would be the same as relinquishing control, to allow herself to be vulnerable. She couldn't bear the hurt again, the anguish, if he should reject her again.

"You do, you know. Love me."

"I never said that."

"You didn't have to. Not in so many words."

"Then why do you think I love you?" The words came out breathier than she'd wanted them to.

He leaned his forehead against hers. "Stubborn woman. When you held Franklin hostage at gunpoint, you told me. When you came halfway across the continent to see me, you told me. And when, in spite of everything—" he stepped closer, nuzzling her hair "—you let me hold you and make love to you at the pool yesterday, you told me."

Her legs went weak.

"You never said so in words, but your actions said it every time." He leaned down and kissed her gently on the lips. "Every time."

She plopped down on the rock. "I intended only to let you know about the baby."

"That's all?"

"You…you hurt me." She looked down at her bonnet in her lap. She felt so exposed. "I never wanted to care again. I just need your help with the baby. I don't want to love anybody. Not ever again."

He tilted her face toward him, studying her face, seeing more there than perhaps she wanted him to. "You'll be a good mother," he murmured. "I've always known that."

His hand, gentle on her chin, made her tingle there. She wanted to turn and meet his fingers with a kiss, wanted to rub her lips against his palm and move into his arms, but she couldn't bear to have him see her so plainly. She turned from his probing, intense gaze.

He stepped back and straightened, drawing in a deep breath. "I have something to say."

Half curious, half scared, she waited.

"I don't like the thought of you being beholden to your parents or your aunt in any way. And I don't want my child growing up on the wrong side of the blanket, Caroline. I want him or her to have my name and every benefit that name might bring, including financial."

Her throat went dry. "What are you saying?"

"I want you to marry me."

She swallowed hard, barely able to breathe. It would take care of all her problems. "Are you asking me to stay here? In Texas?"

"I'm asking you to marry me. To be my wife."

She couldn't help remembering the first time he'd proposed, declaring he loved her. Then he'd left her. He hadn't said anything about loving her today although he'd admitted to understanding her dilemma—to a point. Still, he was offering her help and she would be grateful for that. In her situation she couldn't expect undying love. She had to take what he could give. Even though the proposal this time was less than romantic—no flowers, no boat ride on the canal, no moon. She opened her mouth to accept…

"There is something you should know before you accept—or reject—my offer," he said with a firmness to his voice she'd not heard before.

She waited for him to finish.

"I'm not going back to Charleston—"

So she *would* be staying in Texas. "That's all right. I—"

"—but I want you to."

Chapter Twelve

Her breath caught in her throat, and a coldness congealed in the pit of her stomach. "What—what are you saying?"

"We'll get married tomorrow—in Bexar," Brandon continued. "It'll be small. Quiet. I don't want to take anything away from Jake and Victoria's day. They should have their own wedding as they planned it. Then I want you to go home with Franklin and have the baby there. Your father and mother, with their connections will be able to hire a good midwife."

She couldn't believe it! What kind of strange marriage was he proposing? "And where would I live?"

"Wherever you wish. My home in Charleston, or if you prefer, you could live with your family. Their support will be important for you in your time of confinement."

It was the same thing as him leaving her. Only this time he was sending *her* away! She felt as though she might explode on the spot. "How could you!"

She had to move, had to release some of the agitation that overtook her. Standing, she strode out from under the oak into the heat of the day, then turned around and marched back until she stood before him. "I cannot believe you expect this of me."

He frowned. "I'm trying to consider this rationally. The child will have proper parentage and you will not be ostracized. It's the sensible course."

"Oh, it's quite sensible! With the exception of your sudden departure from Charleston, you have always been so careful to be rational."

He looked genuinely surprised at her outburst. "I thought you'd be happy. You'll be taken care of."

She tried to calm down. Didn't he realize he'd said nothing about love, nothing about his feelings for the baby—his baby?

"I thought you wanted to go back home."

Not without you, came the thought. "The pull isn't as strong as it was at first," she admitted. "I believe I could like it here."

"You can't mean that," he said cautiously. "Here in Texas?"

Her chest tightened with pain. "You don't want me here, do you? You're willing to give our child a name and money for support, but that is all you are willing to give."

His jaw tightened. "Now, Caroline, that's not true."

"Don't you wish to be at my side when the baby comes into this world and takes its first breath? Find out whether it's a boy or girl? Don't you want to see it grow, take its first steps, say its first words?" Her hands clenched into fists at her side. She'd never been so frustrated, so hurt in her life.

Brandon frowned. "Damn it all, of course I do! Seeing you ride away will be the hardest thing I'll ever do in my life."

"Then why are you insisting on it? Why can't we be together?"

"I have my reasons. Look. I'm being honest with you."

"No, you're not. Not completely." If he didn't really want her, didn't really love her, then he needed to say it. She wouldn't hate him for it, but she had a right to know where she stood with him.

"You want to know why?" he asked roughly.

"I deserve an answer—and so does your child."

He pressed his lips together. "You won't like it."

Hands on hips, she waited. She wasn't going anywhere until he explained himself.

"I know you've seen what is happening to me. The unsteady nerves, the shakes, the hallucinations."

She froze. *Hallucinations, too?* This wasn't what she'd expected him to say.

"It started when I was in prison. In Goliad. But it was only nightmares then."

"You have nightmares, as well?" Her thoughts churned back to earlier at the cabin.

He nodded.

"You use liquor to help you sleep, too? I thought it was to help with your leg pain."

The look he shot her way was dark and filled with frustration. "It's so I won't dream. The pain is nothing compared to the dreams." He removed his hat and sat on the boulder. "Every time I close my eyes I see them."

"Who?"

"The men I took care of...their injuries..." He paused a moment, then began again. "The last soldier I doctored in Goliad was a Mexican boy of sixteen. He'd been in the thick of the fighting when his arm was bayoneted."

"Did he survive?"

Brandon huffed. "I wrapped his arm so well that by the next day he was up and helping with the prisoners. By the second day he was back on the line working alongside the men. He was shot accidentally—as it turned out by one of his own comrades. Now tell me what good I did?"

Her heart ached for him. The pain he carried inside was real. "You didn't have a choice."

"When I was sixteen, I hadn't even heard of the Texas territory. I was swimming in the bay and fishing off the dock. That boy had never gone swimming—never seen the ocean."

"You did what you had to do."

"A smart man would have figured out how to save that boy."

"Brandon—stop. Don't torment yourself."

"What? Just let it go? Forget it?" He paced away a few steps and stared up at the sky. "Tell me—how in the hell do I do that?"

She didn't know how to answer, what to say to make it better. There wasn't anything that would help. She waited for him to turn back to her. "I don't know," she whispered. But he had to. It was killing him.

"There's more. You might as well hear the rest."

The way he said it scared her. So calm now.

He straightened his shoulders and finally met her gaze. "I'm going crazy. Not all at once, but little by little. The dreams, the spells—they're getting worse. I don't know how much longer I'll be able to doctor, how much longer I'll be able to function at all. You could have been killed with that bull. I…I don't want you or the baby hurt because I can't protect you. And I won't have you around watching me go slowly insane. That's why you have to leave."

Shocked to the core, her voice came out a mere whisper. "No."

"It's true. I've seen it enough since the war. A man isn't made to go through something like that and survive."

Awkwardly he rose to his feet and with the use of his wooden cane, stepped over and pulled her up. He touched her chin, raising her face so that her gaze met his. "My offer stands. I want to help, to do right by you, but you have to agree to go back to Charleston."

So this was her choice. A woman alone, raising a child. She wasn't that strong—not if her parents chose not to support her desire to raise the baby and she didn't have any reason to think they would. Brandon was right on that account. In the end, the baby would bear the brunt of their poverty and of being an outcast—this baby that she already loved.

She swallowed hard. He'd said nothing about love. At least now any romantic dreams she'd had would have to stay just that—as dreams.

It wasn't about herself anymore. She must think of the child now. "It is a generous offer. And, you have made a good argument. Your name and your money, but not you. A woman could do worse."

She stared up into his blue eyes while inside she broke apart. She felt brittle, as though the slightest breeze might shatter her into a million sharp-edged pieces. Choosing her words carefully, she answered him. "Under the circumstances, it's a reasonable offer. My parents are anxious for me to return, but they made it clear I was not to come back with the baby. I know I won't be able to leave it with my aunt. I already love this child."

"Then you'll agree? For the sake of our child?"

Our child. The words warmed her. She closed her eyes against the look of hope on his face. Agree? To a life without love? A life without him?

She blinked away the tears swimming in her eyes. "Yes. I…I'll agree to your terms."

The relief at her decision was plain on his face. "You won't regret it, Caroline. I promise."

She shrugged from his grasp. Inside, her heart continued to beat, but slowly, insidiously, it hardened and turned to stone. She'd have a marriage in name only. She'd been a fool to hope. Nothing felt right. Nothing at all.

The next morning, she dressed in her best gown—the mint-green one with gigot sleeves and the deep green bodice. She called for the maid to fix her hair high on her head, and thread it with a matching green ribbon. When she descended the stairs, a look of admiration passed over Brandon's face. He wore black pants and a white linen shirt. With his hair wet and slicked back, he was the handsomest man she'd ever seen.

Beside him, Victoria waited. "Dressed so elegantly, you two are sure to set people talking in town. Thank you for seeing to the things I need for my wedding."

Apparently Brandon hadn't told her the true reason for their trip into Bexar. Victoria looked curious, but held her questions, too well-mannered to pry.

The ride into Bexar on the rutted wagon trail was bumpy and rough. Caroline's insides were jarred into new positions and she wondered that the baby didn't come then and there.

Brandon pointed out the charred remains of the Svendsons' barn as they passed. The place looked deserted. Again, Caroline wondered what drove a man to try making a go of it in this desolate territory where no law and nothing could protect him. Finally, after two hours, the sun-bleached walls of the fort came into view.

They passed the Catholic church and Brandon pulled the wagon to a stop in front of a small, square adobe building. He helped her down from the buckboard.

"This is Catholic land. We would have to convert for the priest to marry us. I know you'd prefer a church wedding..."

A sinking sensation filled her. "Who will marry us then?"

"The colonel for the fort." Brandon tucked her hand in his arm, holding tight as though he suspected she might back out at the last moment, and escorted her into the office.

Colonel Parker was a slight, graying man who looked up from his desk when they entered the one-room building. He greeted their interruption with a distinct air of distraction.

It wasn't how she'd pictured her wedding. Her girlish heart had dreamed of a ceremony at the gazebo in White Point Gardens with a proliferation of blooming flowers and the blue waters of the harbor stretched out behind her. Here in this dusty town, with clucking chickens and rutting pigs just outside the door, she was surrounded by stucco walls. Her chest tightened. Everything here was foreign and strange from the pistol on Brandon's hip to the brusque manner of the colonel as he removed a worn leather Bible from his desk drawer.

She had never felt so out of place in all her life. Perhaps Brandon was right and she didn't belong here at all.

Brandon stepped closer and took her hands in his. Her world narrowed to his face, the serious look in his eyes and the tenseness in his jaw. To marry him is what she wanted—had always wanted. The rest—this awful room, her worries about his spells, the baby and their future—she would have to face later. "I am ready."

Was it possible, or did his shoulders relax with her words? Even at this late hour had he been worried she would change her mind?

There was no lecture on the sanctity of marriage, no questions on whether they should wait to make sure their love was real. The colonel simply began the vows.

"Do you, Brandon Dumont, take Caroline Benét as your lawful wedded wife, to have and to hold, from this day forward, for better or for worse, for richer or poorer, in sickness and in health, to love and cherish, until death do you part."

With the words *in sickness and in health,* Brandon squeezed her hands. The change was slight but she felt it—the small pressure of his thumbs against the back of her hands. His face remained as impassive as it had been before. "I do."

The traditional words were ones she'd heard often at the weddings of her friends, but now that it came to be her time to respond to them her heart filled with resolve. She would honor them, honor the love she had for Brandon, no matter that he might send her away. She answered, "I do."

Brandon released her one hand. He dug in his pocket a moment and withdrew a gold ring. Where had that come from?

"Caroline, take this ring as a sign of my love and faithfulness in the name of the Father, the Son and the Holy Ghost." He slipped it on her finger. It fit perfectly.

Still holding her hands, Brandon lowered his lips to hers, she tilted up to touch his—soft, warm, eloquent in tenderness. She trembled and opened her eyes.

He noticed, his lips pressing together almost imperceptibly.

"Remember your vows here today," Colonel Parker said from somewhere near.

She pulled back from the kiss.

"Ahem. Doctor Dumont, you'll need to sign the certificate."

Brandon turned toward the desk. They both signed their names and Brandon paid the colonel.

"Have you heard about the Svendsons' place?" When Parker shook his head, Brandon told him what he could about the renegades. Then, after shaking hands with the colonel and thanking him, Brandon escorted her outside.

"Where?" She held out her hand with the ring.

"It's yours. I had it made back in Charleston."

Then he'd had it over five months! "But how did it come to be here?"

"I asked Franklin to bring it. I thought Jake might want it for Victoria, but he had other ideas."

"So it really is mine," she murmured, stunned.

"It was meant for you from the beginning."

She fingered the ring, twisting it slightly.

"You are pleased with it?" His breath warmed her ear.

She nodded, not trusting her voice.

They walked down the street and ate at the cantina. Her wedding meal, rather than the smoked bacon-wrapped scallops and Johnny cakes with sweet milk she'd once envisioned, ended up being something called enchiladas and almost too spicy for her to choke down. She and Brandon didn't converse much, feeling the curious stares of the bartender and cook.

After their meal, they walked down the street to the parade square. There at the bazaar tents Brandon purchased the items Victoria had requested. When finished, he told her to wait while he retrieved the buckboard.

She watched him stride away as an intense feeling of loss came over her. She didn't want to be separated from him for one moment. How could she endure the rest of her life?

The ride back to the ranch was a quiet affair. Once, when the wagon jostled violently, Brandon reined the horses to a stop and helped her down so that she could stretch her legs. By late afternoon, they reached the hacienda.

Jake strode up to hold the horses while Brandon helped her down from the buckboard. Jake's gaze landed on her ring.

"Welcome to the family." There was no smile of welcome on his face or in his voice. "Guess this is what you wanted all along."

She didn't respond. She hadn't expected anything from Jake. And exhausted from the ride, she couldn't tell if his words were simply an observation or meant to hurt her.

Juan's wife, Gertrudis, had a light early meal waiting for everyone. At the table, everyone offered their congratulations. Victoria, especially, was full of questions that Brandon fielded expertly. Caroline could hardly eat. Her stomach was in knots from the trip and from what would happen next. Would she even have a traditional wedding night like any other bride or was that lost to her, too? Finally, begging fatigue from the trip, she started to head upstairs to take a short nap.

"Señorita?" Gertrudis said softly. "I will have fresh water sent up for you. Diego and Brandon can move your things to the cabin later when you wake."

"That won't be necessary," Brandon said.

Caroline's gaze flew to his.

"But, Brandon," Victoria said. "You will want privacy for a few days."

"Caroline will be sleeping in the same room until she leaves with Franklin."

At his announcement, everyone stopped eating and stared from him to her.

"What's this all about?" Jake demanded.

"It's no one's business but our own," Brandon said, his voice harsh. "Suffice it to say that Caroline will be returning to the coast after your wedding."

"And you?"

"Nothing will change. I'll stay here—in the cabin."

"Then why did you marry?" Jake asked suspiciously.

Brandon didn't answer, yet his hesitancy spoke volumes.

"Why?" Jake asked again, this time his voice more demanding as he rose to his feet and stared at her.

"Because," Caroline began, her gaze meeting Brandon's. Would he not help her? He didn't move or say anything, by his silence agreeing to whatever she would say next. She took a deep breath to continue. Everyone was staring at her. Straightening her shoulders, she willed her voice to be calm, steady. She would get through this. "Because I'm having a baby. His baby."

The sudden quiet in the room was deafening. She felt so alone, so incredibly vulnerable. She closed her eyes to the stares of the others. It was then she heard a chair scrape and felt strong arms go around her—his arms. Relief spread through her and she leaned against his chest.

"You are having his baby and yet you are leaving?" Victoria asked. Caroline opened her eyes to see the woman frowning. "Why must you go? This land, this place is not good enough for you?"

"No…that's not it." She didn't want Victoria to think that. Didn't want her to believe that it was her desire to leave. But she couldn't say anything about Brandon's problems. He was her husband now and that position demanded her loyalty.

"Enough!" Brandon said. "No more questions. Caroline and I have our reasons."

Tired beyond belief in body and in mind, Caroline shrugged from his hold. His eyes held hers a moment and in them she saw his concern for her. It didn't matter. He didn't care enough for her to stay with him, to make a life with him. He didn't think she was strong enough. She turned her back on them and trudged up the staircase to her room.

Chapter Thirteen

Just after sunset, Caroline rose refreshed from her nap and made her way down to the dining room where she heard soft conversation. She felt stronger—better able to withstand the questions now. When she entered the room, Victoria looked up from putting finishing touches on her wedding dress. Her lips pressed together in a thin line before she nodded to a nearby seat.

Caroline sat down and picked up Victoria's wedding slippers from a nearby basket. She had embroidered seed pearls in a delicate swirling pattern on the top of one slipper last evening and now started on the second slipper. Señora Torrez sat next to her, braiding silken cords and beads to make the wedding lasso—something Victoria had said was a Spanish custom.

"I saw Diego take mugs to the cabin," Victoria said, her words clipped. "The men are drinking a toast." She did not look up from sewing buckwheat into the hem of her wedding dress—a last-minute fix in case the day of her wedding was windy.

Caroline watched for a moment and could feel the animosity coming from the woman in waves. She couldn't let things between them continue like this. Still, she wasn't ready to talk about her unusual marriage arrangement with Brandon. Although to another it must look like Brandon had married her out of duty and that leaving was her choice, there was so much more to the situation. However there was one thing she could clear up.

"I don't hate it here, Victoria. I never meant to give you that impression."

Victoria lowered her needle and material.

"Texas is different. It takes some—adjusting."

"Is it that we are not so cultured, so elegant as this place called Charleston?"

"That is not what bothers me." And she realized she meant it. "Everything is rough here, coarser. The men wear guns and even you carry a knife."

"It is necessary."

"After passing the Svendsons' place today, I realized that. But that doesn't make it easy to understand. How will these marauders be stopped? There is no law here. No justice."

"We are the law. We take care of our own."

"But how can I bring a baby into this? Medicine is scarce. What if my child gets sick?"

Victoria's gaze was steady and cool. "Then you see why we wish Brandon to stay."

Afraid her next question would be about Caroline staying, too, Caroline changed the subject. "How many will be attending your wedding?"

Frowning, Victoria answered. "Not as many as I'd hoped for. If we could have had it at my home in Laredo there would be many more cousins attending. But the most important family will be here—Juan, Gertrudis and my parents."

Caroline smiled. "And Jake."

"*Si.* He is the most important of all." A dimple showed on her cheek. She lowered her voice. "It has been hard for him to wait—now even more so since he is staying in the house with us."

A sudden vision of Brandon, impatient with desire filling his eyes, nearly choked Caroline. If Jake was anything like his brother, Victoria could look forward to an exciting wedding night. She envied her that.

Victoria studied her shrewdly. "We are both passionate by nature. Would you say that Brandon is passionate?"

Caroline swallowed. She remembered Brandon's insistent kisses, his constant desire to touch her. Her face grew hot. She wasn't used to discussing such things.

Victoria's eyes suddenly sparkled. "Ah, I see your answer before you say it." Standing, she held the dress up to herself.

"It's beautiful!" Caroline said. And it was—a white silk creation with gold accent thread on the sleeves and bodice.

"It was my mother's wedding dress. I am so proud to wear it. It means much to me." She looked lovingly at her mother, said something in Spanish and then carefully handed it off to the maid with instructions.

The candlelight in the candelabra overhead flickered wildly. A door slammed and Juan shouted in Spanish from the front of the house.

"Something's wrong," Victoria said, rising.

Dropping her needle and thread on the table, Caroline followed her into the hallway along with Señora Torrez.

The door stood wide-open and the odor of smoke, carried by the wind, poured through the front door. Juan strode toward them, a rifle in each hand, his face grim. Drawing a long dueling pistol from his belt, he handed the weapon to Victoria. "The stable is on fire. Keep the women inside!"

Gunshots sounded near the corral. Caroline jumped.

The hair on the back of her neck stood on end. What was happening?

Maria hurried from the kitchen.

A donkey bellowed in the stable and then a horse neighed. The iron gate squealed as someone passed through. Caroline's heart thudded with each new sound.

Victoria closed the door after Juan and turned to the women. "Into the library," she said. "It will be safest there in the chance that the fire spreads. Maria? Please bring the children and Gertrudis."

Victoria ushered her mother and Caroline into the enclosed room. "Into the corner. You'll be safer." She dragged a straight-back chair to the spot for her mother.

Caroline strained her ears, trying to make sense of the noises she heard outside in the yard. Even the stretches of silence sounded ominous. What was going on and where was Brandon? Was he safe?

"What is happening, Victoria?" she finally asked in a hushed voice.

"I know as much as you. Perhaps it is *Comancheros*, perhaps it is *bandidos*."

Alarm heightened Caroline's senses. Her thoughts raced with the image of the burned barn they'd passed earlier that day and the desolation at the ranch. She might never understand why these people stayed here in the face of such danger, yet this waiting and wondering, this cowering in the dark library was worse than actually doing something. She had to find more protection than this.

"My gun is upstairs," she said suddenly.

Victoria read her thoughts. "No!"

Ignoring her, Caroline ran from the library and up the stairs to her room. She threw open her trunk and tossed the items within aside until she came to her brother's pistol. She checked to make sure it was loaded properly and then looked about the room for anything else she might use to protect herself and the other women. Picking up a tall candlestick holder from the bedside table, she then raced back down the wide staircase and into the library.

Victoria pulled her to the corner of the room with the others. "That was very foolish." But approval gleamed in her dark brown eyes.

"What do we do now?" Caroline asked, handing off the pewter candlestick holder to Maria.

"We keep watch."

"But the men!" Caroline worried that Brandon might be in his cabin, unaware that Juan needed help, or in need of help himself.

Victoria nodded, sharing in Caroline's worry. "Stay here. I will check the window." Staying low, and ignoring her mother's hiss of dissension, she maneuvered to the side of one of the two large windows in the library. No curtains covered the glass so that with the candles in the wall sconces flickering, anyone outside could easily see into the room. She blew out the candles near her head.

Caroline crouched low in the shadows and made her way behind the settee and two large chairs to extinguish the other candles. Then she moved to Victoria and peered outside. The night was black with but a sliver of moon.

"Can you see what is happening?"

"It's too dark out there. If only the moon were full."

"Do you see a fire?"

"No. But it could be inside the stable."

As they watched, a familiar figure moved stealthily across the yard.

Victoria gripped Caroline's arm. "That's Jake."

Two figures, unrecognizable to Caroline, emerged from the stand of pines that separated the main house from the cabin. She started to point them out, but Victoria already had her pistol trained on them. The tall one glanced at the hacienda and then watched as Jake slipped through the stable door. He motioned to the other and stealthily moved in behind Jake.

With her heart pounding in her chest, Caroline raised her pistol beside Victoria's. Victoria glanced down, seeing it, and whispered, "I'll go out through the courtyard and circle around the house to come up behind those men. You stay here."

"Juan told you the same."

Victoria's brown eyes flashed. "*¡Él es mi prometido!* He may need my help."

Caroline nodded, realizing she was seeing only a small part of what the woman must have been like during the rebellion. "Go then," she whispered. "Be careful. There may be more than two."

Victoria squeezed her hand and then moved silently from the room. After she left it seemed to Caroline that they waited an eternity in the dark although it could only have been a few more minutes. She wondered if the fire had been put out, wondered who the two men were and wondered if there were more.

A shot sounded. Her heart pounded triple time. A few seconds later the large door to the stable swung wide and two horses charged through ridden by men crouched low on their backs. Caroline saw a swish of deep gold from Victoria's skirt as she ran from the courtyard gates across the dirt yard and into the barn. Caught between keeping her word to Victoria and wanting to help, Caroline hesitated on the edge of the decision.

Victoria screamed.

Caroline ran from the room, threw open the front door and raced to the barn.

Smoke filled the interior.

"Victoria?" She coughed and waved her hand in front of her face in a vain attempt to reduce the amount she inhaled. Her eyes burned and watered.

"I'm here!" Victoria's frantic voice came from a point in the darkness. "Jake is hurt. I can't move him!"

"We need to get him out of this smoke," Caroline said. "Where are you? Keep talking so that I can find you!"

A moment later Caroline bumped against a boot and nearly tripped. Jake moaned. She crouched, feeling up his leg to his hip, to his waist and then his arm. "He needs fresh air. The smoke will kill him. If you can get under that arm we can drag him outside." Victoria's dress rustled while she positioned herself. "Now."

Together they turned Jake around and dragged him out into the clean night air. When Caroline let loose, something sticky coated her fingertips. She held them to her nose. The scent of blood filled her nostrils. "He's bleeding."

"Jake!" Victoria cried out frantically. "Jake. *Háblame!*"

No sound came from his still form. Caroline felt for a pulse as she'd seen her father do countless time before. There. In his neck. Rapid but steady. "He's alive, Victoria, but we must see better to know where he's hurt. I'll run to the house and get candles."

As she rose, a form dashed around the corner of the stable.

"Jake! I couldn't catch them!" Diego yelled.

"*¡Diego! ¡Ven aqui!*" Victoria cried. "Jake's here. He's been hurt."

Diego fell to one knee at Jake's side. "*¡Dios!*"

"Where is Juan?"

"He's smothering the fire on the far side of the barn."

A moan rose from Jake.

"We should take him to the house," Caroline said. "Can you move him? I'll go get Brandon."

"*Si*, Señorita Caroline."

"Do you have your gun?" Victoria asked. "Those men may still be near."

"Yes."

Victoria reached out and grasped her hand. A tremble shuddered through her.

"I'll hurry," Caroline said, and turned quickly away.

Moonlight slashed through the branches overhead as she ran down the path through the trees. The figure of a man loomed before her. Gasping for air, she stopped and clutched the gun in front of her with both hands, aiming at the shadow.

"Caroline. Wait! It's me."

She lowered the weapon. "Brandon. Thank God."

Immediately he was at her side, taking the gun from her shaking hands. "I heard a shot. What's going on?"

"Jake's been hurt!"

The curiosity on his face quickly dissolved into concern for his brother. "Where is he? What's happened?"

"He's bleeding. His chest, I think. Diego is carrying him to the house now. He tried to stop two men from stealing the horses."

Brandon grabbed her arm. "Stay near me. Whoever shot him may still be around." He crouched low and kept a firm grip on her until she was across the yard with him and safely inside the big house.

In the library, Diego laid Jake on the long settee that sat across from the fireplace. Victoria knelt beside him and, grabbing the knife from her garter, cut away Jake's shirt from his wound. Fresh blood ran from a hole in the skin, down his chest. She staunched it with her lace handkerchief which quickly turned from white to red.

Brandon stopped short when he saw his brother.

Jake lay quiet, pale and ashen. His breath was so shallow that the rise and fall of his chest as he breathed was barely discernible. Slowly he opened his eyes.

Victoria looked up at Brandon, meeting his gaze even as tears stained her cheeks. The fear Caroline saw in their depths gripped her heart like a cold band of steel.

Why wasn't Brandon doing something? Caroline glanced at him. He hadn't moved, but stared at his brother, caught up somewhere in his thoughts.

Diego stepped back. "I'll find Juan and see about the fire."

Brandon started, jarred at the sound of Diego's voice. He nodded, then knelt beside his brother and checked his pulse, much like Caroline had done. "Are you hurt anywhere besides your shoulder?"

Jake grimaced, his lips a tight line with the pain. "My head."

Brandon felt over his brother's scalp. "You have a lump the size of a walnut. This is the wrong angle for a fall. Someone struck you."

Carefully he peeled the shirt off Jake's shoulder, the sound of tearing fabric loud in the hushed library. He examined the bullet hole. Caroline remembered that oozing was good—pulsing blood would indicate an artery had been hit which could have been fatal.

"Can you move your arm? Grip?" He took Jake's hand from Victoria's hold. Caroline watched as Jake tried to squeeze Brandon's hand without success. A slight tremor shook Brandon's hand. Her imagination, surely. Or perhaps it was Jake that was shaking from the pain in his shoulder or the effort to squeeze Brandon's hand. Any number of reasons—

"Well, that's the pits," Jake said, training bleary eyes on his brother. "Can't have a wedding night without two good arms to hug my lady."

A sob escaped Victoria as she bent to kiss Jake on his temple. *"Te quiero."*

"You too, darlin'." His mouth quirked up in a smile and then he raised his gaze ever so slightly to Brandon. "Gotta come out."

Brandon took a deep breath. "Yes."

"Then get to it."

Brandon rose. "Franklin. Let's move him to the table in the kitchen. I'll work on him there."

Caroline pulled Victoria away and helped her stand. "Do you have any whiskey? Something to help blunt the pain?"

Victoria nodded numbly, and motioned to Maria to bring the liquor. Franklin and Brandon helped Jake to his feet and half walked, half dragged him to the kitchen. Once there he took a long gulp from the bottle of mescal and then stretched out on the long center table used for preparing meals. Señora Torrez placed a blanket beneath his head.

Brandon rummaged through the kitchen drawers, taking out a small knife, a spoon, two forks. "I need you to get your sewing basket, Victoria," he said, without looking up.

"But Brandon," Caroline said when she took stock of the things on the table. "What about your surgical instruments? Your father's instruments?"

"They were taken in the war. I'll have to improvise."

She saw nothing on the table that could be of service. "But your forceps, your retractors! How—"

"The bullet has to come out," he said. Frustration filled his voice. "I don't have a choice."

Caroline glanced back at Jake and found that what Brandon said was true—bleeding continued despite the pressure bandage Franklin applied to the wound. It was then she noticed Brandon was nearly as pale as his patient. A sheen of sweat coated his forehead.

He was nervous, she suddenly realized. She looked again at his hands.

And beginning to shake.

She couldn't deny it now. The tell-tale evidence was too obvious. A fine vibration seemed to hum through his entire body. In Charleston, his nerves had been as steady as the ticking of a grandfather clock. Steady and sure. He'd handled his cases with care and precision—and confidence. Perhaps his nervousness stemmed from the fact that this was someone close to him—his brother rather than a stranger.

She looked at the others in the room and saw that their concern was focused on Jake, not Brandon. That was good. There was no reason for them to have more worry heaped upon their fear for Jake. Somehow, Brandon must get through this. How could she help? She tried to think what her father had needed at times for his surgeries.

"Maria," she said, turning to the wide-eyed cook. "We'll need warm water to wash out the wound. Please put a pot on the stove. Gertrudis? We need bandages, cloths and towels to soak up the bl…to place beneath his arm and shoulder for support. Señora Torrez? If you could see to turning down a bed for him and lighting the lamp in a room. He'll need rest when Brandon is through."

The women left to do her bidding. As they were occupied, she turned to Victoria. "You'll have to hold his arm. Can you do it?"

Victoria nodded, her face grim but determined.

Caroline stood before Brandon. "What else do you need?"

He looked at her, his eyes clouded with confusion. "There's so much blood."

Caroline looked once more at Jake, assessing his wound. "Some," she said cautiously. "A normal amount for such a bullet I suspect. Less than the longhorn we encountered, a little more than the boy with the fishhook. I've seen similar when at my father's side." She moved closer, lowering her voice so only he could hear. "A normal amount, Brandon. What do you see?"

"A lake. It covers everything."

Shocked, Caroline tried to keep from letting it show in her expression. It was important to stay focused on what Jake needed at this moment.

"I tell myself it isn't real."

"You're right. It isn't. And your brother needs you."

He nodded, his eyes tormented pools of indecision beneath dark brows. "If I nick an artery, I could kill him."

"If you do nothing, he's already dead. The wound will fester."

"I know."

"That's Jake. Your only brother. He moved mountains to get to you here in Texas. You're a good doctor—the best I know and he needs you now."

She suddenly noticed Victoria listening intently and she rotated Brandon so that his back was to her. "You can do this, Brandon. You're a brilliant surgeon. I'm sure you've managed much worse situations than this. Now tell me, what is the first step?"

Still he hesitated and stared at Jake's shoulder, lost in a fog his mind had manufactured without his consent. "No more than the ordinary amount?" he whispered.

"No more," she said. She pinched his hand and forced a sharpness to her voice. "Now, Brandon."

His eyes cleared slightly.

She handed him a sharp knife and grasped his fingers once again, trying to infuse him with her confidence.

Brandon squeezed his eyes shut and when he opened them they seemed clearer, the purpose in them stronger. He moved close and poised the knife above the wound. Jake watched him steadily. "Brace yourself." At Jake's brief nod, Brandon motioned to Victoria. "Hold him tight—and don't faint on me, Señorita Torrez."

Caroline moved the lantern, holding it high to afford the best light for the operation. She dabbed the blood away from Jake's arm.

Brandon probed for the bullet. At the same time Jake stiffened with pain. Even though he'd been less than cordial to her, her heart went out to him. Jake kept his gaze trained on his brother, his jaw tightening with each new probe of the knife. Then she felt his gaze slide to her. The usual cynical look she had come to expect was displaced by his pain. However, she thought she saw something more. What—she wasn't sure.

More blood oozed up, blocking Brandon's view. Caroline dabbed the blood away. Whatever Jake thought of her, it didn't matter now. He had to come through this—for Victoria, and for Brandon, too. Brandon would never recover if something should happen here and Jake didn't pull through. She met Jake's gaze once more, watching him tense for a final time before his eyes closed and he went limp.

Victoria froze. "Is he…?"

Brandon pressed his bloodied fingers against Jake's neck. "He's passed out. A blessing for him. I'll need the spoon," he said to Caroline.

She handed it to him, wondering at its use. The bowled end was entirely too large to fit into Jake's wound. He flipped the spoon around and inserted the handle, scooping down with it. "I see the bullet," he said. "Got it!" He dragged the plug out quickly. "Pressure," he said.

Caroline wadded a clean cloth against the newly flowing blood.

"Needle."

Maria handed a threaded needle to him and he used it to tie off something deep inside the opening, then he sewed shut the edges of Jake's skin. He pressed a new wad of cloth against the wound and wrapped strips around Jake's shoulder to hold it firmly in place.

"Should we move him?" Franklin asked.

"Not now," Brandon said, moving to the stove to rinse the blood from his hands. "Give the blood a moment to clot. When he comes around will be soon enough. He's too heavy to get up the stairs at the moment.

"Stay with him," he told Victoria. "He shouldn't be left alone."

"Where else would I be?" She grabbed his hands in hers and pressed them to her wet cheek. "*Muchos gracias,* Brandon."

He took a deep breath. "I'm going to find out who did this." He left the room without so much as a glance at Caroline.

Startled at his abrupt exit, Caroline followed. She caught up to him in the library.

"I thought you were going to find Juan?"

Brandon ran a hand through his thick hair. "I had to get out of there," he admitted. "When I think about how close that bullet was to his heart vessels. Another inch…" He shuddered and sank down on the settee, staring at his hands. "Please, Caroline. Close the door."

She did as he asked, then stood at the door, guarding it from intruders, and watched the trembling overtake his hands. She wanted to run to him and grab his hands, forcing them to stop shaking, but didn't.

"It's nerves. I can't stop it from happening," he said, not meeting her eyes. He turned his hands palm up. "Ever since spending time in prison this happens. Guess I'd make a good subject to study."

She took a step toward him and then stopped. He didn't need mothering and wouldn't want it. "You did an excellent job."

"Maybe. I'll know more in a day or so, once Jake is up." He rose to his feet and took a deep breath. "It's better now. I need to see Juan and Diego." He started to say more and then thought better of it. Clamping his jaw tight, he strode through the door.

"Caroline!" Victoria called from the kitchen. "Help me, *por favor!*"

Caroline rushed into the kitchen. Jake moaned. He was coming to his senses. Victoria held down his shoulder, trying to keep him quiet as he thrashed about, the liquor still in his system. Maria and Señora Torrez held his legs so that he wouldn't wrench himself off the table.

"Franklin, let's get him up to his room," Caroline said. "Then we can give him more mescal. Take care not to pull the stitches."

Caroline, being larger than Victoria, moved to take Jake's injured left side and with Franklin on his right, they eased him into a sitting position. She spoke to him gently as he blearily came to, his face pale and pasty. Then ever so slowly, they helped him stand and make his way up to the bedroom upstairs. Victoria gave him another gulp of strong spirits, and then he sprawled onto the bed and closed his eyes once more.

Chapter Fourteen

The entryway door slammed open. Caroline stepped to the banister. Juan stood in the open foyer. "We're up here, Señor Seguín."

He looked up, his face dark with soot. It was then that Caroline remembered the smoke she'd smelled earlier and started down the stairs. "Is the fire out?"

"*Si*," he said, taking out a cloth and wiping the black from his face. "Gertrudis? The children?"

"They are safe," Victoria said, coming from Jake's room and, along with Franklin, following Caroline down the stairs.

Diego and Brandon strode inside, rifles in their hands. The determined looks on their faces set her on edge.

"Ready, Juan," Diego said from the door.

Caroline frowned. "Ready for what?"

"To go after the men who did this. They can't be far," Diego answered.

"In the dark? How can you track them?" And hadn't there been enough excitement for one night?

"We'll do what we can." Brandon held Franklin's gaze. "Keep the house shut and pistols close at hand."

Franklin nodded, understanding his place in defending the ranch and keeping the women safe while they were gone.

The plan sounded ludicrous to Caroline. How could they possibly see anything? "Oh, no…those men could be waiting for you. They could easily ambush you in the dark. Why can't it wait until morning?"

"By morning they may be too far away," Brandon answered.

"Good! Let them stay there!" She didn't care if she was interfering. What they proposed was crazy.

"They took two good horses," Juan said. "I must try to get them back."

Caroline knew on a gut level that the men had to do something. They wouldn't sit and let this happen to them without a fight. That's how men were. But she didn't have to like it. Any one of them could be hurt—could be killed!

"It's not just about the horses," Brandon said. "It's about what they did to Jake. About what they could have done to any one of you or Juan's children. They have to be stopped. They can't go unchallenged or they'll do it again and again. As long as they get away with it, they will steal from and hurt good people. Our neighbors."

"Can't the law handle it now?" she asked, although her hope was growing dim that they'd put off this fool-hardy quest.

"There is no law close enough to help. And we're not going to cower in the house with the women," Brandon said. "It's how things are done here."

"In Texas," she said.

"Yes. In Texas." He stepped close to her and lowered his voice. "Enough discussion. Remember, you are only a guest here."

The hope that she could change their minds drained

from her body like sand through a sieve. She'd lost. "Go, then. Just go. You'll do what you want to anyway."

With one more glance at Franklin, Brandon spun around and joined the men.

Caroline slammed the door after them, clenched her fists and turned. Only then did she realize that Victoria had witnessed her lack of composure. The woman stood frozen to her spot at the base of the stairway, her gaze probing as she took in Caroline.

"They won't do anything foolish. You must remember that they've been through a lot together."

Caroline dragged in a deep breath and swiped at her eyes. Victoria's face blurred before her. How could she explain all that was inside her? Her chest tightened with emotion. She loved him. She hadn't meant to, didn't want to. It made everything so much more difficult, more complicated. But there it was. In spite of his problems, in spite of the fact he wanted her to leave, in spite of everything, she still loved him.

"I…" She tried to voice her thoughts and couldn't.

"I know," Victoria said with a small smile. "We have a long night ahead of us, you and I. Let's get some tea."

The bandits headed southwest. Brandon tracked them to the bend in the river near the crossing. He didn't want to think about what had happened with Caroline, but as time dragged on and there were no more signs of the renegades, thoughts of her invaded his mind.

She just didn't understand how things were here. You couldn't depend on anyone else helping you. You had to do things yourself and take the consequences as they came. Of all people, he knew that. Look at his injury—a consequence from running headlong into the Texian rebellion.

Caroline was smart and eventually would figure things

out. Now that she knew of his spells, she'd realize that he couldn't possibly be a husband to her, that he was probably going crazy and it would be too risky to have him around a baby or around her. She'd understand now that he couldn't doctor much longer. It was sheer luck that he hadn't hurt Jake during the surgery.

"I think we lost them," Diego said. He'd been walking rather than riding his horse for the past half hour and studying the ground for tracks.

"They were desperate enough to steal the horses from us while we were all at the hacienda, which means they are probably crazy enough to try to ford the river even though the water level is still high," Juan said. "They won't care if they kill the horses in the process."

"Hopefully they'll fall in and the horses will find their way back home," Brandon said.

Diego mounted. "Start again in the morning?"

Juan nodded and they turned their mounts toward the hacienda.

Near to midnight, they arrived at the ranch. After stabling their horses, Diego and Juan strode to the big house. Brandon stood at the corral and stared at the hacienda. The odor of smoke still lingered in the air although the fire had been put out hours ago. All the windows were dark with the exception of Jake's room where a candle burned, the flickering light dancing through the window. He imagined Victoria sat by Jake's side. They'd nearly lost each other during the rebellion. If their present course continued, their lives would never be smooth. Yet he still envied them. They clung to each other, put each other first in their lives. Their love would be well served.

It was a life he yearned for, a life he could never have. He looked up at Caroline's dark room and wondered if she

slept. This was her wedding night—*his* wedding night…
What would happen if he went to her? Would she welcome
him or turn him away? He had a feeling he could change
her mind easily enough—with a touch, with a kiss, her
body responded to him—but would it be the right thing to
do? And could he ever let her go afterward? He dragged
his hand through his hair, debating to himself. It was best
not to succumb to the temptation, best to keep his distance
until she left for good.

He started to close the stable door when something
flashed silver in the straw piled by the wall. Probably just
shine from a bridle that had fallen from its hook, he
figured, and stepped inside to hang it back up.

It wasn't a bridle, but a knife. He picked it up slowly and
brushed off the few straws that clung to the muddy blade,
studying the handle, the familiar carved crest in the ivory.

His knife—he'd carried it with him to Texas. What the
hell was it doing here? The memory of the prison rushed
back at him—the frigid cold, the constant hunger and the
ill treatment by his guards. A shiver went through him
even now, in the comfort of the warm July night.

He wiped the mud from the blade with his thumb. One
of the bandits must have dropped it. That seemed the only
explanation. He shuffled through the straw and dirt with
his foot, looking for clues as he tried to remember who had
taken the knife from him initially. Most likely it had
changed hands several times. Odd for it to show up here.

Finally, unable to come up with any more information,
he headed for his cabin. In the morning with daylight he'd
check again.

Chapter Fifteen

At dawn, Caroline rose, threw a light quilt over her shoulders and peeked in on Victoria. She sat in the rocking chair at Jake's bedside, her head lolling to the side, halfway between wakefulness and sleep. Jake slept on, his dark hair tousled about his head, his breathing deep and even.

"Señorita?" Caroline whispered.

Victoria roused.

"Victoria!" she said again and Victoria awoke with a start. At first disoriented, she focused on Caroline, but then her gaze swung to Jake. She leaned over and pulled the sheet up under his arms, carefully tucking it in and then checking his forehead for signs of fever.

"I'll sit with him awhile," Caroline said. "You should get some rest."

Victoria stretched, her hand to the back of her neck, and then rose from her chair. "I am tired." A look of concern passed over her delicate features. "But you…you are expecting a *bebé*. How did you sleep?"

"Not well." Caroline grimaced. "Some. I heard the men come back around midnight."

"As did I. They left again just now to look for signs of the bandits."

"Already? I didn't hear a thing."

"Good. Then you slept better than you realize."

"Did…did Brandon check on him? Has Jake been all right through the night?"

"*Si*. He was restless once, but has been sleeping now for a few hours."

Jake stirred and then quieted once more.

Victoria stood and motioned for Caroline to join her at the door. "You don't want to leave Brandon, do you? I see that now—in your eyes."

Caroline took a deep breath. "No."

"Then why must you?"

"It's complicated."

"Tell me," Victoria urged.

Caroline hesitated. She did want to talk about it… almost felt like she might explode if she didn't.

"Whatever Jake may think, I didn't come here to corner Brandon into marriage. I just thought he should know about the child, that it existed. And I needed his help." She struggled to collect her thoughts, to say what needed saying coherently.

"He left me, Victoria. If he'd loved me, he never would have gone. I found out that I was going to have a baby the day word arrived of the fall of the Alamo. I believed Brandon was dead."

Victoria waited quietly.

Her frustration ebbed and Caroline continued, calmer now. "I suppose, if I am to be honest about it, I did hope that on coming here that he would marry me. I was frightened of what others would say, how I'd be treated if I had the baby without being married."

"It is understandable."

"But I would never force him," she hurried to say. "How could I? It is not something a woman can do to a man."

"But surely you had a plan?"

"Yes—to persuade him to come back to Charleston, but I see now that that is impossible. He wants to make his home here." She tapped her hand on the banister, her thoughts going back a few days to when she first arrived, before she knew what was happening to Brandon.

"I want to keep this baby. Once it is born, my parents will not let me bring it home. They've already told me so. I…I didn't know how I would support it. That's why I came here—to see if Brandon would help me."

"Of course he would help! This *bebé* is his own flesh and blood! I don't understand why you must go, then. It is obvious he cares for you."

But not enough. "I don't belong here—at least according to him. You heard him last night. He doesn't think I'm strong enough to make a go of it in Texas."

Caroline couldn't explain about the spells or explain about the true reason Brandon didn't want her to stay, but perhaps Victoria had already noticed. Perhaps she could help.

"I know you did not know Brandon before the rebellion, but have you noticed anything…unusual…about him?"

"Other than his limp? No. He is different than Jake. More serious. Sometimes he thinks too much and it gets him in trouble." The corner of Victoria's mouth quirked up. "Sometimes Jake acts too quickly and that gets *him* in trouble."

Caroline smiled, thinking if the brothers' temperaments had been the opposite Brandon would have been the one who was shot and lying in the bed now. "Has Jake said anything?"

Victoria's eyes clouded. "No. But in many ways I am an outsider between those two."

"At his father's funeral Brandon felt like everyone in his family had deserted him—first his mother left, then Jake took off and then his father died. At the time, I was glad to be there for him."

Victoria met her gaze. "And now he has the chance for a family and he is sending you away."

Caroline nodded, miserable at the thought.

"Perhaps he is afraid to care again. Afraid he'll lose what he cares for."

"He can't lose what he never had."

Victoria's gaze swept down to Caroline's tummy. "Oh, I think he had you."

A blush heated her face. "You are not so proper as I first suspected, Señorita Torrez."

Victoria's eyes filled with merriment. "There are many things you do not know about me, but I think we understand each other better now."

Suddenly Caroline felt the baby kick. She straightened and cradled her stomach with her free hand. "He moved!"

Victoria's smile turned gentle. "Are you frightened?"

"Yes," Caroline answered truthfully. "And happy all at the same time."

"The baby will be here before you know it. Will you have a *dueña* to help at the birthing?"

"What is that?"

"A woman to help at the time the child comes."

"I—I don't know. I suppose a midwife will help."

"But you will have a friend…someone to care for you, to be there with you."

Caroline shook her head. She'd have strangers attending her at a time when she should have family and friends near—when she should have Brandon near. "My aunt will help, but I don't know her well. She's never had children."

Victoria frowned. "You must have—"

A low moan came from Jake as he shifted into a new position. Caroline lowered her voice. "Are you still planning to go through with the ceremony?"

"Yes. If it is what Jake wants."

Caroline nodded. "He's strong. He'll pull through."

Victoria yawned once more.

"Go and lay down." Caroline squeezed her hand. "You are the one who is exhausted. I'll sit with Jake awhile."

"Just a few hours. And you will call me if he wakes?"

"Of course."

"Gracias." Victoria gave a tired smile and tiptoed down the hall.

Caroline pulled the quilt about her tighter and slid into the rocking chair that Victoria had vacated. Jake seemed to be sleeping well, though his breathing sounded more rapid than previously and he'd changed positions—turning from his back to his side. With the amount of alcohol he'd ingested he'd likely sleep until noon. She watched him a moment. In his own way he was as handsome as Brandon—a bit rougher and unrefined perhaps. She wished she were on better terms with him.

She rocked back and forth slowly, the movement somehow comforting, her thoughts on all that Victoria had said. Daylight slowly changed the gray room to a sandwashed white color. The shadows in the corners grew lighter and made her wish the shadows in her life could evaporate as easily.

Drowsy with the rocking, she was nearly asleep when she felt another flutter low in her abdomen. Her hand flew to the spot to cradle it as a warm glow filled her. For a moment, for now, she would enjoy knowing she carried Brandon's child, enjoy knowing it kicked and squirmed inside, strengthening its little body. It would be smart, of course. There was no question regarding its intelligence with such a smart father.

And strong. She remembered how strong Brandon had been, swimming the channel to win the chance to take her home. His powerful arms had sliced through the water, hardly displacing a drop and yet he'd beaten the other two boys in the race by at least three lengths.

A light morning breeze tickled her cheek. She opened her eyes and stared at the curtains, fluttering at the window. Day was upon her again and with it her thoughts plummeted back to earth. She rose and blew out the candle at the window.

When she returned to her seat, she glanced at Jake.

He stared at her, his eyes open, quiet, assessing.

At least the sardonic look was gone from his face. If he'd started in on her, she wouldn't want to stay, but she would have so that Victoria could rest.

"Good morning," she said cautiously.

He didn't answer immediately, but continued to stare at her.

She tried again. "How do you feel? Is there anything I can get for you?"

"Water."

His voice was scratchy—most likely burned from inhaling smoke. She reached for the mug at his bedside and supported his head while he sipped. It seemed strange, the gesture almost motherly considering their ambivalent relationship. Her fingers scraped his day-old whiskers as she held the cup.

"More?" she asked when he'd downed the entire contents and didn't seem to care when some of it dribbled down his chin and chest.

"No. Thank you."

She set the mug aside and though she thought about using the sheet to absorb the small spill on his skin, couldn't bring herself to touch him so intimately. "Anything else?"

"No."

She searched her mind for something to say. "Victoria has just gone to her room to rest. Would you like me to call her?"

"No."

Unnerved by his continued study of her, his eyes so like Brandon's, she picked up the tray at his bedside. "I'll get fresh water."

"Stay, Caroline. I want to talk to you."

At the door, she halted.

"Tell me what happened last night. My head feels like it is caught in a vise."

"You don't remember?"

"I remember getting shot. After that, it's confusing. I remember everyone standing over me—Brandon, you, Victoria. I remember the pain in my shoulder—and my head."

"Yes." She replaced the tray on his table and took her seat again in the rocker. "Men started a fire by the stable. They were stealing the horses. Juan thinks there were only two. You tried to stop them in the stable. One of them shot you. Someone hit you on the head, too."

"Did they get away?"

She nodded. "After Brandon removed the bullet from you, the men went after the bandits. They took off again early this morning, just before dawn." It seemed a bit odd, having a fairly normal conversation with Jake. He'd been so antagonistic before. She leaned forward. "Are you in much pain?"

He tested his shoulder, moving it slightly. "Nothing I can't handle."

"You turned through the night, and the bleeding didn't

start again. That's a good sign. Brandon says you should be fine." *As long as infection didn't set in,* was what he'd said, but Caroline didn't want to load that on Jake now. With his hard life he was well aware of that possibility. "You had a lot of liquor."

Again he was watching her—contemplating her.

Did he need something? Perhaps—did he need to relieve himself? "If you need to use the chamber pot, I...I'll see if I can get Franklin to help." Her cheeks grew warm at the mention of the device.

An amused look passed over his face. "Not just now."

If he felt like talking, she was willing enough. She had never *wished* to be at odds with him.

"I saw it," he said finally. "What you mentioned the other day at the cabin."

She held her breath, letting him gather his thoughts to continue. She was certain Brandon didn't want anyone knowing about his problem, especially Jake, so she wouldn't be the one to blurt anything out.

His brow furrowed. "He hesitated. He's never done that before. Never. The few times I've seen him doctorin', he's always been sure and direct. Fast."

"That's one of the reasons my father offered him the position in Charleston. He's very good at what he does."

"I can see how that would come about. Matter of fact here in Texas he got a name for himself once the troops learned he was a doctor. They depended on him to be quick—especially with amputations. He could cut off a leg in less than a minute. Clean, too. There was less pain that way."

Just imagining what Brandon had had to go through made her stomach roil. Her face must have turned a shade of green, because Jake suddenly clamped his mouth shut. After a moment he continued.

"Sorry. I shouldn't have said that, not to someone in your condition. I just assumed you were used to such things with your father being a doctor and all."

"Does one get used to such things?" She shivered and hugged herself.

"Some things. But not all." His eyes narrowed. "Are you all right?"

She waved away his concern, even though it was the first show of compassion she'd had from him. At this point, figuring out what was going on with Brandon was more important than the nature of her interminably queasy stomach. "It may have been the fact that he was operating on you—his brother. I'm sure that would give anyone pause."

"Do you really believe that?"

She sighed. "No…no. I don't."

"Be honest with me, Caroline. You owe him—and me that much."

She blinked, and a tear escaped.

"Now don't go soft on me," Jake said gruffly. "I want to sort out what went on with Brandon last night. Apparently this has happened before. You've seen it. That's why you said something at the cabin. I just didn't want to hear you."

It wasn't exactly an apology. Few men were good at apologizing, but at least it was an acknowledgment that he'd been rude. "You and I have been at odds for most of our acquaintance."

"Chalk it up to not understanding women. Victoria says I have a long way to go but she's determined to teach me."

Caroline allowed herself a small smile. If anyone could tame this man, it was Victoria.

"Franklin is a good judge of character. I should have been suspicious when he suddenly changed his opinion of you. I'm beginning to see that he was right. There is more to you than just a pretty face. Especially now." He chuckled as his words took on new meaning, and then stopped abruptly when a cough erupted. He grimaced in pain. "Damn smoke. Water. Please."

He had to wait until he could speak without coughing.

"So the question is—why is my brother making you leave? And don't give me that 'I'm not strong enough mash.' You are tough or you wouldn't be here."

"You accept things so quickly. Why does Brandon have to be complicated?"

"Soon as I'm able, I'll knock some sense into him," he said gruffly. "In case you haven't noticed, he thinks way too much."

"I have noticed that tendency," she said teasingly, as though being smart was a deficiency. It is what made Brandon a good doctor. It is who he was. And it's what she loved about him—among other things.

"Don't give up on him, Caroline. He needs you whether he knows it or not. I don't understand exactly what is going on inside him, but I do know you are forcing him to figure it out—something he hasn't done since I found him in that prison."

Jake's expression grew serious. "Something happened in Goliad. He doesn't talk about it. Yet I know it weighs heavy on his mind."

"Victoria said you found him there."

"I found him sick and starving. He won't want to talk about it. But maybe he needs to."

Jake's words stayed with her after she relinquished his care to Franklin and went downstairs to breakfast. During her coffee with Gertrudis and her children, the men returned to the hacienda after searching for signs of the renegades. She heard the frustration in their voices as they left their mounts in the corral and strode up to the big house. Although Diego and Juan joined her, Brandon did not come inside.

Probably to avoid seeing her.

After eating, she walked outside to examine the damage to the stable. The fire, started by the bandits as a diversion, had worked. It was only due to the recent heavy rains that the fire hadn't flared out of control and whipped through the entire stable to destroy it. The bandits had struck it on the shaded northern side of the barn where it had smoldered and smoked more than it had burned. A cold blackened ring of pine needles marked the spot, which was muddy now from the water Juan had used to douse the fire last night.

She walked around the side of the barn. The path through the trees started to her right. She stared at it, mentally following each bend, each exposed root and low-hanging branch, to its end where the cabin stood in the small clearing. Brandon was there, probably eating his breakfast alone. Did he feel any urge to speak with her? Anything at all?

Well, she refused to seek him out. He'd left her alone on her wedding night. That spoke volumes.

With a frustrated sigh, she turned and walked around to the front of the stable. Slipping through the large door, she checked to see which horses remained. The two geldings from Charleston were in their stalls and Victoria's small mare, too. The young filly Diego had been working with was also in her stall. The thieves had escaped with the stallion Juan had hoped to use for stud and another large horse.

At least the stable hadn't burned to the ground. There was that.

The morning dishes had been cleared by the time she returned to the house, determined to help Victoria with the wedding preparations. With only two days left, there was still much to do. She sat down at the massive oak table, and took up Victoria's slipper. It would only take a few more stitches to finish it and then she would begin making favors for the guests that would attend the festivities.

Chapter Sixteen

Brandon rode to the Svendson ranch that afternoon. Lars Svendson was a Swede who had staked his claim here with his wife and young family three years ago. The place was much smaller than the Seguín ranch and Lars worked hard to sustain it, looking forward to the time his sons would be old enough to help him.

The place appeared deserted, but then he saw Lars striding from the direction of the hog pen with an empty bucket in one hand, a rifle in the other. He wore a cotton shirt that had sweat stains at the armpits, and dungarees, blackened from working among the soot and ashes.

Brandon dismounted and tied his horse to the front porch railing. He unfastened his cane from the saddle and walked out to meet him.

Lars deposited his bucket on the ground and shook Brandon's hand. "What brings you here, Doc?"

"Same trouble. Some men stole two of Seguín's horses last night."

"Everyone all right?"

"Jake was shot trying to stop them."

Lars shook his head. "How is he?"

"Mending. I got the bullet out." He glanced down at Lars's gun. "Not taking any chances."

"It's good I don't if they are still in the area."

"I'm pretty sure it was the same men. They went after the stable first, just like here. We ran them off before they got in the house. Did you get a good look at them?"

Lars shook his head. "My wife did. There were three. One older with gray hair, short, no meat on him. The other two were young—in their twenties—and tall as me. Black hair. One tied his back like a Comanche, but he was Mexican."

"They speak any English?"

"Some." He rubbed his jaw where a bruise was turning from purple to green. "I understood what they wanted enough."

"I can see that. What were they after?"

"Anything worth anything. First, they started the fire by the barn. When I ran out to check on it, they circled around and snuck into the house. Frightened my Ilse."

Brandon noticed for the first time that she hadn't come out to greet him. Usually she came quickly out the door when visitors arrived. He checked the house windows, but didn't see anyone peering from the dark interior.

Lars noticed. "She took the boys to Bexar. Wanted to be with family. Those men scared her. Grabbed her around the neck and pulled a knife."

"I'm sorry, Lars." He couldn't blame her for leaving.

"It's harder on women," Lars said. "But she'll be back with the boys. She is strong. She loves this ranch."

"What did the men take?"

"Food, blankets, canteens. What money I had. A gun. My rifle was hidden."

"What about your horses?"

"They left Betsy and Gerta alone, thank *Gott in himmel.* I don't know what I would have done if they'd taken my girls."

Brandon smiled. Lars's girls were his workhorses— shires that did the work of six saddle horses. "Your girls and their broad backs aren't easy to ride and are even harder to hide."

"*Gut* thing, too. But they did take my saddle horse." Lars chuckled, the skin crinkling at the corners of his gray eyes. "What happened at your place?"

"Juan saw two men. They used the same method— started a fire near the stable to draw the men away."

"Did they get in the house?"

Brandon shook his head. "Probably too many people. Victoria's parents are there for the wedding along with a few others. But they did take two horses."

"So, if these were the same men, they now each have a horse. They are probably far from here by now."

"Maybe. I'm not sure." From a sheath on his belt, Brandon pulled the knife he'd found in Juan's stable. "Is this the knife that threatened your wife?"

Lars took the blade and studied it. "I don't know." He turned it over in his palm. "I was trying to put out the fire when Ilse screamed. I ran in the house and one of the men hit me with a board. By the time I got to my feet, the men had gone."

"Your boys?"

"Ilse hid them in a cupboard. I tell you this, Doc…I'm just glad those men were bent on thievery and not on murderin' my family."

Brandon nodded in agreement, sure that Jake had been a sight more threatening than Lars's wife. That's why he got a bullet. Or perhaps the men were more desperate. He took the knife back from Lars. No need to tell the man the blade belonged to him. He most likely wouldn't care for that bit of news.

"Anything I can help you with here?"

A grin split the Swede's face. "Come with me."

He spent the greater part of the day helping Lars move the debris and rubble from the barn and make it habitable for his two shires again. Betsy and Gerta were a formidable team paired together to drag away the charred wood and made short work of the mess. The physical labor felt good and even with his bum leg, he felt like he pulled his weight in work. By the end of the day he was coated in sweat and fine straw dust from the new bed of straw he'd forked into the barn.

Lars walked him to his horse.

"That big brother of yours gonna be well enough to take a wife now?" Lars asked.

"I don't think anything, least of all a bullet, is going to stop Jake from marrying Victoria."

"Ya. She is a fine woman, like my Ilse. They make a good team."

"We'll see you at the house on Saturday."

"We'll be there, Doc."

With a wave, Brandon turned his horse toward the hacienda and kneed him into an easy lope. *They make a good team.* Lars's parting words echoed in his thoughts. To the big Swede, everything came in pairs and it was all about working together—his shires, his sons, and he and his wife. The confidence that Lars had in Ilse's ability to shake off the attack baffled Brandon. He'd never expect any woman to recover from something like that.

He veered west on his way to the ranch to wash the fine straw dust off in the clear pool. Thoughts of Caroline engulfed him as he dismounted and stepped to the edge of the water. She was everywhere here. He could see her rising sleepily from her rock bed, her blond hair tangled and falling down to her waist like some wood nymph from a fairy tale; her eyes widening in alarm at the descending swarm of bees and looking to him for protection; and then her hand grasping tight when he took it to jump into the clear pool.

Did they make a "good team"?

Obviously they did when it came to desires of the flesh. They couldn't seem to keep their hands off each other—at his home in Charleston or here at the pool. Even now, thinking of her, he wanted to feel her smooth skin again, feel him sliding into her warmth as he kissed away the doubts lingering in her eyes. Doubts he'd put there.

He kneeled and cupped water to splash over his arms and neck and face. The straw dust made him itch all over. Rethinking his decision to stay clothed, he removed his shirt and washed his chest and back. And then he sat down, stretching his legs out in front of him to wait for the last rays of the sun and the warm breeze to dry off his skin as he contemplated all that had happened in the past few days.

How he'd helped Jake last night was a miracle in itself. No instruments—no decent place to work. It's a wonder he hadn't pushed the plug further inside and caused more damage. Having Caroline beside him had helped. Even though his hands had started shaking sooner than usual he was able to focus. She'd somehow calmed that part of him that started his nerves to quiver.

They made a good team.

He thought of the moment he'd discovered the baby, of the soft, rounded curve of her tummy as she'd lain on her back. What was it like, he wondered, to feel it move. Would she let him put his hand on her? Let him feel it, too? Perhaps it was a silly thought, and selfish, but did having a part of himself growing inside scare her? Or…or appeal to her?

He pushed himself to his feet. *Get hold of yourself!* That he'd even had such thoughts irritated him. Of course she was scared. Any woman would be. She'd had as much choice in getting pregnant as he had in becoming a father. She'd just had longer to work through her feelings.

A father! He was going to be a father!

How could he support a family or protect them? With the visions, nightmares and shakes he had, how would he make a living? His chest constricted. So much blood on his hands. So many he couldn't save. Could he ever hope to have a normal life after what he'd been through? Did he even deserve one?

Good God—*a baby*. What the deuce was he going to do? It didn't matter whether or not they made a good team. Caroline had to leave. That hadn't changed. Was he strong enough to do what was necessary for the both of them?

A half hour later, when he rode into the ranch, the candlelight flickered through the tall windows of the dining room. Everyone was gathered at the table, finishing their meal under the wrought-iron candelabra. He stabled his horse and then entered the front door of the hacienda quietly. As he climbed the stairs to check on Jake, he listened to the animated conversation between Franklin and Juan, wishing he could join them.

Jake was sitting up in bed, sipping a hot mug of soup. Someone had concocted a sling for his arm to help keep his shoulder immobile.

"I see you are feeling better," Brandon said.

"That's a matter of perspective."

Brandon peeled back the bandage to check Jake's wound. The edges were slightly pink, but did not look inflamed. He placed a clean cloth against the skin and retied the bandage. "Looks like you might live to see your wedding."

"That's encouraging. Victoria will be pleased."

"I expect so."

Jake looked him up and down. "Haven't seen you around today. For a newly married man, you're not spending much time with your wife."

"She's not particularly happy with me."

Jake snorted. "Easy enough to see. Why don't you sit down a mite."

Brandon debated. Jake sounded ready to take him to task on a few things but Brandon didn't have anything better to do. "Guess we'll discuss things sooner or later."

"Darn right." Jake motioned to the rocker.

Brandon plopped down. "Look, she's the one who kept the small fact about her pregnancy from me until I stumbled on it for myself. You might excuse me for taking a second to adjust."

"She was nervous. You haven't exactly welcomed her with open arms. Just put it behind you."

"It's not that easy."

"Sure it is."

"Why are you suddenly defending her?"

Jake raised his brows. "I might ask you the reverse. It sounds to me like there is a lot more going on."

"What could be bigger than finding out you are going to be a father?"

"Finding out you are a mother without a ring on your finger," Jake said flatly.

Brandon rubbed his hand over his brow. "That particular problem is taken care of now."

Jake studied him. "Something is still not right here. How did you act when you got the news?"

"Like myself."

"Well, there's the mistake. You are difficult even at your best."

Brandon scowled. "Spoken like a true brother. I may have to change my toast to you and Victoria."

"You had something decent in mind?" Jake said. "Remarkable."

Brandon ignored the sarcasm and rubbed his brow. "We don't exactly come from great marriage material. I'm probably living up to our parents' expectations."

"That doesn't mean we'll repeat their mistakes. *I* don't plan to anyhow, but it looks like you are well on the way to messing things up."

"She's going back, Jake. Just leave it alone."

"Good God, Brandon! Her blue-blooded friends will destroy her back home."

"Not now. She has a ring and my last name."

"That won't stop people from talking. They're going to wonder why you didn't return with her or why she returned at all. It will create all kinds of gossip—gossip she'll have to deal with by herself."

"I'm hoping Franklin will help her there." Brandon didn't want her feelings hurt by those she considered her friends. She was angry with him now, but he was convinced that this was the best way for both of them.

"That's why her parents were so anxious to marry her off," Jake surmised. "It all makes sense now. There was no guarantee that you'd return from the fighting and as people learned of the baby, Caroline's unmarried state would be an embarrassment to them."

"From their point of view, they were just looking out for her."

"What she did—traveling all the way here—took guts.

She laid her feelings on the line with you whether you choose to acknowledge them or not. The least you can do is treat her with respect."

Guilt surfaced. He knew it hadn't been easy for Caroline and his demands had only made things worse. He dragged a hand through his hair. "I do respect her," he answered his brother. "I love her. But loving each other has never been the problem. From the first time we met, she's all I've thought about. The same can be said of her feelings for me."

"I still don't see what the problem is."

"I'm not what she needs!" Brandon gritted out the words. "I can't support a family, Jake. I can hardly support myself now."

His outburst startled Jake. "What do you mean? You have half of Father's estate waiting in Charleston for you. If you wanted, you could go back and take up father's place there. His patients were loyal to him. And you're the best doctor west of the Mississippi River. You're already making a name for yourself here. It's just a matter of time before you are earning your livelihood no matter where you live."

Before he'd finished, Brandon was shaking his head. "It's not about the money. You don't understand."

"Then explain it."

"I can't, Jake. Just leave it alone. Caroline is going to be all right. She'll be well taken care of once I get the will adjusted to include her and the baby."

His brother shifted in bed. "Did you know she saved Franklin's life? Made some kind of a sling to hold his head above water. There's a lot more to her than I thought at first."

Brandon remembered the cloth he'd slashed away from the wheel, the one that had washed downstream. "It doesn't change anything."

Jake stared at him a moment. "I'm done, Brandon. Figure

it out for yourself, then. You always have to make things more difficult when some things are just straightforward."

Brandon stood. "I'll see you in the morning. We can go over the will with Franklin."

"Does this have something to do with your spells?"

Brandon froze.

"Caroline didn't say anything, if that has you worried. But she did ask a few days ago if I'd noticed anything strange happening with you lately. She was worried about you. I brushed her off—actually I was downright mean with her."

"So why do you think something is going on?" he asked cautiously.

"Something happened when you took out my bullet." Jake paused. "Want to talk about it?"

"No."

"Does it have something to do with Caroline leaving?"

Brandon pressed his lips together. Jake would learn of his spells eventually, but Brandon didn't want that worry on his brother's shoulders—not now, right before his wedding.

"You're among people who care about you, Brandon."

"There's nothing that needs saying."

A furrow formed between Jake's brows. "I went through hell trying to get you out of that prison, but I'd do it all again if I had to. You're my brother. If you can't be straight with me…"

Brandon took a deep breath. He just couldn't talk about his problems. It wasn't something a man did. And it wasn't like Jake, of all people, to press him. The fact that he was, made Brandon realize his brother really was worried for him.

"I'm all right. Just leave it at that. Besides, there's something else we need to discuss."

"What's that?"

"I talked to Lars Svendson today. I have an idea of who shot you."

His brother raised his brows.

"It wasn't random." Brandon pulled the knife from its sheath and twisted it for Jake to see. "Do you recognize it?"

"Father's ivory knife," Jake murmured.

"I found this in the barn. The last time I had it on me was in Goliad."

Jake looked up from the blade to him.

"I think the man was gunning for me, but shot you by accident."

"Then if you're right…"

Brandon nodded. "He'll be back."

Chapter Seventeen

The day of the wedding dawned warm and sultry. The sunlight slashed in harsh relief through the window and across the bedsheets, too bright to ignore even with closed eyelids. With a frustrated sigh, Caroline pushed the sheet off and sat up. Sleep had been impossible anyway. She had tossed and turned until the early hours of the morning, only to rise and pace the floor for another two hours—all because of Brandon.

Why couldn't he see that they belonged together? Not in name only, but in all ways? If it were pride alone that stopped him, she would have argued against him, but it wasn't just his pride. He honestly believed he was slowly going insane. To live with such a burden was incomprehensible to her. To live with it alone…how could she let him do that? He thought it better they parted than for her to witness his spells. Well, maybe that was pride, but she loved him anyway. And she would love him through any illness he might have. Wasn't it better to be together and give each other comfort than to be alone? Trying to quell her frustration by sheer will, she rose from the bed.

A horse whinnied in the stable. She glanced out her window. Diego was up extra early, attending to his chores before the festivities of the day crowded everything else out. She watched him work the filly. The horse circled the corral at his command, dust from its hooves plumed up and shimmered in the morning light. A dog barked nearby, its call answered by the long yowl of a coyote in the distance.

Guests would start arriving in the early afternoon and before that she had promised Victoria to go out to the meadow to pick flowers for the tables and for decoration in the courtyard. She slipped on her cream-colored blouse and brown skirt. Later, she would change into the green dress she'd brought with her, the one she'd worn for her own wedding. For now, she plaited her hair loosely in one long braid down her back. Her parents would be appalled that she'd relaxed her standards so much, that she didn't call the maid to help with her hair every morning, but here in the country, it made more sense to be comfortable.

Today would be difficult. Brandon would be everywhere. But it was Jake and Victoria's day. If she could just focus on that, perhaps she would make it through.

The kitchen bustled with activity and excitement for the day. Two of Maria's cousins had arrived at daybreak from a neighboring ranch to help make the wedding cake, which now sat cooling on a side table. The sweet fragrance wafted through the large room and unsettled Caroline's stomach. Rather than bother Maria, who was already harried with what needed to be done for the day, Caroline grabbed a crust of leftover bread from the cutting board and took it into the dining room.

"That is hardly enough, *señorita*," Gertrudis said as

Caroline sat next to her youngest child. "Let me have Maria fix an egg for you."

"No, but thank you," Caroline said. "Dry toast is more to my stomach's liking this early."

"Perhaps later. You will not be shy to ask for something? You must give the baby something to eat."

Surprised at the easy reference to her baby, Caroline searched her face. Gentle brown eyes stared back at her, waiting only for an answer.

"Thank you. I will be sure to ask if I feel hungry."

"Antonio! You must eat all of that!" Gertrudis said sharply to her eldest, then leaned over and kissed her son on his forehead to soften her words.

Watching the display of affection and glancing about the large oak table at the three children, Caroline decided that, yes, Gertrudis would be much like Victoria. Accepting of Caroline's state, but cautious at first, wanting to protect what was hers.

She heard heightened voices in the kitchen and wondered who entered from the courtyard. All of her senses were on edge as she finished her toast and sipped her coffee. Then Brandon walked into the room and took a seat across from her. Although she'd heard that he had often checked on Jake's progress, it was the first she'd seen of him since their wedding day.

"Mornin'," he said, and fell silent as he ate.

The children were unusually boisterous. To get a word in edgewise among the chattering, excited voices would have been difficult. Brandon's silence seemed almost natural, except for one searching glance her way.

She couldn't help that they'd be thrown together frequently throughout the day with the wedding, but to sit here now grew increasingly difficult. "Excuse me…" She stood.

Gertrudis looked up from wiping a drip of milk from her son's chin. "Victoria said you planned to gather the flowers this morning?"

Caroline nodded.

"Would you mind if the children and I joined you? I am afraid if they stay, they will only get underfoot. And they are eager to help with the preparations."

"Of course they may come."

"Gertrudis!" Victoria called from upstairs. "I need your help!"

The woman smiled apologetically at Caroline. "Perhaps we will join you later."

Up to now, Caroline had been treated as a guest in Juan's home. Her mind had been so preoccupied with what was happening between her and Brandon that she'd ignored much of what was going on around her. She did not want to be remembered by this kind woman and her family as a thankless imposer. She would be leaving soon. It was high time she joined in and helped more—especially on a day like today.

"I'll take the children with me," she heard herself say. "That is if you are comfortable with me watching them. I'm sure you have many things to attend to today and Victoria will need your help in much of it."

"You are sure?" Gertrudis said, a hopeful look on her face.

Caroline surveyed the three fidgety youngsters surrounding her. They ranged in age from two to seven years. Could she keep them together? "I'm not sure at all, but I'll do my best."

"Children," Gertrudis addressed her brood in a no-nonsense voice. When she had their attention, she spoke in a rapid stream of Spanish. After a moment, they glanced from their mother to Caroline. The four-year-old, Josefa, smiled shyly.

"I'll help."

Caroline looked up sharply at Brandon's voice.

"Won't you have things to do with Jake?" Caroline asked.

"At the moment he's with Franklin."

"Gertrudis!" Victoria called again.

"Thank you," Gertrudis said, looking at both of them as she stood. "I will leave them in your capable hands."

Caroline watched her leave and then turned to look askance at Brandon. She didn't know what to make of his offer. Didn't know what to make of him. "I'll…I'll just get my bonnet."

After a stop in her room, she headed to the kitchen, following the sound of laughter and good-natured scolding. The room was hot from the cookstove and the bustling women. "Is there something to gather flowers in?" she asked.

Maria handed her a wide, shallow basket and shooed her from the room with a wave of her arms.

The walk to the meadow took much longer than Caroline had suspected it would due to the shorter strides of the children. Before they'd gone a hundred feet, Brandon scooped up two-year-old Juan and carried him on his shoulders. Walking behind him with the other two children, Caroline noticed that the added weight did not seem to bother his injured leg.

They followed a deer trail in single file through the pines and then Brandon moved to her side once they broke through to the tall grass. They were careful not to touch, not to bump into each other. However, the silence was soon broken—and often—by warnings to Antonio to stop running ahead and to Josefa to quit dawdling.

The meadow, as it had been every day, burst with beautiful, colorful flowers. She used a small knife she'd confiscated from the kitchen to cut through the stems. Brandon returned to her from chasing after Josefa as she wrestled with a particularly fibrous stalk.

She sighed. "This will take all day at the rate I'm going. My knife is dull as butter."

He withdrew an ivory-handled knife, carefully handing her the handle. "Don't cut yourself."

Her work went faster after that.

Antonio picked a handful of tall red phlox before announcing his palms hurt from the thick stems and he wanted to quit. Brandon tried to coerce him to pick a few more flowers but soon gave up and challenged him to a throwing match. They meandered off in search of stones.

No matter that she'd lost her crew, Caroline soon had picked a basket brimming with red, yellow and white flowers. She continued adding to her collection, wanting plenty to choose from when she returned to the house. Josefa helped by picking anything with a petal, pretty or not, and running to show Caroline each and every one. Caroline kept the girl close, worried she'd pluck a weed with thorns or needles and hurt herself.

When she had another bundle of flowers, Caroline stopped to look for Brandon and the boys. She stretched her back and gazed across the rolling carpet to the hills in the distance dotted with oaks. The warm air rustled the tall grass, creating undulating patterns while honey bees droned over the tips of the clover.

She sighed. She wanted to stay here. She wanted to raise her child here, but she couldn't stay and face Brandon every day, knowing he did not want her here. She just couldn't do it.

"Josefa! No more!" she called. "We have enough."

She looked again for Brandon and the boys. They had wandered to the edge of the meadow and Brandon no longer laughed and wrestled with Antonio and little Juan. Instead he stared at something in the trees, then searched along the ground, walking slowly through the tall grass. Finally he looked up and she caught his gaze. She waved. It was time to start back to the hacienda.

He waved back and called to Antonio. The boy raced toward her, followed by Brandon. She picked up the basket in one hand and harnessed the second pile of flowers under the same arm, and then took hold of Josefa's hand. She started off, knowing that Brandon would easily catch up.

After she'd gone several paces an odd feeling overcame her—a prickling sensation at the nape of her neck, as if she was being watched and measured. She glanced toward the line of trees. It could be anything—a bear, or cougar, or a man. Or just a silly feeling and nothing more.

Nothing like this had ever happened to her before. She couldn't ignore it. She dropped the basket and flowers. Crouching down, she pulled Josefa to her and hoisted her on her hip. She wished for a gun as she grabbed Brandon's knife from the basket and held it against her skirt, her body tense, her senses alert.

She waited, anxious for Brandon to hurry. When he finally caught up to her, relief poured through her. His gaze narrowed on her grasp of the knife and he looked up sharply, into her eyes, then across the meadow to the trees.

"I shouldn't have drifted so far off."

"It's fine now," she said, holding out the knife.

"Keep it. It won't hurt for you to have a little protection out here."

"It was probably just a silly feeling, Brandon."

He studied her face and did not look convinced. "You carry Juan—he's lighter. And the basket. I'll carry Josefa and the flowers."

"All right. I'll be able to manage, then." She couldn't help glancing once more at the trees. Her heart still pounded. Once Juan was in her arms and Josefa in his, they struck through the meadow, Brandon keeping close to her back until they arrived safe at the hacienda.

Caroline dropped the children off with their mother and then set the flowers on the long dining table. Hat in hand, Brandon watched her from the doorway. "You'll stay at the house now?"

She heard the concern in his voice and saw it in his eyes.

"What did you see up there?" she asked, keeping her voice down so the women in the kitchen would not hear. "I saw you checking the ground and the trees on the edge of the woods."

When he stepped into the room, the walls seemed to shrink in comparison to his size. "Would you believe Antonio was chasing a toad?"

"No." But she smiled anyway.

"Didn't think so."

He stood in front of her now, close. Without touching her, she felt pinned against the table. She could smell his scent, a mixture of leather and soap. "What then?"

He withdrew a silver coin from his pocket and placed it in her hand. She turned it over.

"A Spanish silver dollar?"

"A peso. Also some spilled gunpowder and an area disturbed by men. I thought it might be those who'd shot at Jake."

"But you're not thinking that now?"

"It wasn't that recent. The gunpowder was half washed away from the rain we had. Did you see anything?"

"No. Just had a strange feeling."

"Maybe it was nothing."

It hadn't felt like nothing when it came over her. It was enough to make her grasp his knife.

"What are you going to do now?" he asked.

"I'll help here at the house. I need to trim these flowers and put them in vases." She turned her back to him and began sorting the flowers.

If it was possible, he moved nearer. "Stay close," he said in her ear. He watched a moment more. She heard him take a deep breath, as though breathing her in. "I like your hair this way. Loose."

Startled, she looked for him over her shoulder but he'd already left.

The first of the guests arrived late in the afternoon as Caroline climbed the stairs to her room to change into her best dress. Juan greeted the family and then ushered them through the house to the courtyard where the ceremony would take place. She searched through her trunk and withdrew the intricate ivory comb and lace handkerchief she'd purchased in New Orleans. Then wrapping the comb in the bit of lace and tying it up with a new ribbon, she knocked lightly on Victoria's door.

"*Si?* Please come in."

Opening the door, she stopped short at the sight of Victoria kneeling with her mother. "Have you lost something?" she asked, looking about the floor, and then stepped forward to help Señora Torrez to her feet.

Victoria stood. "It our way to say a special prayer before the wedding."

"I'm sorry to interrupt. I only wished to tell you that the guests have started arriving. And also, I have something for you." She handed over her gift.

"What is this? Oh!" Victoria cried out as she unwrapped the comb. With delight on her face, she tested it in her hair and checked herself in the mirror. "It is perfect for today! *¡Gracias!*"

Her gaze swept up Caroline's clothing. She plucked a cottonwood seed pod from Caroline's braid and handed it to her. "Gertrudis has left a gown for you to wear. She thought it might be more comfortable."

Caroline turned to go when Victoria grasped her hand. "I am glad you are here to witness my marriage. Whatever happens, I am glad you came. I think Brandon is, too."

She gave Victoria a swift hug. "Thank you. Now, don't concern yourself with my problems. Today is for you and Jake. Today is your day."

A rich smile transformed Victoria's face. "My heart is so full."

Caroline left Victoria and walked down the corridor to her room. A maid curtsied as she passed in the hall and then followed her into her bedchamber. "I was sent to do your hair, *señorita.*"

Suddenly she wanted to be alone, and in a most urgent fashion. "I'm sure Victoria or Gertrudis is more in need of your help. Thank you, but I'll take care of my hair, myself." She shut her door in the girl's surprised face.

My heart is so full. Victoria's words haunted her. Would she ever know that kind of happiness? That kind of love? She swallowed hard against the lump in her throat and dragged in a shaky breath. Hot tears brimmed in her eyes. Everything between her and Brandon had been complicated from the beginning. For her, such happiness would forever be out of reach.

More guests arrived. She could hear the exclamations of delight from Juan and Gertrudis, the children talking excitedly to other boys and girls their age, and the frequent creaking of the large iron gate in the courtyard. It would not be long now and she would have to make an appearance.

She drew her hair up high on her head, twisting it into a circular pattern and then pushed two carved ebony sticks through the mass of waves to hold it in place. The dress from Gertrudis had been pressed and now lay on the bed. Caroline stroked the deep royal-blue silk. It was looser through the middle and would be more forgiving of her expanding waistline than the dress she'd brought with her. The simple style was decorated by cream-colored lace at the neckline and on the sleeves.

"Señorita! It is nearly time to start! Early candlelight is upon us!" The maid called from the other side of her door.

"Coming!" Caroline removed her skirt and blouse and washed off her perspiration at the basin. Then, after powdering herself, she changed into the blue dress. It rustled down her body, the large bow in back perfectly positioned on the bustle. The kidskin slippers she'd packed for this day still fit and so she tucked her feet into them, pinched her cheeks for color and then headed down the stairs to the courtyard.

Beside the center fountain and next to the priest, Jake stood resplendent in a white linen shirt and black pants, with a large silver buckle on his belt. He'd polished his boots, wet-combed his hair and stood holding his black hat in his hand, looking for all the world like an anxious groom. He wore a black sling on his left arm to immobilize his shoulder. Noticing her entry into the courtyard, he winked.

Brandon stood beside his brother, nearly as tall, and with finer features but for the exception of his strong jaw. His dark hair had been trimmed since this morning and slicked back, with a few wayward curls that refused to be tamed at his neck. He wore clothes similar to Jake's—the white linen shirt, the black pants, black boots. No gun belt or gun this time. He was so handsome, he stole her breath away. In his hands he carried a small brass box.

Next to him, Diego whispered something and Brandon laughed in response. Amazingly he appeared relaxed and comfortable—much like he'd been in Charleston. He glanced up from the box and his gaze collided with hers.

He stopped laughing. He didn't seem to hear Diego talking at his side. She felt as though the entire breadth of people between them had disappeared. In his eyes she saw warm appreciation as he gazed from her face to her toes.

The priest spoke to him again, drawing his attention away from her.

"You look lovely, Miss Caroline," Franklin said, coming to her side.

She tucked her hand into the crook of his arm, looking over his dark gray suit. "And you, as well. You're not sitting?"

"Not today. But let us move closer. It's not every day I see a Dumont married off. Remember, I knew Jake when he was a boy."

"Was he as independent and stubborn then as he is now?"

"Absolutely."

"What about Brandon?" she asked, thinking of the child within her.

"Ah, yes. He was much more the 'pleaser' of the two."

"I believe that is something he's gotten over." If he'd cared anything about pleasing her, she'd be staying in Texas.

"Considering his present course, I would have to agree with you." He squeezed her hand on his arm. "There are a few more days for him to come to his senses. Don't give up."

"I won't, but I am losing hope," she admitted.

Caroline looked over the people that had arrived. There were more than Victoria had expected—at least seventy men, women and children gathered under the spreading boughs of the oak. A warm, dry wind swept through the garden and rustled its leaves. Chairs from the house had been placed near the fountain for Victoria's parents and the older guests.

The priest stepped forward and those assembled quieted. A look came into Jake's eyes such as Caroline had never witnessed before and she knew that Victoria had stepped to the open gate. Turning with the others present, she beheld a vision.

Victoria walked slowly forward in the flowing cream-colored gown. Her black hair, artfully coiled on her head was set off by the ivory comb Caroline had given her and half-hidden by the long lace mantilla veil. She carried a delicate white fan edged in gold, a prayer book and a rosary, as well as a colorful bouquet of the flowers gathered that morning. Her steps sure, her eyes glowing with love and seeing only Jake, she joined him.

They knelt on a pillow as the priest made the sign of the cross over Jake's head. Gertrudis stepped forward and dropped a handful of gold coins into the priest's hands. He blessed the coins, and then gave them to Victoria, who, in turn, gave them to Jake. Jake placed them in the box that Brandon held.

The customs were unfamiliar to Caroline. She tried to follow along, but unused to the priest's Latin words, especially with the Spanish accent, she soon found her thoughts and gaze drifting inexorably to Brandon. He would see to it that she was taken care of—and the child. He'd always had a responsible nature. It showed in his relationship to his father and to his profession. He didn't do anything halfway. Pride for him, and a fierce, possessive love enveloped her. *Here*, she told her unborn child in her mind, *here is the man who is your father. He is handsome, stronger than even he can imagine, and intelligent. But more than that, he has a good heart.* She sighed, if only he would let go of his stubbornness and see that they were meant to be together.

Enjoying her unhindered view of Brandon, she realized she would carry this image with her when she left.

Juan and Gertrudis stepped forward and looped the beaded lasso around Jake's shoulders and then Victoria in a figure-eight shape. Jake said his vows in English.

The priest took the box of coins from Brandon's hands. Jake accepted the box, and in turn, presented it to Victoria, pouring the coins into her cupped hands and saying: "I pledge all my present and future goods into your care for your safekeeping." Then he set the brass box on top of the small pile of coins.

Victoria smiled and began her vows. "I, Victoria Torrez, take you, Jake Dumont, to be my husband. I promise to be true to you in good times and in bad, in sickness and in health. I will love and honor you all the days of my life." The words took on deeper meaning in light of Jake's recent injury. Caroline glanced at Brandon and caught him staring at her.

The priest removed the lasso from their shoulders and handed it to Victoria. "This cord is a symbol of the love which binds you and the vows you have made today, that you may share equally in the responsibility of marriage for the rest of your lives. You may kiss now and seal your pledge."

Jake took Victoria into his arms. The kiss, so tender and deep, made Caroline hold her breath. It was right to celebrate their love. She glanced once more at Brandon, wishing that he could see what could be theirs. He gazed on the couple, his jaw tight as the kiss ended. He was the first to step forward and offer his congratulations as the mariachi band started to play.

While Jake and Victoria received the congratulations of the closest guests, the servants began moving the chairs to the perimeter of the courtyard to create a space for dancing. With a twinkle in his eye, Diego dragged one chair into the center and motioned to Jake. Jake helped Victoria stand upon the chair. Gathering the end of her veil together, she handed the end to her husband and directed him to raise it high to form a bridge between them.

As the band began a lively tune, the children rushed forward and, holding hands to make a long, snakelike chain, danced under the bridge. They were followed by the women, and though Caroline felt a strong urge to join in, she still felt like an outsider and so held back. When the music stopped, the women stopped in place also. Victoria threw the bouquet over her head. It was caught by a young woman that Caroline did not know, who, with a wide smile, waved it in the air.

At Diego's urging, Brandon stepped forward and helped steady Victoria while Jake dived under her wedding dress. Caroline watched along with the rest of the guests, surprised that Victoria allowed the intimate thing in front of everybody. She looked at Franklin, wondering what he thought of the display and found him laughing along with the other men. Amid the good-natured taunting of the guests, Jake emerged with a rakish grin on his face and Victoria's ribbon garter between his teeth.

The men fell into line to the beat of the small band and danced between the couple. Brandon did not participate but walked over to a small table and poured himself a glass of mescal. Then he made his way around the perimeter of the guests to her.

"May I get you a drink?"

She shook her head. It was the wafting odor of food

from the kitchen that enticed her. She hadn't eaten since morning, and then only that crust of bread. She was hungry, not thirsty.

While Victoria's father gave a short speech, Caroline fought off a wave of dizziness. But when Victoria and Jake moved out to the dance floor for their first dance as a married couple, the music and their twirling bodies converged until she saw black at the edge of her vision.

"Caroline? What's wrong?" Brandon grasped her arm, steadying her.

"I...don't feel well."

"When did you last eat?"

She shook her head, trying to dislodge the cobwebs that had taken up residence in her brain.

"Franklin," Brandon said, his voice sharp as he helped her to a chair. "Bring a glass of wine and a bit of cheese."

"I'll be fine. Just give me a minute."

"Of course you will. As soon as you eat. You have to take care of yourself, Caroline."

"I do take care of myself," she said, not caring for the censure in his voice. "It's only that today has been a different sort of day with the wedding and all." She sipped the glass of wine that had materialized in front of her.

"Cheese, too," Brandon ordered. He crouched down and held a small square to her lips.

She took his offering and chewed it slowly and then swallowed. Leaning in toward his shoulder, she closed her eyes and breathed in his scent.

"Here," he said, jostling her slightly. "Have a piece of bread."

"You're being attentive tonight."

"I think the wine has gone straight to your head."

His voice was gruff, but then he slipped his arm around her shoulder. She snuggled in closer. They were married, after all.

Opening her eyes, she found that her surroundings were a bit hazy.

His gaze softened. "You look beautiful tonight. Will you save me a dance?"

"Yes," she whispered. Her entire body hummed with his nearness.

"Victoria is dancing with her father now. Juan will go next and then I am expected to dance with her," Brandon said, the corner of his mouth lifting. "I hope she is not expecting graceful."

"You are a good dancer. You'll outshine Jake."

"Can't do that." His eyes twinkled. "Not at his own wedding."

He was teasing! It had been so long since she'd heard that tone of voice from him.

"Are you feeling better now?"

"Yes. You don't need to hover."

"Maybe I want to."

He stayed beside her, quiet, until his turn came to dance. A curious emptiness filled her at his departure. She would have to get used to it, she told herself. Soon, she would be on her own.

Caroline watched him dance, envious of Victoria, remembering how it had once felt to be in his arms, to be led around the dance floor until she was deliriously dizzy, always trusting in his strong arms to keep her from falling. She had always trusted him, she realized. If only he could do the same with her now.

A shadow came between her and her view of Brandon. Jake stepped in front of her. "I think it's time we had our dance. It's traditional for relatives and your recent wedding makes you one."

"Are you feeling up to it?" she asked, worried about his wound.

He shrugged in a way that reminded her of Brandon. "Are you?" A quick grin split his face as he held out his hand. "Right now I want to talk to you—while we dance."

Charmed, she stood.

Jake whispered wickedly in her ear. "If it is a boy, you will name him after me. Right?"

To hear him say it so easily, with a trace of pride in his voice, made her relax as she placed her hand in his. "Absolutely not. Should I bear a son, he will carry Brandon's name."

Jake grinned. "I suppose that's tolerable." He turned her about the floor in the steps of the slow waltz. He was a strong dancer, but not as strong as Brandon.

Knowing she would soon be leaving the ranch, Caroline had one more thing to clear up between herself and Jake.

"If a kiss sent Brandon halfway across the country, what would giving your name to his son spur him to do?"

"You got a strong point there."

"Yes. I shudder to think on it."

Jake's expression turned serious. "Well, I imagine that reaction had a lot to do with his strong feelings for you."

"I want you to know that I am… I never meant to hurt either one of you. I'm so sorry."

His eyes clouded over. He remembered it, too. "Neither one of us knew what that would set in motion. At the time it was a lark—nothing more."

"Is there any way that you can…?"

He studied her face. "Let's put it behind us. I think we've all paid our dues."

"I would take it back if I could."

"Hey! It was a great kiss. Just the wrong man."

They finished the dance and Jake bowed. Coming up from her curtsy, Caroline said, "I misjudged you, Jake. You can be kind."

He grinned. "Don't tell anyone. I have a reputation to uphold."

"Oh, I think Victoria has seen through your reputation."

"Only the parts I let her see."

"Keep dreaming," she said with sugary sweetness. She turned to see Brandon staring at her from across the courtyard. "Thank you for the dance, Jake. Thank you for everything."

His face sobered. "Franklin plans to leave the day after tomorrow."

The sense of hope that had started building inside came crashing down. "So soon?" She couldn't keep the disappointment from her voice. That was not enough time to convince Brandon to let her stay.

"He is nervous to be alone with you in your condition," Jake continued. "He wants to make sure to get you to Virginia before traveling gets too difficult."

"I suppose I understand his position. It's just that I should like to stay longer." *As long as possible.*

"Whatever happens, Caroline, if you ever need anything, you can count on me."

"Then please talk some sense into Brandon. That's what I need." She could barely choke out the last. She was near hysteria herself, not caring if the maids heard or not.

Slightly dizzy, whether from the dancing or lack of food, she hurried from Jake's scrutiny and dashed into the kitchen. What was she going to do? Only one day left for her to change Brandon's mind!

The maids were busy making tortillas, trying to keep up

with the demands of the wedding guests. Caroline kept going, into the hall and out the front door, away from the party and music, away from the prying eyes and ears.

Moonlight illuminated the drive between the hacienda and the corral, bright enough for the pines to cast shadows. Hearing Brandon's uneven footsteps behind her, she stopped and took a deep breath of the night air. One of the horses in the stable whinnied nervously and stomped a hoof.

"You followed me," she said, turning toward him.

"Where are you off to in such a rush? Thought we had a dance."

"Oh." She'd forgotten.

"What did Jake say? Was he giving you a difficult time?"

"That Franklin plans to leave in two days, which of course means I am leaving in two days." She pressed her fingertips to her forehead. "It's just so soon."

He didn't meet her eyes.

"Please, Brandon. Don't send me away. Trust me. Trust us."

"I…can't. Caroline, be rational. The situation is complicated."

"Of course it's complicated. Life is complicated, and I want to share all of it, ups and downs, with you."

He hesitated a moment, but then shook his head. "No," he said. "You aren't facing facts."

It was hopeless. He wouldn't listen. She couldn't change his mind. She walked to the corral where Rosa trotted along the railing. "I've lost you, haven't I?"

"The person you lost died in that prison. But you'll have my name and the funds you need to raise the baby. I spoke with Franklin about it this morning. You're all set."

"But I won't have you," she said quietly, turning to face him.

Brandon raked his fingers through his hair. "Are you coming back to the party? You don't have to dance if you don't want to."

"I need a minute."

"It will be all right, Caroline."

No. It won't, she wanted to cry out.

"Do you want me to wait?"

"No. You go on. They'll wonder where you are."

She crossed her arms in front of her and turned away, waiting for him to leave. Finally she heard his boots against the packed dirt as he strode to the courtyard gate. She wouldn't go back to the party. With her emotions so brittle, she couldn't face the people there.

A horse in the stable nickered softly. The moon was already high in the eastern sky and somewhere beneath it was Charleston. Could she be happy taking up her old life? In the few days she'd been here, she knew she'd changed. Not just because of the baby, but because she looked at life in a different way. What mattered most were the people she loved. In Charleston, her life had consisted of parties and society, of picnics and charity work. Could she go back to any of that now? It all seemed so foreign to her.

She started across the dirt drive. A twig snapped behind her. She glanced toward the sound and came to an abrupt stop. A man stood at the stable door. The moonlight gleamed off the gun barrel he raised and aimed straight at her chest.

She couldn't move, couldn't breathe, couldn't scream even though that's what her mind told her to do. Fear sucked the air from her lungs. His shirt hung dirty and lopsided on his bony frame like the rags of a derelict. A mean smile showed yellow teeth half-hidden by strands of his straggly gray hair.

She glanced about and realized they were alone. All the

others were in the courtyard. The fact that he had been inside the stable while she and Brandon talked unnerved her. It was almost as though he'd been waiting for her. "What is it you want?"

"Cállatte!" he growled, and notched the pistol higher, aiming at her face. He held out his hand, palm up. "Your blade, *por favor.*"

Where had she heard his voice before? "Blade?"

His eyes narrowed. "The one you carry on yourself. Give it to me."

How did he know about the knife Brandon had given her? Unless…she went cold inside. "You were at the meadow this morning."

He didn't answer, but extended his hand impatiently. "Now. Or do you prefer I take it myself?"

The thought of his dirty hands pawing her spurred her to action. She removed the knife positioned in her garter. He grabbed it away before she could straighten.

"Your voice…you spoke to Juan about work." She glanced over his shoulder. "You and another man."

"He is waiting for me. And now for you, too." He stabbed the knife into the stable door at eye level, then motioned for her to go ahead of him. "Do not call out. I have killed many. I am not afraid to shoot one more."

"You wouldn't want to bring everyone running at the noise of a gunshot," she said with bravado.

He sneered and grabbed her arm. "Señorita. You are not in a position to question me. We go." He shoved her forward, into the woods.

Chapter Eighteen

Brandon filled his bowl with *mole,* grabbed a warm tortilla and joined Diego on the ledge that surrounded the fishpond.

"Amigo. You don't look so good."

"I'm good," he said, and shoveled a spoonful of the soup into his mouth, hoping to halt any further conversation.

"¿Dónde está tu esposa?"

"She's inside," he answered.

"I have considered asking her for a dance. Would that bother you?"

Brandon stopped eating and dropped his spoon into the bowl. "As a matter of fact, it might." First Jake and now Diego. Heck if he let Caroline dance with someone else before him.

"She is a relative after all." Diego's dark brows rose, and then Brandon caught the twinkle in his eyes.

Brandon ignored him and finished his *mole* and tortilla. A servant bearing mescal on a tray walked by, and he grabbed a mug for himself. Listening to the beat of the mariachi band and watching the dancers swaying to the music made him think of Caroline all the more. He'd gotten what he wanted, so why wasn't he happy? What was wrong with him?

She would keep to her part of the bargain—he could tell by how frustrated she was. It still amazed him that she was willing to stay here with him. He had never expected that. He'd thought she'd be glad to go home to her parents and friends. Love sure made a person do crazy things.

"Isn't it past your bedtime?" he asked Diego. "How long do these weddings last anyway?"

"Often until dawn. And even the little ones like me get to stay up."

Brandon grunted, watching the couples on the dance area. Jake blew softly on Victoria's neck. "Somehow I don't think my brother is going to wait that long."

Diego smirked and Brandon had the feeling that Diego knew a bit about women.

Victoria reached up to cup Jake behind his neck and pull him down to taste his lips. Brandon couldn't keep from staring at the intimacy of the act. The trust he witnessed in Victoria's eyes made him wish for the same—from Caroline. It was his fault she guarded herself around him. His condition on their marriage had hurt her. Unfortunately he saw no way around it. It was for her own good.

He stood and tugged his hat low on his forehead. "I'm not hanging around. See you in the morning."

"*Buenas noches, Anglo.*"

He walked through the house and stopped at the bottom of the stairway. Resting his hand on the banister, he considered going upstairs, at least checking to see if candlelight flickered under her doorway. He hated leaving things the way he had. Caroline hadn't been herself and it was his fault.

He took one step up and stopped. This was foolish. He was only deluding himself that he just meant to check on her. Once he entered her room he'd desire a whole lot more than that—he'd take her body and soul.

He did want her to stay with him. Here. In Texas territory. And for some unconscionable reason, she was willing. So why couldn't he just relax and let them both be happy?

He climbed the rest of the stairs to the second level. No light spilled from under her doorway. No sound came from within. Probably asleep by now.

A young couple tripped through the entryway, the girl whispering and laughing softly as the man she was with escorted her into the library. They shut the door softly.

Brandon turned once again to Caroline's room. Instead of knocking, he opened it carefully, slowly. If she was asleep, he'd leave her alone.

He waited for his sight to adjust to the darkened room. She wasn't in her bed. He glanced about the room, thinking she must be sitting in a chair. "Caroline?" he whispered, and swung the door open further, stepping into the room. "Caroline!" Not here—that was plain. She must have rejoined the party.

He strode downstairs, through the kitchen and out into the courtyard looking for her among the guests. Still he couldn't find her. A sliver of alarm snaked its way up his spine. He tamped it down. As he walked through the gate heading for the stable, Diego joined him.

"What is it?"

"Probably nothing. Just looking for Caroline." But he couldn't let go of a growing feeling of dread inside him. The corral was empty. "Rosa's gone."

He nearly missed it—nearly entered the stable but for the sudden gleam of white at the door. He stopped. There, pinned to the wood at eye level, was the ivory-handled knife he'd given her.

His gut clenched.

"What's this about?" Diego asked.

"She wouldn't have left it here like this. Something is wrong." He wedged the knife free.

"Should I get Jake and Juan?"

"No." Brandon had a feeling this was personal. Somehow, this knife held the key.

"Maybe it is only a lover's quarrel?"

Brandon shook his head, convinced that was not the case. He checked inside the stable—no other horses were missing. "Caroline knows Rosa is only green-broke. She wouldn't chance riding her—not if she had a choice."

He studied the vague footprints in the dirt. In the moonlight, Caroline's small prints were recognizable going toward the pines, but now she was probably on horseback. "I think she's been kidnapped. Get your rifle and meet me at the cabin."

It'd take a miracle to find her at night. He was banking on the fact that the person who had taken her wanted him, not her. She was the bait.

At the cabin, he grabbed his rifle and a powder horn. By the time he'd stepped outside again, Diego had joined him.

Diego's gaze flicked to Brandon's rifle. Brandon ignored him. This was Caroline who'd been caught in the crosshairs. She was in trouble because of him. He couldn't let her get hurt, couldn't let their baby be hurt.

"We are looking for the same person who shot Jake," he told Diego. "He was aiming for me."

Diego took the information matter-of-fact, his young face grim and determined. He gripped his own rifle. "I'm ready."

"We won't have far to go. He wants me to find him—on his terms."

They tracked the horse until they lost sight of the hoof-prints in the thick pine needles. That gave him a direction at least—toward the river.

"Rosa is unpredictable," Diego murmured. "Especially with strangers. I hope the *señorita* is not riding her."

Brandon placed a finger to his lips, signaling Diego to keep quiet. He'd heard something as they neared the rushing water. On the alert, he pressed forward slowly, cautiously.

The whinny of a horse sounded, upwind and much further away. At the same time Brandon saw trampled grass in front of him. Were there two men? Had they separated or was this a trick?

It made sense for Brandon, being the slower of the two, to stay on his original course and let Diego chase after the faster bandit. He hoped Caroline would slow her captor and could only trust that he would find her in time. He motioned to Diego to follow the sound. Diego nodded once and disappeared silently into the brush.

Brandon waited. Listening.

The sound of a hoof pawing the ground caught his attention. Slow and stealthy, he parted the branches of the mesquite brush. He surveyed the area just beyond where the trees lined the river. Rosa stood in a small clearing. She snorted once, stomped her hoof and turned in a circle, straining against her reins which were tied to a low branch. He couldn't see Caroline anywhere.

"So you found us, *Médico*."

Fear prickled up his spine. He jerked his head around recognizing the voice. Where? Where had he heard it before?

And then he saw her. Caroline stood with her back against the trunk of an oak, her wrists lashed behind it. Relief shot through him. At least she was alive. Her blue party dress was torn at the shoulder now. With the exception of her light blond hair and that one white shoulder, it was difficult to see her in the dark.

Next to her stood a man with gray straggly hair and clothes that hung loosely on him. Brandon squinted, trying to make out his features better, trying to read what he saw in his eyes.

"An old friend has come to call," said the man, and raised his pistol to wedge it in Caroline's ribs.

His stomach knotted with fear. He had to do something, anything to help Caroline. The man looked vaguely familiar. He had to keep him talking if possible. The raspy voice—Brandon was sure he'd heard it before. He racked his brain trying to place it. Not a neighbor. Not a friend.

"You have me at a loss, sir," he began and took a cautious step forward.

"Move no closer, *señor!* Drop your rifle."

Suddenly it all rushed back at him. He let out a long breath. "Goliad."

"*Si, Médico.* You remember now."

A chill went through him. His guard. The man who'd shot him.

"The rifle. I said drop it."

Brandon lowered the gun slowly to the ground and then straightened.

"You are not so proud now, I see. You must use a stick when you walk." He narrowed his eyes.

"Thanks to you."

"Still you walk—which is more than my boy can do. I will not miss again."

Brandon's thoughts jolted into place. The knife. The last time he'd seen it he'd used it to dig out the plug in his ankle.

He'd tried to hide it again but had passed out. "It was you in the stable. You are the one who shot my brother."

"The bullet was meant for you. I will not make that mistake again."

"You blame me still?"

Malevolence blazed in the man's old eyes. "Because of you my Luis is dead. Because of you, I have no one to care for me in my old age. No one to carry on my name."

"Your son's name was Luis."

"*Sí*—as is mine."

"What do you want with me?" He asked, but he had an ominous feeling he knew.

"I want to take from you what you took from me—someone you care for."

The hatred in the man's face—a malice bordering on insane—struck fear in Brandon. Luis's eyes bulged, his neck veins protruded. Where the heck was Diego? Brandon couldn't take his eyes off the renegade for a second to check the surrounding foliage. "The war is over now. We all lost things important to us. Why would you want to take anything more?"

"Because you have it all and I have nothing!" Luis raged, waggling the gun carelessly in his direction.

Everything inside Brandon screamed to leap forward and wrestle the gun from the man's grasp, but to do so would surely mean his own death. Not that he cared so much about himself. It was Caroline he didn't want hurt. He took a step forward.

The renegade stiffened. "Stop. I will not wait to shoot."

Brandon held himself in check.

"I have eyes. This woman—she is your woman. She carries your child. You deserve nothing—no woman, no *bebé*. Not when you have killed my son."

Fear lodged in Brandon's chest. "She deserves to die as much as your son did, which is not at all. Infection killed Luis. Infection brought on by his wound—a wound I did not give."

"The wound came from a soldier."

"True." He took a deep breath. He would not remind Luis it had been a Mexican soldier who shot the boy by accident. "If you must have your revenge, your retribution, then someone must die. It should be me—a soldier. Not this woman."

"Killing you is not enough. That will not make you hurt the way that I hurt. Every day I must carry this pain. I want you to know the pain that I feel from the loss of my son."

Brandon glanced at Caroline while Luis spoke. She watched wide-eyed. In them he saw fear—a controlled fear—the kind that made a person's thoughts and reflexes fast. He marveled that she wasn't reduced to begging or crying as some women—and men—would be. He *would* see her clear of this, he vowed.

"How old was your son?" Brandon asked, stalling for more time, hoping Diego was nearby—or coming.

"Sixteen."

"I remember him. He was very brave."

The bandit quieted, as if he, too, were thinking back, remembering.

"He did not want to die there in that cabin, but he faced it like a man. He asked…" Brandon took a shaky breath as his throat thickened. He'd done everything in his power not to remember, not to care about that boy…about Luis. He had a name now. Brandon forced himself to continue.

"Luis had trouble breathing in the cabin with all the smoke and the stench of old blood. He asked me to take him outside. It was a clear night like it is now. Cool.

Scarcely a breeze. I was weak from my own wound but found the strength to help him."

Brandon closed his eyes, remembering it more closely than he wanted to. The boy's wound had putrefied. Even now, Brandon remembered the odor of the rotting flesh. "His body burned with fever. I took him to the riverbank. The guards tried to stop me once, but on seeing that Luis had a uniform like them, they simply followed to see what was happening. When I laid him on the ground, he opened his eyes and stared at the night sky."

The pistol hung limp in the man's hand. "My son liked the stars."

Brandon stepped closer as he spoke. "A smile came to his face. A look of peace. He asked if I saw the big dipper. He said it in Spanish and it took me a minute to understand him. He gripped my hand, said *gracias* and died."

Brandon stood before the man now, near enough to reach out and jerk the gun from his hand. The renegade realized it, too, and stepped back, grasping the handle firmly with both hands, again aiming it at Caroline's chest.

Brandon's heart lurched. "You don't want to do that."

"But I do." An unhealthy light came into Luis's eyes.

"It will not honor your son and it will not bring him back."

The man's lower lip trembled. The gun wavered in his hands. Brandon saw that now the end pointed down—at the baby within her. His luck was going from bad to worse.

"Luis would not want this of you. He was brave. Is what you are doing brave?"

The man's shoulders slumped.

Brandon moved swiftly, ripping the gun from the man's hand and turning it on him.

Luis, his eyes wild, yanked a knife from his waistband. He knocked the rifle to the side and lunged toward Brandon.

They grappled and went down with a heavy thud, rolling in the dirt, straining against each other for control. Despite his size, Luis wielded the knife with an unnatural strength. Like a maniac he bore down on Brandon, one hand gripping Brandon's throat and pressing his windpipe, the other hand grasping the knife and hovering inches from his jugular.

Would it matter if he died? The thought came to Brandon in the flash of a second. What future did he have with the madness slowly taking him? His life could be over so quickly and then he would have peace. No more worrying about how he would make a living, no more striving to fight a sickness that couldn't be stopped, no more pain. The thought paralyzed him in its intoxication. In its simplicity. Inside, a low, insistent voice urged: *Just let Luis finish this. Let it happen. Let this be over.*

Jake would understand eventually. He had Victoria now. He would be angry, but he'd get over it. Better that than the worry Brandon had last seen in his eyes. He was beginning to suspect the spells Brandon had although he wasn't completely sure. Brandon didn't want him finding out for sure. He was already the weaker brother—the one who'd gotten himself captured. Jake shouldn't have to keep rescuing him, but he would unless Brandon was out of his life completely.

All Brandon had to do was relax his grip on Luis's wrist, let him slide the knife closer. The man's rotten breath made him gag and in that instant the knife dipped and nicked his skin. It could all be over in one flash of silver. So easy. Perhaps cowardly, but he wouldn't be around to see Jake's disappointment—or even Caroline's. He wouldn't be around...

To see his child. To help him or her into this world, God willing. To watch him grow and teach him about life.

Intense longing filled him, replacing the despair. And Caroline—Caroline most of all. Lord knew he loved her. He didn't know what his future held, but she had to be in it. Somehow he wanted her safe, even if it was across a thousand miles.

The heel of Luis's hand pressed down on his windpipe. Blackness formed at the edge of his vision. Lack of oxygen, Brandon thought clinically. Even in the middle of a knockdown fight, his education, his mind, invaded his thoughts. What a fool.

From somewhere beyond the small circle that had become him and Luis, Brandon heard Caroline cry. She sobbed his name, the anguish and fear thick in her voice.

She was still tied to the tree, he realized. Still a prisoner to whoever won this match. He couldn't let Luis have her. She needed him to best this maniac. She needed him to be strong. Letting Luis kill him was the coward's way out. He'd been thinking like a coward, and damn it, he'd never been a coward in the past. He wasn't about to start now.

A low growl rumbled in his throat. With his thumb, he pressed the man's inner wrist hard—right there where the nerves supplied the hand. Harder…harder still.

Pinpoints of fear entered Luis's eyes and the possibility formed that he might not win, might not be able to carry out his plan. He tensed, the veins in his neck bulging; with renewed force he pushed harder yet.

"Don't do this, Luis. Your son would not want this."

"You know nothing about my son!" Luis grit out the words.

The blade dropped from Luis's hand, slicing Brandon's neck as it landed point down in the dirt. In that second, Brandon jerked up his knee and sent the man toppling over his head. He dragged in a deep breath and pushed to his feet, turning to face Luis again. Somehow, Luis had regained the blade and now strode toward Caroline with a wild, determined look in his eyes.

Brandon reacted without thinking. In a flash of movement, he grabbed the rifle from the dirt and pulled the trigger.

Luis jerked midstride. His eyes went wide. He lunged toward Caroline and then collapsed, the knife scoring down her dress on his descent. He fell with his head against her foot, his eyes blank—the stare of a dead man.

A scream pierced the air. Caroline's scream.

Brandon threw the rifle aside. "It's all right now. Caroline, it's over."

"Oh, God. Oh, God," she cried, her breath coming in jerky sobs as she stared in wide-eyed horror at the man on her feet. "Brandon, please, get him off me."

He grabbed Luis under both armpits and dragged him a few feet away. Then he found the knife in the dirt and cut the ties that bound Caroline. She fell into his arms and clung to him, her body shaking uncontrollably.

"It's all right now," he said again, trying to soothe her. "You are safe."

"I was so scared!" She sniffled. "You could have been killed."

"The thought crossed my mind. Maybe…maybe God wants me around awhile longer."

"Don't make light of it, Brandon. I want you around. I need you around." The words came out jerky and halting.

"Now who is the one with the shakes," he said, rubbing her arms. "Come here. Sit down." He helped her to the ground, her back against the oak, and sat beside her. As he did, the tear in her dress opened and a fresh smear of blood caught his attention.

He pushed the material aside, examining her leg. "He

cut you!" An angry slash from her thigh to her knee oozed bright drops of red.

"It stings, but it is no more than what happened to your neck."

"Quite a bit longer and deeper. I'll have to watch that it doesn't get infected."

She reached out and touched his chin, pulling his gaze to her face. "Always the physician."

He grimaced. "I should have been faster. You wouldn't have been hurt, then."

"Don't try to analyze it this time. It's over and you…you were wonderful." Her eyes brimmed with unshed tears and held such a look he'd never seen before, as if he were a hero—her hero.

"Is the baby…?"

In answer, she moved his hand to her abdomen. He stilled at the intimate gesture. Swallowed. Through the silk layer of her dress he could feel her changing contour. The baby pushed against his hand's added weight. Relief washed over him.

"By the way," she said softly. "You believed you couldn't take care of me."

Slowly he pulled his hand away.

"Tonight you proved yourself wrong."

"This doesn't change anything. It can't."

She sighed. "Just hold me. Till the shaking stops. Please."

His ankle ached. He shifted to move closer to her. "I should get you back to the hacienda." But already he was wrapping his arms around her shoulders, pulling her to him, his mouth pressing a kiss to her temple.

He could hold her like this forever, he realized. Keeping her safe, protecting her. He breathed in her scent, remembering it all over again, and slowly trailed his lips down her cheek until he met the corner of her mouth. He hovered there, waiting, wanting to kiss her—wanting her to want it, too.

She turned her face toward his, her eyes searching his, their breath mingling. It seemed so natural to kiss her. He molded his lips against hers and felt them tremble. If he could, he would give her what strength he possessed—anything to help her get through this.

She opened her mouth and he touched her tongue with his—tentatively at first, and then bolder. Hold her like this forever? Who was he trying to convince? The stirring in his groin made him realize he'd only last so long. He was a young, relatively healthy male and holding led to other things, especially with a woman as giving as Caroline. She didn't need that now. She was probably on the edge of shock from all that had happened. He moved his lips away from hers and kissed her lightly on the forehead. With a sigh, she relaxed against his chest.

Twenty minutes later, Diego found them. He took in the situation in a glance, his gaze moving from them to the man laying dead on the ground. *"Híjole,"* he said as he surveyed the scene and blew out a breath. "Are you all right? Señorita Caroline—are you well?"

She pushed away from Brandon and brushed a strand of hair from her face.

Reluctantly Brandon let go and brought his mind back to the present. Caroline was no longer shaking. He covered up her wounded leg with the edge of her dress and turned to Diego. "Where have you been?"

"I chased the other *bandito* across the river."

"Did you catch him?"

Diego shook his head. "But I found his camp and our

horses. When I heard the gunshot I headed back. I thought you might need help. Doesn't look like you did."

"It could have gone either way for a time," Brandon said, taking his proffered hand for help up.

"It took a while to find you." Diego gave him a quick slap on the back and then turned to help Caroline, but Brandon brushed him aside and grabbed Caroline's hand. Diego took the hint in a flash. He grinned. "I'll get the horse."

"What now?" Caroline said. "We can't leave Luis to the buzzards."

"No," Brandon said, staring at the body. "He was crazy with grief. He didn't deserve to die."

Her brow furrowed. "But he would have killed you or me if you hadn't stopped him."

"I know."

She leaned against his chest and he felt an overpowering urge to keep her there, pressed safely against him. He circled her with his arm.

Diego brought the horse around. Together, he and Diego lifted the body over the horse's back. Rosa shied a bit, and then quieted under Diego's hand.

"Are you able to walk?" Brandon asked.

In answer, she slipped her hand in his.

He gave her fingers a squeeze, pulling her along as they started back to the hacienda.

Chapter Nineteen

Caroline heard a faint knocking through her dream. She'd slept poorly, reliving the events of last evening over and over. Now someone dared to wake her up?

The knocking came again. "Caroline?" Brandon said.

"I'm not awake."

"I'm coming in."

"No!" she cried, sitting up against the oak headboard. "I'm still abed!"

He cracked open the door. "I want to check your leg."

He stepped into the room looking as though he'd been up and working for some time. His body radiated heat. A sheen of sweat covered his face and drops trickled down his neck, wetting his cotton shirt.

She drew up the sheet feeling modest in spite of the fact they were married now. It wasn't a true marriage by her definition. "What have you been doing?"

"Digging."

She thought at first he meant in his garden and it struck her as an odd thing to do after last night, but then realized he probably had been seeing to a grave.

He sat on her bed, careful to keep clear of her legs.

She flexed her ankle. The laceration burned as she stretched. A line of fire raced up her leg.

"Does it hurt much?"

She remembered asking him the same question about his leg and getting a snarl for an answer. That had been days ago—when he'd just learned of her pregnancy and was angry. Much had happened since then.

"Some. I'll be ready to travel in a day or so as long as infection doesn't set in."

His jaw tensed. He swept his gaze down her length and as he did so, his mien became all doctor. "Let me have a look." He readjusted on the bed and rolled the sheets back, taking care not to expose anything more than her leg. A dark red scab ran the length of it, the edges of her skin puckered at places, pink but not unusually reddened. He spread his hand over the cut, checking methodically up her leg for heat and the tell-tale sign of induration or redness that would herald infection.

Slowly he moved his hand up her thigh. Her heartbeat quickened. Knowing his intent didn't stop the tendrils of desire that curled in her abdomen at his gentle touch. He reached the top of her cut, so close to the apex of her legs. His fingers trembled, hovering over the last bit of scabbing.

She looked up into his face, inches from her own. A question lingered in his blue eyes, along with a look of intense wanting.

He expelled a ragged breath. "Caroline…?"

He leaned close, his lips hovering near hers and she remembered how soft they were, how they sent chills through her body and left her begging with need. It broke her heart to deny him. She closed her eyes and willed herself to be strong and resist the temptation that was and always would be—Brandon.

"You want an answer I can't give. Not if you are still set on sending me away," she murmured, wishing her voice was stronger. Only if he asked her to stay would she say yes. And he didn't want that.

"You know I want you, Caroline. It's always been you and only you. Last night when I thought I might lose you and the baby..." His voice trailed off as he searched for the right words. "I've never known such a deep fear."

"Not even in the prison?"

"No. Not there. I've never worried much about myself, but you—you have to live. You are what keeps me going. Thinking of you has always given me hope."

"Yet not enough to ask me to stay."

"You know why I can't let you."

"I've heard your reasons. You're afraid I'll think less of you when the nightmares get worse, when the spells rob you of your mind." She struggled with her thoughts. They were harsh. But it was how she felt. "But you are a coward, Brandon. No matter that you survived last night's ordeal. No matter that you saved me from Luis. You are a coward because you won't trust me. Not with your whole heart. You won't trust me to stand by you through the good days and the bad."

"I've been through bad days—with my father and my mother. I don't want that for you—for us."

"But, Brandon—" She grasped his hands. "Your name will not keep me warm in bed at night. It will not stop me from...from loving you as, God help me, I still do. Beyond reason, beyond life itself, I still love you. And I want to be with you. I believe in you, Brandon. I believe in the strength of the love we share, but only if we are together."

He was shaking his head while she spoke. Unwilling—

or afraid—to believe her words. His face blurred before her. She blinked away the tear.

"I need someone who believes as much as I do. I need someone who will be there for me and for the baby. Someone I can count on." She struggled against the thickness clogging her throat. She had to get this out, had to make him understand that she wasn't giving up on him, but what he asked—to leave him—was near impossible for her.

"I'm not turning my back on you or the child. You'll be taken care of."

She shook her head. "That's not enough for me anymore."

"It's all I have to give."

"I don't believe that. Whatever happened in prison changed you, Brandon. I don't understand you anymore. Perhaps I never did. You had better leave now." She said it to hurt him even though she didn't really mean it. She would always love him.

He didn't go—but remained sitting on the bed. "Have I told you how I got my position in Santa Anna's army?"

She stilled. He'd never spoken of his time in the battle. As far as she knew, he'd never told anyone. She shook her head.

"I was heading toward Goliad with another soldier, Richard Blalock. I carried orders in my pack for Colonel Fannin from General Houston. On the road the Santanistas captured us. Richard knew we didn't stand a chance but he knew the orders had to get through. He pointed at me and yelled, *'Médico! Médico!'*"

"I don't understand."

"Santa Anna gave orders to kill everyone but doctors. Those he needed to tend the Mexican wounded. Richard knew of it. I didn't. The Santanistas shot him and let me live."

"Oh, Brandon! What a horrible thing to witness, but it

was brave of him. If not for him and his quick words, you would have both died."

"Richard had a wife and two children waiting for him in Washington-on-the-Brazos."

"Have you contacted her? Does she know?" It would help, she thought, and not just the woman. It would help Brandon to speak to her, explain how her husband had died and how the man had been a hero to the end.

"I tried, but she'd moved on by the time I was well enough to travel."

"He saved your life. I…I will always be grateful to him." Brandon didn't comment.

"What happened after that?"

"The soldiers took me to Goliad to doctor their troops. There was nothing to work with—no stethoscope, no bandages. Infection set in constantly. At first I figured that if one of the men died in my care, the soldiers would shoot me. When that didn't happen, I couldn't decide whether I should be relieved or whether death would have been the better choice."

It hurt to hear him talk like this. She reached out and put her hand over his.

He stared at it. "There wasn't enough to eat. If I was lucky, I'd get a bowl of beef broth once a day. Sometimes the broth would have pieces of raw meat in it. Wormy, gamey—I won't speak to what that did to my gut. But it was all I had so I ate it."

Caroline held her midsection. "Please, Brandon. No more. I can't stand to hear it."

"I lost weight. It's a wonder Jake recognized me when he found me."

She swallowed convulsively, trying to quell her rising stomach contents. He was finally opening up to her—if she could bear to listen. "How did that happen? How did Jake find you?"

"My guard thought I was trying to escape and shot me in the ankle."

"Luis?" The words the bandit had said last night rushed back to her.

"After his son died, I wasn't any use to him anymore. Luis moved me to a room with the other Texian soldiers. We were pretty much forgotten there. We'd get water if we were lucky. My wound festered. I grew delirious. Victoria happened to see me as I was being transferred and got word to Jake. That's how he found me—burning up with fever and half out of my mind."

She couldn't help it. She was crying now. Crying for the innocence he'd lost in that prison, crying for the inhumanity of man, and crying with relief that he'd survived at all. She knew war was ugly, but she'd never been this close to it. "I had no idea…" she murmured. "No idea at all."

"I'm glad you don't. No one should."

He fell silent, his gaze on her hand covering his.

"About last night," she said. "I was proud of you. You were amazing in your strength—and in your capacity to forgive a grieving man."

"He shouldn't have died. Shouldn't have charged me."

"You did the only thing you could. Luis was worn-out with grief for his son. I hope that now he is in a better place."

Brandon didn't comment, but continued to look at his hand in a way that she suspected he was seeing something else—either last night or his time in Goliad.

A new thought came to her and she leaned forward. "Afterward, there was blood—on my leg and dress, and on Luis's chest. Brandon, did you see anything?"

"You mean another hallucination?" he asked cautiously.

She nodded.

"I was only concerned with you."

"Have you noticed that the spells are less, not worse since I've arrived? You don't dare admit it, but it is happening before my eyes. Last night, I was the one shaking after the attack, not you."

He shook his head, refusing to believe her.

"And when you removed the bullet from Jake, you started to shake, but it wasn't like the time with the fishhook. You controlled it, Brandon."

"It still happened."

The more she thought about it, the more she was convinced she was right. "Perhaps it means you are healing— at least you have some control over the symptoms. You focused. You did what had to be done. Don't you see? You are getting better, not worse."

For a moment, she thought he believed her, but then he frowned. "You're grasping at straws. It doesn't mean anything." His voice sounded harsh, strained, as if he couldn't bring himself to think it—to believe it.

She felt hollow inside. Why was it so hard for him to believe anything good about himself? "You don't want to heal, do you? It would change all your plans."

"Caroline, you're not making any sense."

"I know exactly what I'm saying. If you were to heal on the inside, you might actually have a future. Trouble is—you don't believe you deserve one."

He pulled his hand away.

She'd tried her best. There was nothing more she could say. Turning her attention back to her leg, she asked, "Do you note anything to worry about?"

He cleared his throat. "No. It's healing well."

"Will it scar?"

"Probably." He huffed. "You're worried about a scar in a place no one will ever see?"

"Only my husband."

His gaze flew to hers. He sat straighter on the edge of the bed, remote. "You've had no cramping? No bleeding? The baby moves?"

She drew the sheet back over her leg. She felt betrayed by her own body, by the way it yearned for him even now. "The baby is fine. If you'll leave now, I'll get dressed."

He stood and took a step back. "Of course." When he got to the door, he didn't walk through.

"What is it?" she asked.

"It is past noon. The last of the wedding guests are leaving." He sighed. "I buried Luis this morning. Juan is having the priest say words over the grave before he departs."

She swallowed hard.

"We don't have the luxury of waiting for another day, Caroline. The priest is here now."

"I understand," she murmured. But understanding couldn't hold back the conflicting emotions rolling through her. To have the funeral so close to Jake and Victoria's wedding seemed somehow to taint the day.

"I'm sorry it has to be like this," Brandon said.

"It needs to be done. If things had turned out differently last night…" She didn't finish. The words were too difficult to say, too horrid to even consider.

"It would have been me lying out there in the meadow," Brandon finished for her.

"Yes."

"You needn't worry. I've already talked to Franklin. My will has been altered to provide for you."

Anguish ripped through her. "Oh, Brandon. It's not about the money. It's you I need. Only you."

His jaw tightened while his face closed into a mask. "Gertrudis is worried about you. She's made tea and is waiting downstairs. I'll be back later."

He turned on his heel and left. Through the window she saw him join Juan and the priest. Of course he needed to be there, needed to hear the words of absolution for Luis—absolution perhaps for himself, too.

Brandon headed for Luis's grave, shutting out Caroline's words. He knew she'd try to change his mind about making her leave Texas, but he couldn't think about that now. Thoughts of her were too tangled, and he needed to see to Luis.

That morning he'd buried the man who was guard, soldier, renegade...and father and put a simple cross at the head of the grave. Juan and Diego waited for him there.

The few words the priest said brought a sense of finality to Luis's life. At the end, Brandon grabbed a handful of dirt, dropped it on the grave and said, "Have peace, Luis. Go with God."

The others headed back to the hacienda, but Brandon couldn't bring himself to join them. He stared at the grave awhile, thinking about Luis and his son. Thinking about all he'd been through since coming to Texas. He sat down and rested his arms on his legs.

He should take comfort in the unending sameness of this land, the permanence of it, but when he let down his guard, the thoughts that came to him were not peaceful, but chaotic. They were the sounds of men who had at first yelled out their battle cry only to have it end in a wild-eyed scream of pain, watching them fall as a lead plug found a vital organ—or a bayonet penetrated their flesh. The blood. The loss of life. The cries of agony.

He closed his eyes, dropping his head between his arms, no longer willing the images to retreat but examining each one in his mind, holding them up to the light of day and accepting them for what they were—horrific and ugly. He'd asked for it when he came to Texas to fight. He knew there'd be death. That was the price of Texas' independence. He thought he could handle it. After all he'd been around death before as a doctor. How different to see it from the perspective of a soldier. He hadn't counted on the sheer numbers lost in the rebellion or the unnecessary loss of life because of lack of food and water, or bandages, or medicine.

He'd believed there was nothing left of himself to give Caroline. The war had taken his hopes, his dreams and his health. He'd felt hard on the outside, unable to feel anything anymore. And here she'd shown up and proved him wrong, breaking through his shell until being near her, holding her, was all he wanted. He needed her softness, her light, in his life.

In spite of all his worries, last night he *had* protected her. The blood from the fighting and from her leg hadn't triggered a spell. She'd been right about that.

Telling her about his time in Goliad had been hard, but once he started, he couldn't stop. The words poured out of him from deep inside where they'd been locked. Knowing that she would sit there and listen and accept whatever he said without judging him somehow made him want to keep talking. The more he said, the more it felt like a weight fell from his shoulders.

Could he trust that he was getting better? Could he trust that the spells were subsiding? Or would he live forever in fear of them coming back worse than before.

He stood and looked down the small knoll to the hacienda in the distance. From here he could see Diego starting to work Rosa in the corral. Smoke from the chimney spiraled up and drifted north in the light breeze. By now, Caroline would be finished with her tea. She'd probably be ready for another nap after all that had happened. Would she look out the window and wonder what kept him away? He dragged his hands through his hair.

He wanted her. In her room today, he had wanted to pull her body against his and kiss her soundly, completely, until she gasped for air—until she drove every last memory of the war away and left only her love in its place. What would happen if he went back to the house now, knowing they were married and he had every right to touch her, to hold her...

Would she let him stay with her tonight? Would her heart have softened toward him since earlier when she turned him away? He hadn't pressed her before, but perhaps now he would. He wouldn't force her—yet he didn't want her to accept him as though it were her duty. He'd sampled the fire in her and that's the only way he wanted her—burning for him as he burned for her. Anything less would be a corruption of their feelings for each other. Yet could he enjoy her body as a husband could and then send her away?

He turned away, his back to the hacienda, and started walking, putting one foot in front of the other. He strode through the meadow and entered the woods on the far side before he realized he hadn't brought his cane with him. He tested his weight on his leg at a different angle. Except for being sore from the fight with Luis, it didn't hurt much today.

He continued through the woods. If he couldn't put distance between himself and Caroline in his thoughts at least he could do so in space. Until he had a grip on his emotions, on his thoughts, he couldn't be near her.

He had told her that Texas was too tough for her, that

she wouldn't survive here, yet she was the one who had held Franklin hostage to force her way here. She was the one who had climbed out on that tree limb, turning back only when he'd insisted. And it was she who had withstood kidnapping with more spirit than he believed possible. All while her baby—his baby—grew inside her.

Trouble was, some of her ideas made sense. He did want to be around to help when the baby came. He did want to know if he had a son or daughter—and not just from a letter. He wanted to hold the baby, be there for the first smile, the first word. If he truly was getting better why was he forcing her to leave? It was beginning to make no sense—even to him.

The woods became denser and he heard the sound of water over stones. The river. He'd walked a far distance and without his cane. He picked his way through the foliage along the bank and stood for a moment, watching the water race past. The level had decreased in the past few days. The current flowed and eddied over boulders along the bank. Toward the center it was deep enough to mask the swift speed. Only a person unaware of the river's distinctive personality would knowingly challenge it.

He glanced downstream, his eye drawn to the white cloth Caroline had been so adamant about rescuing. It remained tangled on the half-submerged branch in the middle of the river. What was it about the material that triggered such a strong response in her? A wedding present for Jake and Victoria—that's all she'd said about it. Franklin was the one who had admitted she used it to gird him up when he'd been caught under the coach.

He was amazed the cloth hadn't washed away by now. He considered the pros and cons of going after it. He'd like to get it for her. Was he being a complete fool? Last night, his past had challenged him and he'd survived. Perhaps, he thought as he stared at the cloth, perhaps today he would challenge the river.

He walked along the bank, studying the current, the distance to the branch, and the flow of the water in the curve upstream. A snake slithered out from a decaying log by his foot. He ignored it, caught up as he was in the possibility of retrieving the fabric. He would have to enter the river a generous one hundred yards upstream from the branch if he were to make his way to it and not get swept past.

Enough thinking! If he was going to do this before nightfall—or winter—he'd just better do it.

He made his way to the calculated entry point and pushed through the thick brush. Bracing for the moment his injured leg would feel the sting, he stepped into the drink. The water swirled around his thighs, pushing him. He took an unsteady step. His ankle held, and he took another step, and another—the water up to his waist now. He pushed off, his strokes strong and hard as he swam, overcorrecting his path to allow for the pull of the current.

He was adjacent to and nearly past the cloth in a flash. His leg caught on part of the branch and he went under. His heart pounded. He struggled and freed himself, then floated beyond the cloth, only to grab the top of the tree branches to hang on. Dragging in great gulps of air, he paused a moment to let his heart return to normal.

Slowly, against the current, he inched his way back to the fabric. Holding on to the branch, he carefully untangled the cloth. Then folding it so that it didn't trail and catch on anything else, he pushed off into the center of the river.

In comparison, it had been easy to swim toward the cloth. The river flowed fastest in the center and the current sucked him there. To get out of the pull—the very grip of the river—

proved to be the difficult part. He swam hard, gaining only small success in making his way back to the bank. The water swept him onward. His limbs became leaden weights as he tired, but still he struggled. He gasped for air, and then gave up the fight, letting the current take him.

Chapter Twenty

"Señora Dumont? Is Brandon back yet?" Diego called from outside the cabin.

It was the first time she had heard herself addressed that way. A pleasant warmth spread through her, much like drinking hot chocolate on a cold winter's night. She cracked the cabin door. "He hasn't returned."

"Should I look for him?"

"Not yet."

His dark eyes flashed. "It isn't right for him to leave you. Are you sure this is what you want?"

She was glad twilight had come and Diego couldn't see her blush of embarrassment. She wasn't sure how to answer him.

"You have the *pistola?*"

She glanced at her brother's gun on the mantel. After what had happened last night, she felt better having it near, loaded for protection. "Yes. Don't worry. I…I'll come to the house if he doesn't return soon."

"*Si.* Or I will return to check on you again." He headed back to the hacienda.

She closed the door and paced the length of the floor. Where was Brandon? Had something happened to him? After he'd left with Juan and the priest, she had berated herself for turning him away. What kind of foolish pride was it that made her refuse him earlier? If, as his wife, all she would have to remember was one night in his arms, then she would make it count.

Her gaze fell on the wooden bed in the corner where once the straw pallets had been. This afternoon when she had announced her decision to move to the cabin, Victoria had asked Juan and Diego to move the bed and her trunk from the hacienda. A braided cord held aside the curtain, revealing the bed and the wedding bouquet on the pillow. She had been touched by their gift and thanked them, although she wondered now if she would even have a wedding night.

She looked out the window for the millionth time. The full moon painted the landscape in shades of gray. A dying wind rustled the pines and the tall prairie grass beyond them. The red flowers swayed, their petals already closed up for the night. In the distance, a man walked toward the hacienda, his stride steady, yet favoring his right leg. He glanced at the cabin and paused, and she knew he was taking in the smoke coming from the chimney and the candle flickering in the window.

Caroline held her breath.

She grabbed the door latch, but couldn't bring herself to open it. Although she wanted to go to him, something inside told her no. She should stay. Wait.

Wait for him to come to her. After all, she'd been the one to travel fifteen hundred miles to see him. Now it was his turn.

She waited.

She spun on her heel and paced—to the bed to readjust

the bouquet for the hundredth time, then to the hearth to stir the soup in the kettle. She stopped moving about and held her hands clasped before her, waiting by the small fire she'd started.

He didn't knock. He simply strode in and shut the door. And dropped the latch.

Something had changed. She could feel it as sure as fresh rain coming in on the afternoon breeze. The air was charged with a current running between them. She could tell by the way he looked at her—a fierce tenderness in his eyes. Her breath caught in her throat.

He crossed the distance in four strides and pulled her to him, his mouth swooping down on hers, firm and demanding. His fingers tangled in her hair, sending tingles over her scalp and down her spine. In the back of her mind she realized his clothes were cool and damp. It mattered little since heat emanated off his body in waves.

Her muscles turned to liquid. How had she denied him this morning? She could deny him nothing. Not when every part of her yearned for his touch.

He released her lips and stared down at her, his face now unreadable, his deep blue eyes boring into hers. "I have something for you."

He turned back to the door. It was then she noticed a cloth hanging from the latch. Something white and dirty and wet. She went still, knowing without further examination what it was.

He held it up for her. "It's not for Victoria and Jake."

"No."

"It never was."

"It's for the baby's cradle and later, the bed." She turned the fabric over, examining the holes and the destroyed edges.

Brandon turned her hand, bringing a portion she'd embroidered to her view and read out loud the words she'd stitched around the perimeter in gold thread. "Love is patient and kind. Love is not proud. Love bears all things, believes all things, hopes all things and endures all things. Love never fails."

She spread her hand over the fancy cursive letters, some a little crooked, but each painstakingly made. "I've never been much of a seamstress. I don't have the patience for sewing, but I wanted our child to always know he or she was loved."

He stepped closer—so close she felt his breath on her cheek. "There's no doubt the little mite will know he's loved with you for a mother."

She tried to absorb his closeness, afraid it might be all she would get. Tonight of all nights that would be horrible. She wanted a wedding night.

"I've been doing some thinking."

Oh, dear. "I don't know if I can handle much more of your thinking, Brandon," she warned, bracing herself.

"Now hear me out. I figure that if I can survive what happened in Goliad, perform surgery on my brother despite one of my spells, best a deranged renegade bent on killing the both of us and swim the river at its peak for a piece of cloth, then I can handle just about anything I get served in this life. And crazy as it sounds, for some reason you seem to want to share it with me."

"Of course I do. I love you."

"Simple as that?"

"It is for me."

"Then stay with me, Caroline." His voice was insistent, urgent in her ear. "Don't leave."

"Don't leave?" she repeated. She had to be sure she understood. "You mean for tonight?"

He shook his head. "I mean ever. Don't leave ever. I want you at my side when I'm working. I want to help bring our baby into the world. And I want to hold you in my arms every night starting with tonight, starting with now. I'll never let you go."

She hesitated, wanting so badly to trust his words.

"You said some things this morning, things I hadn't faced before. You were right—I was able to remove that bullet from Jake's shoulder because of your help. And the spells, they are easing up since you came."

Her vision blurred.

"I don't know if they'll go away completely," he warned.

"Whether they do or not, you have to trust that I'll be here for you. You can't send me away."

His gaze burned into hers. "In *sickness* and in *health,* from this day forward…"

"I meant those vows," she whispered.

"I do, too, Caroline."

He captured her lips with his. If there were any lingering doubts, his kiss brushed them away. He *was* strong—strong enough to confront the demons that had haunted him.

She pulled back and studied his face once more, finally letting herself believe his words.

The corner of his mouth quirked up in that smile she loved. His blue eyes twinkled. "Guess you're my hostage."

She took a deep breath, letting the joy spread through and fill her. "No. You're mine. And just think—I didn't even have to hold a gun on you."

She released herself from his embrace and stepped back. Turning to the hearth, she took the pistol from the mantel and carefully released the cocked lever before setting it back down. She spun around to face him, enjoying the slightly stunned look on his face.

"Now, Dr. Dumont, I believe I'm ready to start my life in Texas with you."

* * * * *

We'll be spotlighting a different series every month throughout 2009 to celebrate our 60th anniversary.

Look for Silhouette® Nocturne™ in October!

Travel through time to experience tales that reach the boundaries of life and death. Bestselling authors Lindsay McKenna, Cindy Dees, P.C. Cast and Merline Lovelace join together in a brand-new, four-book Time Raiders miniseries.

TIME RAIDERS

August—*The Seeker*
by *USA TODAY* bestselling author Lindsay McKenna

September—*The Slayer* by Cindy Dees

October—*The Avenger*
by *New York Times* bestselling author and coauthor of the House of Night novels P.C. Cast

November—*The Protector*
by *USA TODAY* bestselling author Merline Lovelace

Available wherever books are sold.

Silhouette®

Romantic
SUSPENSE

Sparked by Danger, Fueled by Passion.

The Agent's Secret Baby

by *USA TODAY* bestselling author
Marie Ferrarella

TOP SECRET DELIVERIES

Dr. Eve Walters suddenly finds herself pregnant after a regrettable one-night stand and turns to an online chat room for support. She eventually learns the true identity of her one-night stand: a DEA agent with a deadly secret. Adam Serrano does not want this baby or a relationship, but can fear for Eve's and the baby's lives convince him that this is what he has been searching for after all?

Available October wherever books are sold.

**Look for upcoming titles in
the TOP SECRET DELIVERIES miniseries**

The Cowboy's Secret Twins by Carla Cassidy—November
The Soldier's Secret Daughter by Cindy Dees—December

Visit Silhouette Books at www.eHarlequin.com

SRS27650

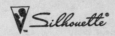

In 2009 Harlequin celebrates
60 years of pure reading pleasure!

We're marking this occasion by offering
16 **FREE** full books to download and read.

Visit
www.HarlequinCelebrates.com
to choose from a variety of
great romance stories
that are absolutely **FREE!**

(Total approximate retail value of $60)

We invite you to visit and share the Web site
with your friends, family
and anyone who enjoys reading.

You're invited to join our Tell Harlequin Reader Panel!

By joining our new reader panel you will:

- Receive Harlequin® books—they are FREE and yours to keep with no obligation to purchase anything!
- Participate in fun online surveys
- Exchange opinions and ideas with women just like you
- Have a say in our new book ideas and help us publish the best in women's fiction

In addition, you will have a chance to win great prizes and receive special gifts! See Web site for details. Some conditions apply. Space is limited.

To join, visit us at
www.TellHarlequin.com.

REQUEST YOUR
FREE BOOKS!

Harlequin® Historical
Historical Romantic Adventure!

2 FREE NOVELS PLUS 2 **FREE GIFTS!**

YES! Please send me 2 FREE Harlequin® Historical novels and my 2 FREE gifts (gifts are worth about $10). After receiving them, if I don't wish to receive any more books, I can return the shipping statement marked "cancel". If I don't cancel, I will receive 6 brand-new novels every month and be billed just $4.94 per book in the U.S. or $5.49 per book in Canada. That's a savings of 20% off the cover price! It's quite a bargain! Shipping and handling is just 50¢ per book.* I understand that accepting the 2 free books and gifts places me under no obligation to buy anything. I can always return a shipment and cancel at any time. Even if I never buy another book, the two free books and gifts are mine to keep forever.

246 HDN EYS3   349 HDN EYTF

Name	(PLEASE PRINT)	
Address		Apt. #
City	State/Prov.	Zip/Postal Code

Signature (if under 18, a parent or guardian must sign)

Mail to the **Harlequin Reader Service:**
IN U.S.A.: P.O. Box 1867, Buffalo, NY 14240-1867
IN CANADA: P.O. Box 609, Fort Erie, Ontario L2A 5X3

Not valid to current subscribers of Harlequin Historical books.

Want to try two free books from another line?
Call 1-800-873-8635 or visit www.morefreebooks.com.

* Terms and prices subject to change without notice. Prices do not include applicable taxes. Sales tax applicable in N.Y. Canadian residents will be charged applicable provincial taxes and GST. Offer not valid in Quebec. This offer is limited to one order per household. All orders subject to approval. Credit or debit balances in a customer's account(s) may be offset by any other outstanding balance owed by or to the customer. Please allow 4 to 6 weeks for delivery. Offer available while quantities last.

Your Privacy: Harlequin Books is committed to protecting your privacy. Our Privacy Policy is available online at www.eHarlequin.com or upon request from the Reader Service. From time to time we make our lists of customers available to reputable third parties who may have a product or service of interest to you. If you would prefer we not share your name and address, please check here. ☐

HH09R